KILL PLAN

EVA HUDSON

KILL PLAN

EVA HUDSON

First published 2014 by Two Pies Press
This edition published by Venatrix

ISBN 978-0-9926357-6-3

KILL PLAN

For Steve Murray - a true fan

Come on you Swans!

ONE

Special Agent Ingrid Skyberg peered more closely at the dead man. His light brown hair fell loosely across his forehead. His haircut had been styled by an expensive hairdresser rather than a barber. His suit jacket was open, revealing the deep maroon lining: a touch of flamboyance in an otherwise somber gray two-piece. Ingrid supposed he was trying to prove he had a personality. His right hand was shoved up into his left armpit. He must have fallen clutching that side of his chest. His left arm was flung over his head, the hand bent into a claw-like curl. His face was unlined, his skin clear. His lips already had a bluish tinge to them. He couldn't have been older than late twenties.

She pulled a pair of nitrile gloves from her pocket, quickly snapped them on and stepped over the makeshift cordon of blue and white police tape strung across three office chairs.

"What do you think you're doing! You can't touch him!" A uniformed police officer lunged forward and grabbed Ingrid's arm.

Ingrid stared into the woman's face. It was criss-crossed with deep lines. Her cheeks were flushed. No doubt a result of years working the beat in all weathers. "I have no intention of compromising your crime scene, officer," Ingrid said.

"Who said it was a crime scene?" The middle-aged officer glanced toward her youthful male colleague, as if she wanted his support. But he didn't seem to be listening. He'd been staring at Ingrid from the moment she'd shown the two cops her FBI badge.

"If it's not a crime, why are you here?" Ingrid asked.

"The paramedics called us in." The cop gestured toward the two EMTs who were standing near the elevator, deep in conversation with a gray-haired man dressed in a suit even smarter than the corpse's.

"Why did they call you in?"

The cop puffed out an irritated breath. "Why don't you ask them?" She started to walk away and beckoned to her colleague to follow her. They disappeared around a corner at the far end of the corridor.

Ingrid stood up, pulled off the gloves and looked through the glass wall separating the corridor from the large open-plan office of Fisher Krupps bank. The morning sun was streaming through the floor-to-ceiling windows. There had to be about seventy or so individual work stations on the trading floor. Over two-thirds of those were currently occupied by traders. Most of them had a phone cradled between shoulder and ear, their hands moving fast over computer keyboards. They were clearly still working despite the fact that the dead body of their colleague was lying just yards away in the corridor outside.

She approached the two men in green jump suits, an empty gurney standing between them.

"Hey," she said and flashed her badge at the EMTs and the smart-suited man they were talking to. "Special Agent Ingrid Skyberg, from the US embassy. Can I ask you a couple of questions?"

The man in the smart suit shoved out his hand. "Richard Wennstein, I'm the manager of the trading floor—I called the embassy." His accent was East Coast, probably New Jersey.

Ingrid shook his hand. "Thank you for your vigilance, sir."

He shrugged. "It's company policy here at Fisher Krupps. Anything happens to one of our US employees, we call the embassy." He stood back a little and unashamedly scrutinized her from head to toe. "I saw you just now looking at the body. What's an FBI agent doing here anyway? I expected some administrative clerk to arrive and make me fill out a dozen forms."

"We should really get going," the first EMT said.

"I'm sorry, Mr Wennstein. Would you mind if I spoke to these gentlemen before they leave?"

Wennstein shrugged again. "Be my guest."

One of the EMTs glanced at his watch.

"I promise I won't keep you," Ingrid told them. "Why did you call in the police?"

"Standard procedure," one of them said.

Ingrid nodded at him. "It is?"

"If someone dies unexpectedly we always inform the police. It's up to them to decide how to proceed."

"What are the options?"

"There are basically two: call the coroner's office to request an autopsy and let them come and collect the body. Or, if foul play is suspected, call in the detectives. Full forensics examination of the victim and the scene."

"You think this could be foul play?"

"I couldn't tell you one way or the other."

"Any idea what he might have died of?"

"It's down to the pathologist to determine the cause of death," the other EMT chimed in and glanced toward Wennstein, who was hovering a few feet away, well within earshot.

"How about an educated guess? Help me out here, fellas."

The first EMT leaned toward her, almost conspiratorially. "If I was a betting man, I'd put fifty quid on it being a massive coronary."

"Based on what?"

"The sudden onset, the way he was clutching his chest when he keeled over."

"He's a little young for a heart attack," Ingrid said.

"Which is why we called the police."

Ingrid glanced down the corridor. The two uniformed cops still hadn't returned to the body. Where the hell were they? "Thanks for your time, guys," she said.

They looked at one another, said goodbye to Wennstein, then shoved the gurney toward the elevator. The first EMT punched the down button and let out a long sigh.

Ingrid turned to Wennstein. "You manage the trading floor?" she asked him.

He nodded.

"So that's maybe seventy, eighty people?"

"Ninety-two."

"How well did you know Matthew Fuller?"

Wennstein glanced over her shoulder down the corridor and toward Fuller's stiffening body. He sniffed. "No better than anyone else here. He worked hard, always made good numbers every month. He was a stand up guy. What do you want me to say?"

"Was he healthy?"

"I guess—he worked out."

"The bank must have something on file about his medical history."

"Sure. Look—he was a fit, young guy. Not heart attack material if that's what you're asking." He took a step backward. "Exactly what are you asking? I mean, why is a federal agent getting involved with something like this?" He stuck a finger between his collar and his neck.

In Ingrid's experience, the presence of a Bureau agent often had this effect on people. Especially those working in financial institutions. It was as if they were all hiding some guilty secret they were worried was about to be exposed.

"Unexplained death of a US citizen in a foreign country? An FBI agent from the Criminal Investigation Unit always gets involved."

"Criminal? You think somebody killed Fuller?"

"I'm not saying that at all." Not at this stage, Ingrid thought. "Whatever this is, I'm here to represent the embassy and the Bureau. If there's a criminal investigation into Mr Fuller's death, I'll be assisting the police any way I can. I'll also write a report on the way the investigation is handled."

"Is that something we get to see?"

"It's more for the family of the deceased."

Wennstein closed his eyes for a moment.

"What is it?"

"Fuller's girlfriend. She works here at the bank. She's in New York, working at HQ for a couple days. How am I going to tell her about this?"

"Would you like someone from the embassy to contact her?"

"Could they?"

"Sure—I'll take her details before I leave. What about his parents?"

"I… I don't know anything about them. Maybe you should talk to Kristin."

"His girlfriend?"

He nodded.

"Would it be possible to see Mr Fuller's medical records? Would he have had a medical exam before he started at the bank, for insurance purposes?"

"Every employee does."

"So, can you get me the records?"

"I should really be getting back to the floor, see what's going on."

"Maybe you could make a couple of calls? Get the personnel department to do the legwork?"

Wennstein stared forlornly through the glass wall of the corridor toward his busy team of traders, like an anxious father peering into a room full of newborns at the hospital. He reluctantly pulled his phone from his pocket.

Ingrid was about to return to Matthew Fuller's body and continue the examination she'd started before the uniformed cop told her to stop, when she heard a loud crash sound from further down the corridor. She looked up to see a man wearing dark blue coveralls stagger out of a door. For a moment she was transfixed by the six feet tall man's strange lurching gate. She glanced at Wennstein, who was speaking in hushed tones into his cell phone. He shrugged back at her.

The man in the coveralls leaned a hand against the corridor wall to steady himself. Ingrid ran toward him. As she approached she could see he was blinking rapidly and sweating like he'd just stepped out of a sauna.

"Hey, are you OK?" Ingrid asked him, just a few feet away now.

The man dropped heavily onto his knees, remained in a kneeling position for a few moments, then pitched forward onto his face.

TWO

Immediately, Ingrid hollered back to Wennstein, "Call reception downstairs. See if those EMTs are still in the building. We need them back up here fast."

"What's wrong with him?"

"Make the call, goddammit!"

Wennstein tapped a number into his phone.

Ingrid turned her attention back to the guy on the floor. She pushed two fingers into the soft flesh of his neck, trying to feel for a pulse. It was fast, but faint. His eyes flickered open. "Hang in there, buddy," she said.

"Help me," he said feebly.

"Don't worry. Help is on its way."

"Help me get up."

"You just rest there, the ambulance guys will be here any second."

He ignored her, and, still lying face down, reached out his right arm and leg and hauled himself a foot or so sideways. He writhed, snake-like across the tile floor until he reached the wall of the corridor. Then he started to haul his upper body upright. Ingrid pulled one of his arms around her shoulders and together they managed to get him into a slumped sitting position, propped up against the wall.

He looked down toward his hands and flexed his fingers, then relaxed them. Then he started tapping the tips of his fingers against his thumbs. He swallowed. The perspiration had made his hair stick flat against his head.

"Pins and needles," he said and took a sharp, shallow breath. "My arms are going numb too. My legs feel like rubber." He turned his head to one side and stared into Ingrid's face. "I'm so cold." The sweat continued to drip from his eyebrows into his eyes. He shivered. "Freezing."

Ingrid glanced up toward the elevators. She saw Wennstein standing with his hands on his hips, looking up at the illuminated display above the elevator doors, no doubt thinking the same thing she was: where were the goddamn EMTs? Behind him Ingrid could see the prone body of Matthew Fuller. She bent close to the sweating guy's head.

"Do you have pains in your chest?" she asked him.

He nodded. "Can't breathe."

A few moments later Wennstein stepped back from the elevator as the doors opened. The gurney came crashing out ahead of the two EMTs. They ran toward Ingrid who was waving frantically at them. When they reached her, Ingrid quickly described the man's symptoms.

"So cold," he said again and his torso slid sideways to the floor as he passed out.

Ingrid stepped away and let the medical guys do their thing. One EMT was shining a light into the man's eyes while the other snapped an oxygen mask over his mouth and nose. There was nothing she could usefully do, so she set off in search of the two uniformed cops. The last time she'd seen them was at the opposite end of the long corridor. She started to hurry toward it. A few feet from the end she heard the raised voice of the female cop.

"For God's sake, Mark, it's not murder just because you think it's exciting."

She turned the corner to discover the two police officers sitting on a low window ledge, steaming cardboard cups of coffee in their hands. They looked up at her, guilty expressions on their faces.

"You have to call in your homicide detectives," Ingrid said. "Right now."

"Have you been listening to our private conversation?" The female cop stood up. Coffee slopped over the edge of her cup.

"Come with me." Ingrid headed back around the corner, hoping the police officers were following.

When the female cop finally appeared at the end of the corridor her mouth dropped open. The EMTs were lifting the tall man in the coveralls onto the gurney. "What's happened to him?" She eyed Ingrid suspiciously as if she'd had something to do with it.

"I guess the same thing that happened to Matthew Fuller," Ingrid told her.

"Bloody hell," the male cop said and started to jog toward the elevator.

"You need to call in your homicide and serious crime team, CSIs, pathologist, whoever else needs to be here. And get somebody to go with that poor guy to the hospital."

"I'll be the judge of that." The female officer hurried toward the moaning man strapped to the gurney. "What's wrong with him?" she asked the EMTs.

"I've got no idea." The lead man in the green jumpsuit pushed her out of the way and dragged the gurney to the elevator.

"Maybe you should get the whole building evacuated," Ingrid told the policewoman.

"I don't have the authority to do that."

"Then get somebody who does. You've just watched a second victim get stretchered out of here. Don't you think it's time to call in a little help?" Ingrid looked up and down the corridor in search of Wennstein. Maybe the manager of the trading floor could close down the building for her.

A few moments later the door to the men's restroom opened and Wennstein appeared. Ingrid strode toward him.

"We need to get this floor evacuated," she told him.

"Stop trading? There is no way that's going to happen." He winced a little.

"Are you OK?"

"I'm perfectly fine." Beads of sweat had broken out across his top lip.

"Do you know what that maintenance guy was doing here?" Ingrid asked him.

Wennstein ignored her question. He seemed distracted. "What?"

The guy the EMTs just took away—what was he doing here in the building?"

Again, he didn't answer. He was staring at his hands. "That's the weirdest thing." He started to shake his hands, as if he were flicking water off them. "Hey—didn't that guy say his hands were tingling?" There was a definite strain of panic in his voice. He balled his hands into fists then folded his arms.

"The maintenance guy?"

He blinked at her. "Servicing the hand driers in the restrooms."

Ingrid glanced at the restroom door. Wennstein had emerged from there just a few moments ago. "What were you doing in the restroom?" she asked him.

"What do you think I was doing? Taking a crap, if you must know."

Ingrid ran to the restroom and flung open the door. A man was standing at one of the urinals at the far end of the room.

"Get out of here—now!" she hollered.

He didn't move.

"I said now." She marched over to him.

"Jesus Christ—I'm mid-piss. I'm not going anywhere."

Ingrid kicked open the doors of each of the three cubicles in the washroom. All the stalls were empty. She raced over to the wash basins just as the man was zipping his fly. "Forget about washing your hands."

He raised his eyebrows at her. "Don't tell my mom."

Ingrid hurried him outside into the corridor. "I want the restroom sealed off," she told the policewoman. "And the floor evacuated."

"No way!" Wennstein said. He was rubbing his fingertips together. "I can't lose a day's trading."

"You can't lose any more of your employees either."

THREE

Thirty minutes later the trading floor was still trading, but at least the men's restroom had been cordoned off. Five minutes after that, the detectives emerged from an elevator, together with a half dozen CSIs already suited and booted.

The man leading the team of four detectives had a determined expression on his face. He looked like a quarterback squeezed into a suit two sizes too small. His biceps were bulging through the cheap material. Beneath a close-cropped beard, Ingrid noticed his chiseled jaw and cheekbones. The hair on his head was even shorter, no more than a black stubble against his dark skin. Ingrid hurried toward him.

"Special Agent Ingrid Skyberg, from the US embassy." She extended her hand.

The detective glanced toward the policewoman, who was currently standing sentry outside the men's restroom. Her colleague had gone in the ambulance with the maintenance guy. The cop pulled a face then looked down at her shoes.

"Detective Inspector Patrick Mbeke," he said and shook Ingrid's hand. "You're from the embassy?"

"Standard procedure," Ingrid said, and smiled warmly at him. "I work out of the Criminal Investigations Unit."

"And your role here?"

"To assist in the investigation, any way I can. I report back to the embassy."

"You don't trust the City of London Police to get the job done?"

"It's not like that at all. I'm just looking after the interests of American citizens."

"And American banks?" His tone was sarcastic.

She chose to ignore it. "City of London Police? Is that part of the Met?"

"No it bloody well isn't. The Met have no jurisdiction in the City."

Dammit. Why didn't she know that already? Since she'd arrived in the Capital, four and a half months ago, she'd been aware the Met weren't exactly the most popular police service in the country. With the public or the media. Now she'd pissed off a potential ally.

"Hey—can I use the excuse that I'm new here? Shall we back up and start over?" She smiled her broadest grin at him, hoping it might work some magic.

Two of the CSIs were moving the temporary cordon surrounding the corpse of Matthew Fuller, and had started to create a new, much larger no go zone around the body. Two more disappeared inside the men's restroom.

"How much have you been told already?" Ingrid asked Mbeke.

"Practically nothing—I only got the call from my DCI ten minutes ago."

"Are you the senior investigating officer?"

"No—DCI Simmons is. She'll be here shortly."

Ingrid quickly got Mbeke up to speed as they both quickly pulled on protective overshoes and gloves and ventured into the restroom.

"So you think the problem is in here?" Mbeke said when Ingrid had told him everything she knew. He glanced around the bathroom. "Should we even be in here? I mean—it might not be safe."

The two CSIs, who were busy bagging up anything that wasn't bolted to the floor or the walls, froze and glanced at one another.

"I'm guessing we're not dealing with an airborne pathogen, otherwise every guy who'd had a piss today would be in the hospital by now." She raised her eyebrows at the CSIs, who got back to work. "Just as long as we don't touch anything, I think we'll be OK."

"There are three casualties, is that right?"

"One fatality, one hospitalization."

"And the third?"

"He seems OK now. At least, he refused to leave the trading floor."

"He's still here?"

"I get the impression he thinks he's indispensable."

Mbeke turned in a slow circle then headed for the door. "We'll let them get on with it, shall we?"

Back in the corridor, Mbeke stared through the glass wall toward the busy trading floor. "It's a bank holiday," he said. "Don't they get any time off?"

"It's not a public holiday in Japan, or Hong Kong. The New York Stock Exchange will be opening in a few hours."

"There's a dead man in the corridor."

"Hey—I'm with you on this one. I want to clear the whole floor. But I need you guys to authorize that for me."

"That's a bit above my pay grade, I'm afraid. I'll have a word with the DCI, but I wouldn't be surprised if Fisher Krupps won the argument. Got to keep our international corporations happy, otherwise they might just up sticks and move somewhere else."

Ingrid thought it wise not to comment.

"You've been on the scene the longest. Come up with any theories?"

"Maybe some kind of anti-banking extremist? Or a disgruntled investor."

"You think someone would go this far to make a point?"

20

"I've seen people do a lot worse, just because someone pissed them off in the post office line."

Mbeke ran a hand over the stubble on his head. "But this would have taken some planning. I mean, how did they even get into the building?"

"You've sealed it off?"

"No one in or out unless I've personally approved it."

Ingrid was relieved someone was taking things seriously, even if Fisher Krupps didn't seem to be. She turned in response to the elevator doors pinging open. A woman dressed in a navy blue suit and pink shirt stepped into the corridor. She glanced left then right, spotted Mbeke and hurried toward him. "Patrick, what have you gleaned so far?" She ignored Ingrid completely.

"This is Agent Skyberg, boss. FBI, from the American embassy. Agent Skyberg this is DCI Anna Simmons."

The woman looked at Ingrid with narrowed eyes. "I'm sure you've done absolutely sterling work, agent. Rest assured, we have everything under control. You can return to the embassy."

"I'd rather stick around, assist if I can." Ingrid glanced at the team of CSIs buzzing around Matthew Fuller's body.

"That really won't be necessary." The DCI turned to Mbeke. "Do you have any business cards on you, Patrick?"

Mbeke reached into his breast pocket and handed Ingrid a card, his face a picture of apology.

"I'm sure Patrick will be in touch just as soon as we have anything to report." DCI Simmons smiled blankly and planted her hands on her hips. "Would you like one of our uniforms to give you a lift back to the embassy?"

"Thanks for the kind offer, but that won't be necessary, Anna." Ingrid reluctantly made her way to the elevator. She could have chosen to hold her ground, do a little flag planting, but if her experience of working with UK cops had taught her anything, it was when to choose her battles.

FOUR

The embassy seemed eerily quiet when Ingrid returned there from Fisher Krupps. Apart from a little congestion around the main shopping streets, traffic had been pretty much non-existent and she had made it back to the underground parking lot beneath the nine story building in Grosvenor Square in under fifteen minutes. She jogged up the emergency stairs two steps at a time, feeling the need to give her heart rate a little jolt. Since her motorcycle accident two weeks ago, Ingrid's lack of regular training was making her body feel heavy and sluggish. Any extra exercise she could incorporate into her day was very welcome.

She reached her floor and carried on up until the pleasant burn in her legs was matched by the one in her lungs. Rather than turn around and go straight back down again, Ingrid took the opportunity, seeing as the building was emptier than usual, to take a peek at the view from the top floor. She'd only made it halfway down the dark wood-paneled corridor before a woman's voice called after her.

"Hello there. You drew one of the short straws, huh?"

Ingrid spun on her heels and found herself face to face with none other than the US Ambassador. "Yes, ma'am. I mean… I guess…" Ingrid doubted she'd have been more tongue-tied if the president himself had stopped her in the corridor.

The ambassador took pity on her. "It's such a lovely day to be cooped up inside."

"Actually, ma'am, I just got back. I've been working on a new case. I came up here to take a look at the view."

"I find myself staring out of the window all the time. Especially during particularly tedious teleconferences!" Smiling, she walked toward Ingrid. Then straight past her to the end of the corridor. "Well come on then, if you want to take a look at the view."

Ingrid hurried to the window.

"And you are?"

"Special Agent Ingrid Skyberg, ma'am. Criminal Investigation Unit."

"Ah yes—you pretty much hold the fort all by yourself, I hear."

"I work with a great team."

"That's very loyal of you. I meant you're the only investigating agent."

"Yes, ma'am. I like to keep busy." Ingrid was surprised the ambassador had the first clue about her role.

"And what is this new case of yours?"

Ingrid wasn't sure how to respond. Right now she didn't know exactly what she was dealing with. "Sudden death of a young trader in the City."

"Oh dear. Do the police suspect foul play?"

"Yes, ma'am. It's possible that Fisher Krupps bank has been targeted by some extremist organization."

"Oh my." She stared directly into Ingrid's face, her clear, brown eyes filled with concern. Up close the woman looked more like Jackie O than Ingrid had noticed before. "I suppose the police have notified other major investment banks in the City?"

Although Ingrid was tempted to explain how she'd been thrown out of the bank, and didn't know if it had even occurred to the investigating team to inform the other banks, she knew it would be totally inappropriate, not to mention unprofessional, to complain about the City of London Police's obstructive attitude. She gave the ambassador a noncommittal nod.

"How young is the victim?"

Ingrid hadn't gotten chance to see Matthew Fuller's personnel records before she'd been dismissed. "Late twenties," she said, hoping she didn't sound too vague.

"Tragic." The ambassador turned toward the window. "His poor family."

"Yes, ma'am." Ingrid stared through the glass. She'd only seen the view once before—on her second week at the embassy, when Sol Franklin, her boss, had finally gotten around to giving her the guided tour. It was so clear today she could see all the way across town to the City, where she'd just been.

"I mustn't keep you from your work. It was lovely meeting you, Ingrid." The ambassador held out a small, pale hand. Ingrid was careful not too squeeze it too hard.

"The honor is all mine, ma'am." She trapped the ambassador's fingers inside hers for a fraction of a second too long and awkwardly pulled her hand away.

Goddammit.

Ingrid turned and moved as fast as she could down the corridor without actually breaking into a run. Her hands were sweating and her heart was beating hard and fast. When she reached the stairway she silently cursed herself for being such a klutz. She'd been even worse with the Secretary of State a few months ago. The memory of her clumsy interactions with her sent a shiver across her shoulders.

Jogging down the stairs, she managed to shake a little of the tension from her limbs. She was thirty-one years old, for God's sake. What was she doing feeling like a teenager at their first pop concert?

She reached the office a little flushed and forced herself to take a couple of deep breaths before opening the door.

Jennifer, the Bureau's civilian administrative clerk, was at her desk, speaking animatedly to someone on the phone.

"I know, I know! She was so nice to me! Said I was making a big difference. Said US citizens could sleep a little easier in their beds with me here to support them. Can you imagine that?" She glanced up and finally spotted Ingrid. "Listen, mom, I gotta go." She gave Ingrid an embarrassed smile. "No, of course I didn't ask for her autograph! I'll call you later, when I get home." She slammed the phone down. "Hey! Can I get you anything? Coffee maybe?"

"I'm fine. I'm guessing from what I just overheard you were graced by the presence of the ambassador?"

"Sorry about that—I just couldn't wait to call my mom." Jennifer suddenly looked much younger than her twenty-four years. She could have been fresh out of high school.

"I don't care who you call." Ingrid was a little relieved someone else had reacted to an audience with Frances Byrne-Williams the same way she had.

"She was so charming. Came right in here, and introduced herself to me. Can you imagine?"

Only too well.

Ingrid glanced around the office. It looked pretty much as she'd left it. Jennifer hadn't taken the opportunity to switch desks in her absence. Even though she had been making noises about a reorganization of the office furniture since the departure of her fellow clerk a few days ago. They were still waiting for his replacement to arrive. For some reason it was taking a while for the State Department to assign one of their embassy clerks to the FBI Criminal Investigation Unit. "Apart from the excitement of meeting the ambassador, how have things been here?"

"Oh real quiet. A couple stolen credit cards to deal with. A road traffic accident—no serious injuries. Nothing you need to worry about." She stood up. "Sure I can't get you that coffee?"

"Actually I'd like you to run a check on the trader who died this morning."

"How'd it go at the bank? How did the trader die?"

Ingrid wondered if the pathologist had arrived at the bank by now. "Too early to say." She fired up her desk computer. "I should know more later."

Jennifer tapped something into her keyboard. "Matthew Fuller... social security records, school records, college... employment... medical. Have I forgotten anything?"

"Criminal," Ingrid added helpfully.

"You said he was the victim?"

"Still worth looking into."

"Of course. I wasn't thinking." Jennifer, always eager to please, twitched an embarrassed smile in Ingrid's direction.

Ingrid's online search was a little less clearly defined. She wanted to know which substances might trigger a heart attack in an otherwise healthy victim.

After ten minutes of surfing, she had compiled such a long list of possible agents, some everyday innocuous household substances, some rare and highly toxic chemicals, that it would take a lab months to test Matthew Fuller's tissue for all of them. She got up and wandered over to Jennifer's desk. "Have you checked his medical records yet?"

Jennifer swiveled in her chair to another computer screen. "I can do that for you right now." She ran her fingers over a second keyboard in a blur of typing. A moment later a half dozen windows opened on the monitor. Ingrid started reading over the clerk's shoulder. When she was halfway down the first list of information, Jennifer closed the window.

"I hadn't finished," Ingrid told her.

"Sorry—I can scan text stupidly fast. You want me to bring it back up?"

"No—you carry on."

"What am I looking for exactly?"

"Any evidence of heart disease. Or a history of it in his family." Ingrid had been wondering why Matthew Fuller had died and, as far as she knew, the maintenance guy had survived. An underlying weakness in Fuller's heart might explain it.

"Not getting any indication of that so far."

"Let me know when you're done."

Ingrid returned to her desk and did a little research into the organizational structure of the City of London Police. As far as she could work out, the force's main responsibilities within the Square Mile were investigating cyber crime and corporate fraud and dealing with threats of terrorism.

"Ingrid? Can you take a look at something?" Jennifer was frowning at her computer screen. "I haven't seen anything like this before," she said. "I don't know what it means."

Ingrid hurried to the clerk's desk. "What is it, have you found something in his medical records?"

"Nothing connected to heart disease. But look at this." She pointed at her screen. "In 1992 the records just stop. There's nothing here about him before he was eight years of age. Looks like it's all been redacted."

"No record of his place of birth? Inoculations? Childhood illnesses?"

"He had chicken pox aged nine. From birth to seven, your guess is as good as mine. Have you seen records just stopping like this before?"

"It's weird, isn't it?" Ingrid said innocently and peered more closely at the information on the computer monitor. She had indeed come across something very similar before. But never for someone so young. In her experience, there was usually just one explanation for it, but it certainly wasn't something she wanted to share with Jennifer right now. Not until she had more information. "And no sign of heart disease after 1992?" Ingrid asked.

"Nope."

"Family medical history?"

"I've only been checking on Matthew Fuller himself up till now—so the information I have is what appears on his insurance applications. His dad died in 2003, but he was involved in an accident. Nothing to do with his heart. I guess Matthew Fuller was a pretty healthy guy." Jennifer gazed eagerly at Ingrid. "So if he wasn't sick, does that mean he was murdered?"

"Ask me again tomorrow, when we have the autopsy report."

Jennifer's shoulders slumped a little.

Ingrid searched the FBI database and brought up the same records for Matthew Fuller that Jennifer had, plus another couple that the admin clerk didn't have the security clearance to access. Ingrid stared at the screen, wondering what this revelation meant to the investigation into Fuller's death. The records she was looking at now, from the US Marshals database, confirmed her hunch. For some reason, at the ripe old age of seven, Matthew Fuller had been enrolled into the Federal Witness Protection Program.

FIVE

Ingrid had eventually asked Jennifer to fetch her a coffee from the local Italian coffee shop, rather than the embassy cafeteria, hoping that in the time it would take the clerk to walk there, wait for her order, and walk back again, she would have gleaned all the information she needed from the US Marshals Service. She'd been wrong. Fifteen minutes later, she was on hold, having been transferred a half dozen times. Each person she'd spoken to had refused to give her any details about Matthew Fuller's former identity, or the reason he'd been enrolled in the Witness Protection Program in the first place. Every time she'd been rebuffed she'd insisted on speaking to that person's superior. Now she'd just been left hanging. She was just about to slam the phone down when Jennifer appeared at the door. Ingrid listened to another second of hold music then gently returned the handset of the phone to its cradle. She smiled up at Jennifer.

"They insisted on calling it an Americano, even though I asked for a long black," the clerk said. "But I watched the barista as he was making it. He poured the espresso into the water, just the way you like it." She carefully placed the cardboard cup on Ingrid's desk.

"Thanks, it's exactly what I need. Now you're back, I might stretch my legs." She shoved her cell and DI Mbeke's card into a pocket, picked up the coffee and strode toward the door. "I won't be long."

She made her way to the emergency stairwell at the end of the corridor, where she knew she wouldn't be disturbed, and sank onto a cold concrete step. She tapped Mbeke's number into her contacts list—she had the feeling she might be speaking to the man a lot—and called him.

"DI Mbeke." He sounded a little irritated. Maybe he was having as frustrating a time as she was.

"Hello, this is Agent Skyberg, from the embassy?"

"I don't really have any developments to report, I'm afraid," he said, his tone mellowing a little. "I'll get in touch just as soon as I do."

"Actually I have something to tell you," Ingrid said quickly, concerned Mbeke was just about to hang up on her. She told him everything she'd uncovered so far about Matthew Fuller.

"Witness Protection?"

She'd kept that morsel until last, hoping it would pique his interest.

"Why was he put into the program?" Mbeke asked her.

"I'm still waiting for the US Marshals Service to get back to me on that." It was only the smallest of lies.

"You think he may have been specifically targeted?"

"It's a possibility, right?"

"But if someone wanted Fuller dead, why go to those lengths? Why not choose a baseball bat to the back of the head on a dark street? Why endanger other people?"

"Maybe the killer doesn't care about collateral damage."

"Do you really believe that?"

"I'm not ruling out any possibilities at this stage of the investigation."

"You think I am?" The irritable tone was back.

The last thing she wanted to do was piss off the investigating detective. "Not at all. I just thought I should let you know about anything I dig up, Stateside."

He paused a beat before answering. "Look, it's been a long day, we've got dozens more people to interview… I didn't mean to be short with you."

"Has anyone else complained of the same symptoms as Wennstein? The tingling fingers, numb hands?"

"Not to my knowledge. Could be we just haven't spoken to them yet."

Ingrid grabbed the handrail and pulled herself up. "How is Wennstein?"

"He seems fine. He's still working."

"And the maintenance guy?"

"Still waiting to hear back from the hospital about him. I'll let you know when I get an update." He hung up without saying goodbye.

Ingrid wandered back to the office, an untouched cup of coffee in her hand.

"Matthew Fuller has no criminal record," Jennifer announced as soon as Ingrid stepped in from the corridor. "No misdemeanors, major or otherwise."

"Good work, Jennifer, thank you."

The clerk smiled a self satisfied grin. "So, what's next?"

"Find out everything you can about Fisher Krupps Bank. The police are working on the assumption that someone has targeted the bank. I need to know why Fisher Krupps may have been singled out. What have they done that's any worse than any of the other banks? I need you to find out everything you can about them."

"You know for sure no other banks have been targeted?"

Ingrid thought about calling Mbeke back to confirm, but there was no way he would have forgotten to mention something like that to her. "Concentrate on Fisher Krupps for now—we can widen the search later if we have to."

Ingrid then trawled FBI intelligence herself to see if any anti-capitalist threats had recently been intercepted. After about an hour of intensive searching, she discovered that apart from the usual general social media chatter, no specific threats, about either Fisher Krupps, or the City of London in general, had been issued. Which made her more inclined to believe Matthew Fuller had been the target. For some reason, someone had decided to kill him in the middle of his place of work, using a method that meant collateral damage would be pretty much unavoidable.

"Ingrid?"

She looked up to see Jennifer had swiveled in her seat to face her.

"Something to report?"

"Thought I'd give you a little summary of what I've found so far."

Ingrid found a notebook and pen in her desk drawer. "OK—go for it."

"Fisher Krupps are a little different from other banks."

"Really?"

"If it hadn't been for a buyout back in 2011, they wouldn't even exist today. They were on the verge of bankruptcy."

Ingrid tried to square that statement with the expensive interior decor she'd seen at the bank. Fisher Krupps must have recovered significantly in the past two years. "The banking crisis was in 2008. Why did it take so long to hit Fisher Krupps?"

"Their trouble wasn't caused by the meltdown in '08—they survived it almost unscathed. In 2011 they almost went bankrupt because of a rogue trader. He lost the bank nearly a billion dollars through bad investments. Then Wall Street lost faith in them and their share price bombed."

"So what saved them from going under?" Ingrid wasn't at all convinced Fisher Krupps' previous financial troubles had any bearing on what had happened today in their London office.

"A shale gas billionaire bought the company for a dollar. From what I've read, it seems he'd always dreamed of owning a bank."

"The way some guys want to own a football or baseball team?"

"Oh, this guy owns those things too. He's very, very rich."

"And in all your research, have you discovered any reason why somebody might want to target his bank?"

"Not so far. But I'm just getting started."

"Thanks. Let me know if you do dig up any major enemies who might want to see Fisher Krupps suffer."

"Sure." Jennifer turned back to face her computer and started typing.

Ingrid felt a little sorry for the clerk, it would be a long and tedious task. Unless Jennifer dug up some specific threat to the bank, Ingrid was still more inclined to suspect Matthew Fuller was the intended victim. Discovering the reason for his involvement in the Witness Protection Program was vital to prove or disprove her hunch. Tomorrow she would speak to her boss about the situation. The US Marshals Service might be able to decline her request for information, but they'd have a much tougher time denying an official request from the assistant deputy chief.

SIX

At 7.30 p.m., after putting in a call to DI Mbeke and learning the man had nothing new to report, Ingrid decided there was nothing more to be usefully done and started to pack up her things. Hopefully tomorrow would yield more success. Right now she was too frustrated and hungry to concentrate on anything more than getting back to her hotel and ordering something from room service.

She had been staying at the four star hotel in Marylebone ever since she'd arrived in London, back in December. It was convenient more than luxurious, and lately she'd seriously been considering looking for an apartment to rent. The Bureau offered a pretty generous relocation package and she figured it might make sense to take advantage of it. But first she had to decide whether or not she was planning to stay.

A decision she had managed to avoid making for the last four and a half months.

She grabbed her jacket from the back of the chair and headed to the exit. Her cell phone started vibrating before she'd reached the underground parking lot. She hoped it was Patrick Mbeke, calling to tell her about some vital new piece of evidence his team had uncovered, but when she glanced at the screen she was disappointed to discover the call was from an unlisted 'out of area' number. Which meant it was an international call. She hadn't given her cell phone number to

Witness Protection, so it was most likely her fiancé calling. She quickly dismissed the call. A conversation with Marshall Claybourne on a poor quality trans-Atlantic cell phone connection wouldn't be good for either of them.

As she reached her motorcycle in the parking lot, the phone buzzed again. Again the unlisted out of area number. She thought about switching off the cell, but in a moment of rashness answered the call.

"Hey, Marsh. I'm kinda in the middle of something. Can it wait?" She opened the box on the back of the bike and removed her helmet and gloves.

"I need you to get some place fast. Do you have the bike?"

Ingrid looked down at the Triumph Tiger 800 and thought about telling Marshall it was at the garage for a repair. Instead she said nothing.

"Something's being flagged over here," Marshall continued, "somebody's trying to access a bank account that's on a watch list. I need you to check it out. I have an IP address and a location."

"What kind of watch list? Are we talking terrorism? If we are, then you should go through the counter-terrorism division. Those agents would be better qualified than me to—"

"He's not a terrorist."

"Who is he? What's he done?"

"I can't get into the details right now. Just trust me, OK?"

In Ingrid's experience, whenever Marshall asked for her unquestioning trust, things never turned out well.

"We're wasting time. Check it out—don't identify yourself as a Federal Agent, come up with a cover story."

"What?"

"Report what you find and we'll decide how to proceed. No need to alert him the FBI are on his trail."

"Shouldn't I get some back up?"

"It's probably nothing. Just check it out. I'm texting you the address."

And with that he hung up.

Less than a half hour later, Ingrid had arrived in Dulwich, an area in south-east London roughly seven miles from the city center. She kicked down the prop stand and climbed off the bike. She'd parked fifty or so yards from the address Marshall had texted her, in a regular residential street. As far as she could see, the houses were a mix of large, smart detached properties with well-maintained gardens and even larger double-fronted buildings that had been converted into apartments. Some of the houses had shiny new SUVs parked on their driveways.

Once she'd stored her helmet and gloves, she made her way slowly up the street, doing her best to look like a lost tourist. According to her GPS, the property she was looking for was around the next corner. She approached it cautiously, checking the street for any signs of activity. Apart from a dog walker at one end and a guy washing his car at the other, the street was surprisingly quiet for a sunny evening on a public holiday. She sniffed the air and detected a definite tang of grilled meat and supposed people were enjoying barbecues in their backyards.

Marshall had called her back just after he'd texted her the address and reminded her that under no circumstances should she identify herself as an FBI agent. But he still refused to answer any of her questions. She'd worked out a fairly lame cover story on the ride over. Hopefully it wasn't so lame it would arouse suspicion.

Number twenty-three was the third property on the right. She walked purposely up the driveway of the wide, white stucco house and rang the door bell for apartment two. She waited for thirty seconds or so then rang again, keeping her finger on the buzzer. After another half minute the door creaked open a crack, a suspicious face peered at her through the gap. The woman at the door was probably late twenties or maybe early thirties, thin and very pale. Her hair was piled on top of her head in a haphazard French pleat. It was the color of cherry Kool-Aid. A small, dark green tattoo of a crucifix decorated the left side of her throat. It was a classy look.

Marshall had told Ingrid she was looking for a man in his mid-thirties.

"What is it? Who are you?" The woman's accent was eastern European, one of the Baltic states, Ingrid reckoned. Estonia or Latvia, maybe. The crucifix tattoo danced as she spoke.

"I'm so sorry, ma'am. I wonder, could I use your bathroom?"

The woman looked Ingrid up and down and narrowed her eyes until they were no more than heavily mascaraed slits. Then she looked over Ingrid's shoulder, toward the street.

"I wouldn't ask, only I'm desperate. You're the fifth house I've tried. Seems no one is in."

The look of suspicion still hadn't left the woman's face.

Ingrid reached into her purse and retrieved a tampon and held it up between thumb and forefinger. "You see, it's kinda embarrassing."

The woman raised her eyebrows. "OK—you make it quick, yes?"

"Thank you so much."

The woman ushered her into the house, pointed toward the half-open door of her apartment a few feet away, then stuck her head outside again, before she finally came in and closed the door.

"Quickly!" the woman told her. "Through door, bathroom is on right."

Ingrid scurried toward the tiny room and locked the door. She quickly checked the cabinet above the sink. It was full of the usual bathroom paraphernalia, a collection of various painkillers, deodorant, depilatory cream, tampons. No sign of any male presence. She unlocked the door as quietly as she could, and opened it a crack, half expecting to see the woman waiting for her outside. Thankfully she wasn't. Ingrid stopped for a moment and listened. She heard the woman's voice coming from another room. Then the talking stopped, there was silence for a few beats, and then the machine-gun fire Latvian—Ingrid was pretty sure that was the language she heard—started up again. The woman was having a very one-sided conversation on the phone.

Ingrid crept out of the bathroom and along the narrow, dingy hall and peered into the kitchen and discovered no one lurking inside. The room next to it, a bedroom, was also unoccupied. She was just about to check the closet for men's clothes when she heard the woman's voice call from the only room she hadn't seen inside. "Hello? Are you OK?" came the thick accented voice.

Ingrid hurried back to the bathroom, flushed the toilet and closed the door noisily. Then she strode down the hall and met the woman in the doorway of the sparsely decorated living room.

"Thank you so much—you are a life saver." Ingrid noticed an open laptop sitting on a table at the other end of the room, together with four cell phones of varying sophistication.

The cherry-haired woman followed her gaze, the suspicious expression on her pale face deepening. "You must go now."

"I'm just so glad you answered the door, rather than your husband." It was a long shot, but Ingrid thought she may as well try.

"Husband?" The look of suspicion was quickly replaced by one of confusion.

"You see, in the circumstances I would have felt too uncomfortable to ask a man for help." Ingrid smiled innocently.

"No husband."

"Oh—my mistake—I just assumed you lived here with your husband, or boyfriend. I didn't mean to pry."

"Please—you go now. I am very busy."

Ingrid glanced at the laptop again, its sleep light gently pulsing bright white every second or so. Why did this woman need four cell phones?

The Latvian redhead spread her arms wide and ushered her unwanted visitor to the door of the apartment.

"Thank you again. You're very kind." Ingrid was hustled to the main front door of the building and out onto the driveway. The woman stood at the open door and watched Ingrid return to the street before she went inside.

When Ingrid got back to the bike she called Marshall back.

"Well? Did you see him?" he barked at her as soon as he picked up.

"Can we work this another way? You know, the way where you're really grateful for all my help and ask me nicely."

There was silence at the other end. Then a noisy inhale. She knew Marshall was busy counting to ten to control his frustration.

"I'm sorry, honey. I'm just a little pressured at the moment." Another deep exhale. "Of course I'm grateful for any help you can give me. I really appreciate your taking time out to—"

"Enough! Now you just sound phony." She reached into the box on the back of the bike and pulled out her helmet without saying anything for a long few moments.

"Honey?" She could hear the strain in Marshall's voice. "Honey? Are you still there?"

"I'm here. I met a woman at the property. Latvian, twenty-five to thirty, dyed red hair, tattoo of a cross on her neck. Description mean anything to you?"

"Zip. No man at the address?"

"No man and no sign of one."

"Notice anything interesting at all?"

"The woman was using an expensive laptop. I saw four cells too."

"Four?"

"As far as I could tell, one was a smart phone, the other three no-frills bottom of the range. I assume they were burners."

"Did you ask her about them?"

"There wasn't exactly a way to work them into the conversation."

"See what was on the laptop?"

"It was on sleep mode."

Marshall went quiet.

"What do you want me to do? Call for reinforcements?" she asked him eventually, tired of waiting while he devised her next move.

"No. Seems you may just have stumbled on an internet scammer who got lucky with one of the accounts on the watch list."

"Is that likely?"

"It's not impossible."

"If she's a scammer, the local cops might be interested in her. I should call them."

"No—stand down. Do nothing."

"So who is this guy you're so interested in?"

"It doesn't matter, I don't think you found him."

"What are you doing monitoring watch lists, anyhow? Have you been demoted?"

"Demoted? Very funny."

Marshall's meteoric rise up the ranks was almost legendary. He had a knack of being in the right place at the right time, willing and eager to scoop up any glory on offer.

"So what are you doing? Looking for easy wins?"

"Look, I have to go. We'll talk later, OK?" He hung up.

Ingrid stood for a moment just staring at her phone. She must have hit a nerve. Marshall had to be trawling intelligence for fast turnaround cases. More notches to add to his belt. She wondered for a moment why that notion made her more mad than envious. Then she remembered just how hungry she was.

SEVEN

The next day Ingrid left her hotel shortly after dawn. She jogged around the Outer Circle of Regent's Park: a simple run followed by a few reps of squat thrusts, lunges and chin-ups. It felt good to really test her muscles.

As she headed back to Euston Road, running along the eastern edge of the park, she realized she was running toward Winfield House, the official residence of the US ambassador. She relived her awkward encounter with Frances Byrne-Williams. An embarrassed glow warmed her cheeks. Automatically, her speed increased as she passed the armed cop on the gates—she wasn't exactly dressed for another impromptu meeting with the ambassador.

She managed to maintain the same speed all the way back to the hotel and by the time she stepped out of the shower, she felt a little more human, and ready for the day ahead.

After a breakfast of Bircher muesli and a double-shot espresso, she was pretty much ready for anything the day could throw at her. She arrived at the office to discover Jennifer already at her desk. In her four or so months at the embassy, Ingrid had never seen the clerk so keen. Perhaps her conversation with the ambassador had made her more eager to impress. She was tentatively poking a dessert spoon into a bowl. Ingrid peered at the gray-tinged mixture specked throughout with bright crimson pomegranate seeds.

"What have you got there?" Ingrid asked her.

"Quinoa and fruit porridge." She lifted the spoon to her nose and sniffed. "It's super healthy."

"Are you supposed to spread it on your face or eat it?"

"I was talking to Frances about it yesterday."

"The ambassador is taking an interest in what you have for breakfast?"

"Not exactly. We got on to talking about the new chef. And how all the food is organic now, and locally sourced. It's a passion of hers. She wants the embassy staff to stop eating junk."

"Locally sourced?" Quinoa and pomegranate—most probably from South America and northern Africa.

"Wherever possible." Jennifer prodded the gray mixture again. The spoon seemed to bounce back at her. The porridge was showing signs of resistance.

"Good luck with that. What's for lunch?"

"There's a tofu stir-fry I liked the sound of."

Ingrid felt her own breakfast stirring in her stomach. Thankfully her phone started to ring to take her mind off it. She snatched up the receiver, gave her name and waited for a response, but all she heard was a strange mumble at the other end of the line.

"Hello? Is there someone there?"

She heard a cackling laugh, following by a cough. "Agent Skyberg! How are you this fine spring morning?" It took Ingrid a few moments to place the voice. Once she had, she wished she'd let the answering service take the call.

"Ms Tate?" Angela Tate was a grizzled investigative journalist working for the main London newspaper, the *Evening News*. She had an uncanny knack of turning up at a crime scene just moments after the police. The woman had a fierce reputation for getting the story she wanted, no matter what she had to do to get it.

"I'm calling to claim my prize."

Ingrid closed her eyes. Tate played a major role in her last big investigation. Such a major role that Ingrid owed her a favor. This was payback time. "What do you need?"

"You!" The cackling laugh erupted again. Ingrid wondered if maybe Tate were drunk. The woman seemed to go nowhere without her own private supply of alcohol. "You promised me a fly-on-the-wall, unfettered access, day-in-the-life profile. And today's the day! Aren't you the lucky one!"

"Not today—I'm way too busy."

"Busy's great. I can work with busy. It'd be no fun for me watching you catch up with your paperwork, would it?"

"Call me tomorrow and we'll fix a date. I'd need to clear it with security."

"But I'm here now, why not just throw protocol out of the window and go for it?"

"You're here?"

"Downstairs, sitting on the desk of a very handsome man in uniform. Oh look—I've made him blush."

"I'm sorry—it's just not convenient today."

"Wait a minute." Tate dropped her voice. "I do hope I don't have to remind you of our little agreement."

Ingrid clamped her bottom lip between her teeth. Tate could cause so much trouble for her, if she set her mind to it. The journalist's role in her last case was unconventional to say the least, downright dishonest and immoral might be a more accurate description. Tate had a reputation for tenacity and dogged determination. Once she sank her teeth into a project she wouldn't let up until she was good and ready. Ingrid would have to succumb to her demands eventually. But maybe she could put her off just a little longer.

"Of course you don't need to remind me," Ingrid responded in a whisper, keeping her eyes trained on Jennifer, hoping the clerk's breakfast was enough of a distraction to stop her listening in. "I promise you we'll fix up proper access at a later date. I just really can't do today."

There was a long silence at the other end of the line. Then a lengthy intake of breath. "Oh, all right! But I want you to understand—I won't be fobbed off a second time. Is that clear?"

"Crystal."

Tate hung up, leaving Ingrid listening to the dial tone for a moment, wondering how the hell she was going to handle Tate when the time came.

"Hey, everyone! If you have a moment."

Ingrid looked up to see her boss, Sol Franklin, standing in the doorway of the office with his arm around the shoulders of a tall, slim black man in his very early twenties.

"Listen up, folks." Sol removed his arm and took a step away from his young companion. He cleared his throat. "I'd like to introduce you all to Isaac Coleman. Isaac here is part of the International Mission Graduate Program. He's aiming to specialize in the personal safety of US citizens abroad, and he has the good fortune to have been assigned to the Criminal Investigation Unit for the next part of his training. Say hello, people," Sol ordered.

Jennifer jumped up from her desk and warmly shook the new arrival by the hand. "I'm Jennifer Rocharde. Good to have you on board, Isaac."

"Thank you." Isaac smiled broadly as Jennifer pumped his arm practically off his shoulder.

"Welcome to the embassy, Isaac. I'm Ingrid." Ingrid's gaze switched from the new recruit to Sol. She raised her shoulders at him in an almost imperceptible shrug. Another pair of hands to help Jennifer would be great, but she had an uncomfortable feeling there was more to it than that. A moment later Sol made his intentions plain.

"Isaac here has completed the victim counseling training course and he's eager to apply what he's learned to a 'real-life' situation. So, next US citizen in peril, I want Isaac in the thick of the action. OK?" He turned from Jennifer to Ingrid then quickly looked away. "Good. That's all settled then." He put his arm around the new man's shoulders again. "Now—as promised—the guided tour. And you must remind me to fix a date for you to come to my house for dinner. It's customary for new recruits. And I won't take no for an answer." He swung Isaac around and back through the door, hurrying away before Ingrid or Jennifer could ask any questions about Isaac's responsibilities.

Ingrid supposed her request for Sol to contact the US Marshals Service would have to wait until after he'd completed Isaac's tour.

Jennifer closed the door behind them. "No one has ever asked me if I want to learn victim support skills. The closest I get to supporting US citizens is passing on their temporary passport requests or arranging for a money wire."

"If you want to get more training, I'm sure you can put in a request."

"I get rejected every time I ask for training. It's like I don't count or something."

Ingrid grabbed her purse and jacket. She didn't have the time or the patience to stay in the office listening to Jennifer complain about the shortcomings of the embassy's professional development program.

"Where are you going?"

"Back to Fisher Krupps."

"The dead trader?"

Ingrid nodded. She'd decided to tackle the obstructive DCI who had thrown her out of the bank head on. If the detective complained, Ingrid would escalate the matter with Sol or someone higher up the food chain. "Can you arrange for a driver to meet me in the parking lot?"

"You need him to wait at the bank for you till you're finished?"

"No—I could be there a while."

By the time Ingrid had skipped down the stairs to the underground parking lot, a driver, dressed in traditional G-man garb—right down to the dark glasses, even though the lighting was dim in the basement—was holding open the door of a black BMW sedan. He was embassy rather than FBI personnel, but the black suit and white shirt look was pretty much universal. They were out of the embassy compound and onto the street less than a minute later.

It wasn't Ingrid's habit to use an official vehicle to carry out her tasks, but finding a convenient place to park the bike in the City of London would have been more hassle than she needed. After ten minutes or so the driver let out a heavy sigh and hit the steering wheel with the flat of his hand in frustration.

"It's not just me then," Ingrid said.

"Ma'am?"

"Please—call me Ingrid. I'm guessing you've noticed the tail too?"

"I've been trying to shake him off for the past five minutes. If he's a genuine taxi driver, he's in the wrong business. He's pretty damn good."

Ingrid stared into the passenger side mirror and took a good look at the black London cab. She could barely see the driver. No way could she make out who was in the back.

"Let's just continue to the destination, shall we? I'll deal with our unwanted escort when we get there."

EIGHT

As soon as she'd spotted the cab herself, Ingrid had a pretty good idea who might be tailing her. If it was supposed to have been a covert operation, then the mission had failed spectacularly. Fifty yards from the entrance of Fisher Krupps on Leadenhall Street, Ingrid told her driver to pull over.

"Will you need any assistance?" he asked, turning to her as he switched off the engine.

Looking at him, Ingrid saw two miniature versions of herself reflected back in the dark rectangles of his shades. She needed a haircut. Her hair was hanging limply over her ears. "I think I'll be able to manage," she told him. The driver seemed to deflate a little. Even if she'd needed help, no way would she get a non-Bureau member of embassy staff involved. "You can get back to base now." She opened her door and climbed out, flagging down the cab as she walked into the road. The taxi pulled in just in front of the embassy sedan. Ingrid strode toward it and rapped on the nearside window.

After a long pause, the door opened and Angela Tate stuck her head through the gap. "How'd you know it was me?"

"I took a wild guess." Ingrid should have known Tate wouldn't just accept being fobbed off without putting up more of a fight. "What exactly did you hope to achieve, following me here like this?"

"I thought there was a chance you'd change your mind."

"Trust me—I haven't forgotten our… arrangement. I'll do what I can. Please, just leave it with me."

Tate sniffed in a long breath, obviously unconvinced.

"I'll call you just as soon as I can with an alternate date. I promise."

Tate peered over Ingrid's shoulder, to the street beyond. "Square Mile? What is it? Cyber fraud? Anti-terror? Give me a clue at least."

Ingrid was surprised the sleuthing reporter hadn't already heard about the mysterious death of an American trader. "Nothing so interesting. Please, Angela. Cut me a break here."

Tate pursed her lips and screwed up her face. "I've got a lunch meeting anyway. So I can't stop. But I warn you—I won't let you off the hook."

"Believe me, of that I have no doubt." Ingrid stepped back and watched as Tate slammed the door. A moment later the cab pulled into the busy stream of traffic. A few seconds after that, the embassy car did the same. The driver flashed his rear warning lights at her to say goodbye.

Already later than she had wanted, Ingrid jogged toward the entrance of the bank, glancing around the street as she approached, just to make sure the journalist wasn't still spying on her. After checking in with the main reception desk and collecting a visitor badge, she made her way straight to the trading floor in search of Mbeke, hoping she wouldn't run into DCI Simmons first.

She stepped out of the elevator on the third floor and checked up and down the corridor. The place where Matthew Fuller had died was still cordoned off, as was the men's restroom. Ingrid peered through the glass wall of the corridor into the open plan trading floor area. She spotted Mbeke addressing a group of five detectives in a small conference room immediately opposite her position. She waited for him to finish up before approaching. The grave-faced detectives— three men and two women—filed past her in silence.

"Hey," Ingrid said, "are things going that badly?"

Mbeke blinked at her.

"Your team look a little low. Has something happened? Is the maintenance guy OK?"

"What are you doing here?"

"My job. How's the maintenance guy?"

"His doctors have decided to put him into an induced coma, until they find out what's wrong with him."

"Poor guy. When is Matthew Fuller's autopsy happening?"

Mbeke paused before answering, as if weighing up whether he should even answer her at all. "This afternoon. The mortuary's a little backed up because of the bank holiday."

Ingrid scanned the trading floor. "No DCI Simmons today?"

"She's coordinating back at the station. I'm managing things here."

Ingrid nodded slowly, relieved she didn't have to get into a messy, time-wasting battle with the senior detective. "And you're OK about my being here?"

Mbeke folded his arms. He scrutinized her face. "You promise you won't interfere with my investigation?"

"Interfere? How about assist and consult?"

The merest hint of a smile flickered across Mbeke's face.

"How many staff members are yet to be interviewed?" Ingrid asked him, pleased he might be a little more amenable than his boss.

"We've already interviewed all of the traders on this floor. We're spreading out to the rest of the building today, concentrating on anyone who was in the building yesterday. More staff are in today. The process will take a while."

"What about the maintenance and cleaning staff who had access to the restroom?"

"There's just one man we haven't been able to talk to. He didn't show up for work today."

"And he is?"

Mbeke consulted his notebook. "Miguel Hernandez, thirty-five, originally from... actually, nobody is completely clear about his country of origin. The cleaning agency say Columbia, but a couple of the cleaners here think he's from Spain."

"He was here until when yesterday?"

"Still trying to pinpoint the exact time."

"And he would have had access to the men's restrooms?"

"Just like everyone else in the building."

"You've tried his home address?"

"A couple of uniforms visited his flat about an hour ago. There was no answer."

"Do you have any more intel on him?"

"Surprisingly little. He doesn't have much of a profile on any level."

Ingrid felt a knot tighten in her stomach. "Are you treating him as a potential witness or suspect?"

"Witness at this stage."

She tried to disguise her surprise. "Are the uniformed cops staking out his place?"

"I'd need to put in a special request for a surveillance team. Jump through a lot of hoops. I thought I'd just send them back out there later." He shoved his hands in his pants pockets and stuck out his chin, as if he were challenging her to question his decision.

Ingrid chose not to rise to the bait. "So what's next?"

"According to the cleaning agency, one of the cleaners is quite close to Hernandez. I was just about to speak to her."

"Mind if I tag along?"

"In an observational capacity?"

"Whatever works for you."

A few minutes later, the elevator doors opened onto the eighth floor, bright sunshine flooded the corridor, coming from a floor to ceiling window at one end. Halfway toward the other end, Ingrid spotted a cleaning cart. The cleaner couldn't be too far away. Mbeke picked up pace a little so that he was a couple of steps ahead of Ingrid.

"Hello!" he called. "Patience Toure?"

A heavy, middle-aged woman appeared from a doorway next to the cart. She was dressed in dark pants that were too tight for her and an unflattering sage green tee shirt. "Who is looking for her?"

Mbeke introduced himself and showed her his badge.

Immediately the woman narrowed her eyes and drew in a sharp breath. "Is this about the man who died?"

"I'd like to ask you a few questions," Mbeke said, his voice softening noticeably.

"I wasn't here yesterday—I don't know anything about what happened." She glanced toward Ingrid.

Ingrid stepped forward. "Agent Skyberg, American embassy," she said. "The man who died was a US citizen." Ingrid sensed Mbeke wasn't happy about the interruption. She smiled at Toure and shuffled sideways, leaving the floor to the detective. She glanced into the room Toure had just come out of. It was some sort of closet for storing cleaning materials and equipment.

"We're interested in speaking to one of your colleagues," Mbeke continued, "Miguel Hernandez?"

"So?"

"I understand you know Mr Hernandez quite well."

"Who told you that?"

"Do you have any idea where he might be today?"

Toure shrugged. "How would I know?"

"Is he your friend?"

"I hardly know the man. Why are you asking me about him?"

Mbeke blew out a frustrated sigh. "He's not in any trouble, we just need to ask him a few questions."

"He is in the country legally. You have no right to harass him."

"Like I said, he's not in trouble. I just need to know what he saw when he was here yesterday. I'm not interested in his immigration status."

Toure snorted a laugh. "I need to get back to work. I don't have time for this. I don't know him and I can't help you." She turned away and ducked back into the cleaning closet.

"Mind if I try?" Ingrid asked Mbeke under her breath.

"Be my guest." Mbeke turned and headed back toward the elevator.

Ingrid stepped into the cramped space of the cleaning closet and lightly touched Toure on the arm. "Patience… may I call you Patience?"

Toure shrugged back at her.

"I really don't care about Miguel's immigration status. That has nothing to do with the embassy. The only thing I'm interested in is Matthew Fuller—the young man who died yesterday. Miguel may have some information about what happened."

"Miguel is a good man. He wouldn't have anything to do with the man's death."

"I'm not saying he does, but he might know something that helps us. I promise you, if you can tell us where we might be able to find him, I'll make sure the police don't pursue any immigration issues."

"You expect me to believe you? He speaks to the police and the next thing he knows he's at Heathrow airport waiting for the next flight home."

"I promise you that won't happen."

Toure shook her head. "I don't know where he is. I can't help you." She bent down and picked up a large plastic container from a low shelf and heaved it onto the cleaning cart. It landed with a thud. "I have to work now." She started to push the cart toward the ladies' restroom.

Ingrid looked at the large container Toure had just dumped onto the cart. According to the label it was a ten liter box of liquid soap. "Do you refill the soap dispensers in the restrooms every day?" she asked.

Toure stopped. "Why?"

"Is fresh soap added every day?"

"In the ladies' toilets I refresh the dispensers twice a day. Men don't wash their hands so much. Maybe once every other day."

"It's possible new soap would have been added yesterday to the restrooms on the third floor?"

Toure nodded and looked at Ingrid as if she were crazy.

"Thank you for your help." Ingrid raced toward Mbeke, who was still waiting for her at the elevators. "Call your forensics lab," she said when she reached him.

"What?"

"Get them to test the soap dispensers as a priority. We may have found the source of the toxin."

NINE

Mbeke turned away from Ingrid as he put in the call to the forensics laboratory. She clearly heard him make the request that the soap dispensers should be tested first. She felt as if maybe they were actually starting to make some progress.

"What do you mean?" Mbeke raised his voice. "Are you telling me they've been lost?" He turned back toward Ingrid and momentarily made eye contact with her, raising his eyebrows. "Then what are you saying?" He started to shake his head. "Dear God, what a balls-up. Who's responsible for this?" As he listened to the reply the muscles in his jaw flexed. After a few more seconds he hung up.

"What's happened?"

"There were no soap dispensers," he said and shoved his phone into a pocket.

"I don't understand."

"The lab can't test them because they were never recovered from the scene."

"They had to be."

"All the evidence from the gents' toilets was carefully bagged up and labeled by the CSIs. According to the forensics manager, there were no dispensers to bag up."

Ingrid tried to remember what she'd seen in the restroom when she'd gone in there herself. She would have noticed if the dispensers had been missing, wouldn't she? If they were there when she was in the restroom, what the hell had happened to them? "They must have been removed by the perpetrator, some time between Wennstein visiting the restroom and your uniformed officers sealing it off."

"That wouldn't have been much of a window—ten, maybe fifteen minutes?"

Ingrid pulled a face. She wasn't one for telling tales, but she couldn't just let it go.

"What is it?" Mbeke pressed the down button with a knuckle.

"I'd say closer to twenty minutes, maybe a half hour. I had to do a lot of persuading to get the restroom sealed."

"Do you remember seeing anyone going in or out?"

"I didn't have my eye on the door all the time. I was a little busy fighting with the police constable."

"Which one?"

"I don't want to get anyone in trouble."

"It's OK, I can find out without you telling me."

The elevator arrived. Ingrid glanced up and down the corridor, looking for CCTV cameras. "Is there footage some place of the corridor on the trading floor?"

"I've got a DC with security right now running through all the footage for yesterday morning. There's nothing for the exterior or interior of the toilets." He stepped into the elevator and Ingrid followed him. "But there are cameras in all the lifts." He pointed toward the shiny black hemisphere attached to the center of the ceiling of the elevator. "And the reception area and all the exits have good coverage." He punched the button labeled 'LG'. "Let's go and see what they've uncovered so far, shall we?"

The elevator doors seemed to take an age to close.

"If the toxic agent that killed Fuller and put the hand drier engineer in the hospital was in the soap," Mbeke said, "that blows your theory about Fuller being targeted specifically. Unless you've heard something from Witness Protection?"

"Still waiting for them to get back to me." Ingrid hated having to admit she didn't have the necessary intel. As soon as she got back to the embassy she'd insist Sol Franklin contact the US Marshals Service.

"So there's just as much chance that the hand drier man was the intended target. But still more likely that Fisher Krupps has been targeted in general."

"The maintenance engineer is still alive. Fuller's dead."

"That makes him unlucky, not a target."

The elevator doors opened and two smart suited young men stepped in. Ingrid made sure to drop her voice. "If it was the soap, then we have to assume the toxin was absorbed through the skin. Maybe that might speed up the process of identifying it."

"We'll hopefully find out more after the autopsy." Mbeke looked at the two men, obviously uncomfortable about discussing the case. He remained silent until the elevator doors opened again and they exited. "If it was in the soap, anyone could have been affected. Surely there would have been more casualties."

"Maybe not." Ingrid braced herself to ask an awkward question. "Tell me—and I really need you to answer honestly—do you wash your hands, with soap and all, every time you use the bathroom?"

Mbeke shifted his weight from one foot to the other. "Maybe not *every* time."

"Wennstein complained about tingling in his fingers after he went for a crap. I'm supposing he washed his hands. The maintenance guy would have gotten pretty dirty hands pulling apart a hand drier and reassembling it, so he must have used plenty of soap to clean up afterward."

"And Fuller? What possible reason would he have for being so meticulous about his hand hygiene?"

"That I haven't worked out yet."

"So either the hand drier engineer was the intended victim, or Fisher Krupps was targeted."

"Why remove the soap if someone wanted to do as much damage as possible?" Ingrid felt as if they were chasing around in circles, getting nowhere. "I guess you should look into the background of the maintenance guy. I feel bad calling him that all the time, what's his name?"

"Colin Stewart."

"So—a full profile of Stewart might help."

"I'll get one of the DCs onto it."

The elevator finally reached the lower ground floor. Ingrid followed Mbeke down a maze of corridors to a dimly lit room full of TV monitors, a different image of part of the building on each one. A uniformed guard was showing a plain clothes detective some footage.

"How's it going, Craig?" Mbeke asked the cop.

"Not sure we've got anything worthwhile yet."

"Can we take a look at the elevator footage between 10.20 and 10.50 a.m.?" Ingrid asked.

Rather than answering her, both the security guard and the detective looked at Mbeke for approval.

"In your own time," Mbeke said.

Within five minutes the appropriate footage was lined up on the monitor. The image was split in two—the left side showing footage for 'elevator north' and the right side displaying what was captured in 'elevator south'. All four of them crowded around the screen as the guard ran the recordings at eight times normal speed.

"Stop it there!" Ingrid said, after she saw a figure appear dressed in dark pants and the same color long-sleeved green tee shirt Patience Toure had been wearing, a baseball cap pulled low over his face. The still image on the left hand side of the screen clearly showed a bag shoved under the man's arm.

"Ten thirty-seven," the young constable read from the screen.

"Dammit—I might have been able to stop him." Ingrid shook her head. "You think it's Hernandez?"

Mbeke peered at the screen and shrugged.

"Outside agency staff are issued with temporary security passes," the guard told them. "So that means we don't have a photograph of him on the system."

"You can't see his face, anyway," Craig said.

"But it's enough to keep his place under surveillance?" Ingrid turned to Mbeke. He had already pulled out his cell phone.

"Just about to get that organized," he told her.

It seemed Miguel Hernandez had just switched from being a potential witness to a possible suspect.

TEN

Ingrid ducked out of the way, narrowly avoiding a group of three tottering women who had burst through the door of the tequila bar. She checked her watch. It was already a quarter after nine. Her friend was late, as usual. If Detective Inspector Natasha McKittrick didn't turn up in the next ten minutes, Ingrid would head for the Tube at Old Street. She'd already worked out her route: Northern Line to King's Cross then Circle or Metropolitan to Baker Street. Her hotel was five minutes away from Baker Street Tube. She moved a little further away from the door and, to keep her mind occupied, replayed the events of her day.

Before she'd left Fisher Krupps, she had discovered a few things that she wasn't sure helped the investigation into Matthew Fuller's death or hindered it. On the surface, DI Patrick Mbeke's request that she liaise more closely with his team should have been a good thing. Unfortunately, the reason for his sudden desire for cooperation didn't leave her feeling too confident that the case was in entirely safe hands. After he'd sent a surveillance team to Miguel Hernandez's apartment, Mbeke had taken her to one side for a private chat.

"I'd like you to be more hands on with the investigation," he'd said.

"Great—the Bureau will do everything we can to assist."

"Do you know how many murders there were in London last year?"

Ingrid saw the earnest look on his face and waited for him to tell her.

"Ninety-nine."

That seemed pretty low. She hoped he wasn't going to move on to a discussion about gun control. She preferred to avoid politics in the workplace at all costs. It only ever ended badly.

"Do you know how many of those were within the City of London?"

Again, Ingrid waited to be enlightened.

"Just one. And I didn't investigate it."

She wondered where the conversation was going.

"How many homicide investigations have you worked on?" he asked her.

"Really not that many. The cops only call in the Bureau under special circumstances."

"How many, ball park figure?"

"Twenty-five, thirty, maybe. I've been working in the Violent Crimes Against Children program the past three years. I haven't worked any murder cases there."

"This is my first. Same for DCI Simmons too."

At the time, Ingrid hadn't been able to understand Mbeke's sudden confessional mood. But now she'd had time to think about it, she supposed the reality of a potential suspect had brought his insecurities to the surface. She felt a little sorry for the guy. Their little tête-à-tête had been abruptly curtailed when the detective inspector took a call from the pathologist. As the EMTs had suspected, Matthew Fuller had died of a massive coronary. However, the pathologist's initial investigation had found no evidence of poisoning in Fuller's major organs. But they would know more tomorrow.

Ingrid checked her watch again. McKittrick had precisely three more minutes to make an appearance. She crossed the narrow cobbled street and took a good look at the exterior of the bar. Apparently, it had only opened the weekend before and had created quite a buzz. Ingrid had been reliably informed that it was situated in the 'Williamsburg of east London'. That was Williamsburg, New York, rather than Williamsburg, Virginia, she presumed. Even if it were true, she wasn't sure it was recommendation enough. She just hoped it sold a good range of tequilas. After her nights out with McKittrick, she was becoming quite a connoisseur.

"Hello!"

Ingrid turned to see her friend ambling toward her.

"You look vaguely suspicious loitering on the pavement like that," McKittrick said. "Different shoes and a short skirt and you might get arrested."

"That's hilarious." Ingrid grabbed McKittrick's arm and dragged her across the street. "Let's get inside, I'm really ready for a drink."

"I can't stay long."

"What?"

"Sorry—I've got more crap to deal with from Internal Investigations. They sprang a seven a.m. meeting on me just as I was leaving tonight. I've got to get to bed at a reasonable time. And I can't get too bladdered either."

Ingrid let her silence tell McKittrick how disappointed she was.

"I'm sorry OK? If it had been anything else I'd say sod it, let's party. But we are actually talking about my future career here."

"Are we?" Ingrid pushed open the door into the bar. Immediately the noise of dozens of excitable twenty-somethings swallowed up McKittrick's reply.

It took a full ten minutes to get served at the bar. After nine of those, Ingrid got so pissed off with the wait that she stooped to using what her dad was fond of calling her "feminine wiles" to jump to the front of the line. She felt a little pathetic, flirting her way to a jug of margarita and two large salt-rimmed glasses, but at least it got the job done.

"We're not doing shots then?" McKittrick sounded disappointed when Ingrid arrived at the table the detective had secured in a slightly quieter corner of the bar. Ingrid suspected McKittrick had used her warrant card to stake her claim to the bench and two stools.

"You said you didn't want to have a big night. Margarita is a good compromise." Ingrid found herself shouting against the din. Was she really so old the atmospheric trance track sounded more like noise than music? She hoped to hell she wasn't.

"There's big and there's enormous." McKittrick filled their glasses.

"So are you finally going to tell me what Internal Investigations are actually investigating?"

McKittrick shrugged. "It's just a pain in the arse. A suspect I arrested has made an allegation about me. Says I pocketed some of the drugs we recovered. Claims he saw me slip a few packs into a pocket before we bagged up the evidence."

"Why are your bosses taking him so seriously? Surely they won't believe his word against yours."

"They have to be seen to take every allegation seriously. The Met's had enough scandal to deal with lately, they can't take any chances."

"What was it? Cocaine? Heroin?"

"God no, just some prescription drugs—your usual range of uppers and downers. We weren't even arresting him for possession. He's an accessory in a murder investigation. The drugs were just a distraction."

"When will it all be over?"

"Tomorrow may be my final grilling before they finally accept my word over the scumbag's."

"I had no idea you were going through so much crap." Ingrid squeezed McKittrick's arm. "You should have told me."

McKittrick quickly pulled her arm away. "The irony is I've been clean for ages. I wouldn't have taken his poxy drugs if he'd paid me."

Ingrid stared into her friend's face, not sure how to take that last statement. McKittrick's expression was deadpan. The she smiled a little, a twinkle in her eyes.

"I'm kidding! God—you need to know when you're being wound up." She topped up Ingrid's glass. "Anyway—enough about me and my crap, how's your latest case going?" McKittrick quickly swiped a dish of tortillas from the tray of a passing waitress. Ingrid scowled at her. "I'm sure they're complimentary," McKittrick said. "They bloody well should be, upmarket place like this. Besides, I'm ravenous."

Ingrid quickly updated her with everything that had happened so far.

"And what's the DI like to work with?"

"He's fine. I get the impression he's feeling a little out of his depth."

"Well it's a bit beyond your average credit card fraud or case of embezzlement, isn't it? Out of his depth? I'm surprised the poor bugger's not drowning."

"It's his first homicide. Twelve years a cop and never seen a murdered body before."

"You need to be gentle with him, then." She wiped a little chili powder from the corners of her mouth.

"It's not my job to hold his hand."

McKittrick raised her eyebrows. "What's he look like? Is he fit?"

"Why are you even asking?"

"Might add a little more interest to the investigation."

"I'm engaged to Marshall."

"But he's over three thousand miles away. A bit of harmless fun while you're in London would hurt no one."

Ingrid lifted her glass to her face and swallowed a large mouthful of margarita before she felt able to comment. "I'm not about to betray Marshall's trust, how many times do I have to tell you? I still haven't forgiven you for trying to set me up with your DC."

"But Mills is practically besotted with you. I thought you might appreciate a little adulation."

"Well your little matchmaking exercise didn't work. We had a perfectly pleasant brunch and went our separate ways."

"What did you talk about, work?"

"Actually, I spoke a lot about Marshall."

"Well that explains Mills' stinking mood for the last week. You really know how to crush a bloke's dreams."

"I didn't want him to think I was... available."

"Well you've obviously made that quite clear."

Ingrid wasn't sure how the conversation had veered in this direction. She attempted to get it back to neutral territory. "From everything I've told you about the case, what's your hunch? An attack on Fisher Krupps or something more personal?"

McKittrick chewed thoughtfully on a nacho for a few moments before answering. "This Witness Protection fella... when did you say he entered the program?"

"Nineteen ninety-two."

"I bet you didn't share that particular nugget of information with Mbeke. Doesn't exactly promote your theory, does it? How likely would it be that someone would have been holding a grudge against him all these years?"

"It's not impossible."

"What about the engineer who's in the hospital? Would anyone want to target him?"

"We haven't uncovered any information to suggest that. I think the poor guy was just in the wrong place at the wrong time."

"Why would the toxin have affected the City trader so badly? Is it possible he had an undiagnosed heart condition?"

"I'm hoping the full autopsy report will offer some kind of explanation."

"And you're no nearer locating the missing cleaner?"

"Even his neighbors don't ever remember seeing the guy. Apart from the cleaning agency, no one seems to have heard of him."

"So he's got to be the prime suspect?"

"I'd put money on it."

"I never had you pegged as the gambling type."

"I'm not—I'm just so damn sure Hernandez has to be responsible."

McKittrick drained her glass and refilled it. "Enough shop talk. There must be something else we can discuss."

Ingrid raised her eyebrows.

"OK, OK, I realize we both have nothing else in our lives. What a couple of saddoes. It's what happens when you dedicate fifteen years of your life to the force."

"Fifteen? That beats my eight. I feel like an amateur in your company." Ingrid lifted a glass to her.

"And just you remember that—treat me with the respect a senior law enforcement officer deserves."

"Yes. Ma'am." Ingrid sat to attention.

"But don't take the piss."

"What made you join the police in the first place?"

"Oh God—that's far too boring a story."

"Try me."

McKittrick gulped another mouthful of margarita. "OK, the edited highlights: parents wanted me to be a lawyer—my dad's one—he works for good causes, you know, Amnesty International, Liberty, Reprieve. All a bit too worthy for my liking at the time—I decided I wanted to be the opposite of an idealist, whatever that's called, and I rebelled. I studied criminology at uni then went straight into Nottingham Police graduate scheme and got fast tracked. Never looked back." She was staring blank-eyed into her half-empty glass. "Your turn."

Ingrid got the impression McKittrick had edited the story just a little too rigorously, but the forlorn look on the detective's face warned her not to pry.

"Me… oh now that's too long a story. You said you needed to get home early."

"Just give me the headlines."

Ingrid could feel her nose tingling. She thought it might be the chili powder on the tortillas, but suspected it was the usual cause. She took a deep breath. "I lost someone close to me when I was a teenager. A schoolfriend. My best friend. After she went I promised I'd do everything I could to prevent what happened to her happening to any other fourteen-year-old girl. When it comes to clearing the filth of the streets, I guess I haven't even scraped the surface during my eight years as a Fed."

"She was murdered?"

"Abducted. Never found. The Bureau ran the investigation into her disappearance. But they came up with no leads at all in over eighteen months of searching. After three years they wound the case right down." She shoved a triangle of deep-fried corn into her mouth and started to chew slowly.

"Still hard to talk about?"

"Always—that's why I avoid the subject."

"And here I am asking you to rake over it." She filled Ingrid's glass. "Sometimes though, getting it out of your system is the best thing you can do."

"I was in therapy for years afterwards. Believe me, the only thing that made me feel better was being accepted into the Bureau Academy."

"Well here's to that achievement." McKittrick chinked glasses with her. "Just make sure tomorrow you kick arse with this new case of yours."

ELEVEN

Up a little later than usual the following morning, Ingrid tried to convince herself it wasn't the margaritas making her limbs feel sluggish and her head as thick as cotton, but the high dose of deep fried corn. Whatever the cause, she nevertheless forced herself to complete a three mile run, and felt a little better at the end of it. Skipping the strength and flexibility workout was her one concession to the factory of hammers pounding in her head.

When she reached her desk at the embassy, there was already a message waiting for her. She unstuck the Post-it from her computer monitor and tried to decipher Jennifer's handwriting. Jennifer herself was conspicuously absent. The new recruit, Isaac, was studying something intently on his computer screen in the far corner of the room.

"Hey, Isaac—you came back today, huh? We didn't scare you off."

"Good morning, Agent Skyberg—I'm sorry I didn't see you come in."

"Call me Ingrid." She wandered over to his desk.

"Sure."

"How did you enjoy the grand tour of the embassy yesterday?" she asked him.

Immediately he grew more animated and his eyes lit up. "It was awesome. I didn't realize there are actually *three* basements under the building. Have you seen the bunker?" He paused a beat then carried on without waiting for her reply. "Stupid question, of course you've seen it. Agent Franklin showed me this huge closet of canned and dried foods. It's got its own independent air and water supply too. I'm sure there must be preppers back home who'd go green with envy for all that stuff!"

Ingrid smiled at his enthusiasm. Hopefully the crushing reality of boring admin work wouldn't squeeze it out of him too fast.

"Then we went to visit the gym and the steam room," Isaac continued, almost sounding a little breathless, "Agent Franklin said I should ask Jennifer to organize a pass for me—he said I can use the facilities any time I want—even on the weekend."

"I'd give it a couple of days before you ask for that. Jennifer's a little busy doing work for me at the moment." Ingrid remembered just how pissed Jennifer had seemed at her own lack of training opportunities. No point in adding salt to the wound.

"Sure. OK. I don't use the gym much anyhow." Already a little of his enthusiasm seemed to have leaked out of him. "I'm worrying maybe I've upset Jennifer in some way. She was a little... distant with me yesterday."

"I'm sure she was just concentrating a little too hard on her work. Don't take it personally."

"OK." He sounded anything but convinced.

"Hey, how'd you like the view from the top floor?" she asked, hoping to get him a little excited again. It seemed to work.

"The views are amazing. You can pretty much see the whole of London from up there. Agent Franklin took me up onto the roof. The roof! I stood right next to the flag pole. I wanted to take a photograph, but Agent Franklin said it wouldn't be a good idea."

Ingrid felt a slight twinge of envy. Sol hadn't taken her onto the roof when she'd done the tour. Maybe he'd only recently added it to the itinerary—after all, it'd give him the excuse to smoke a cigarette. Sol rarely missed an opportunity to get a nicotine fix. "Sounds like you got the VIP tour," she said.

"I'm just so pleased to have the chance to work here. Let me know if there's anything I can do for you. I really want to help."

"I'll be sure to." Ingrid smiled at him and returned to her desk. She stared at the message Jennifer had written but was no nearer deciphering it.

The phone on Jennifer's desk started ringing. Isaac jumped out of his seat, eager as a puppy to do something useful. He reached the phone at the precise moment Jennifer reappeared. She threw him a glowering look. He backed off.

After Jennifer was finished with her phone call, Ingrid wandered over to her desk. She bent low and leaned in close to the clerk's ear. "I don't know what is going on with you and Isaac, but you need to get a grip. He's young, inexperienced. He needs our support. He's done nothing wrong."

"But I've been working here for two years and every request I've made for professional development has been denied."

"So you told me yesterday."

"You think I'm complaining too much?"

"You need to speak to human resources about training. If you need me to approve a request, I'd be happy to do that for you."

"You would?"

"Sure, but in the meantime, we've all got to get along, OK?"

Jennifer nodded reluctantly, still keeping her eyes trained on her new rival.

"Good." As Ingrid straightened up, something on the 24-hour news channel Jennifer had playing permanently in the corner of her monitor caught her eye. It was an artist's impression of a young woman with a ghostly pale face and a peculiar shade of red hair. Ingrid pointed at the player window. "Can you make that full screen and turn up the volume?" Jennifer's fingers flew over the keyboard and suddenly Ingrid was staring at a large portrait of the woman she'd seen two nights ago in Dulwich.

According to the reporter, the police were appealing for anyone who might know the identity of the victim of a vicious knife attack. The picture changed abruptly to show divers on a river police boat peering into a murky, churned up River Thames.

"What is it?" Jennifer was staring at Ingrid rather than the news report.

Isaac was hovering uncertainly next to Ingrid. "You know her?" he said tentatively.

Ingrid ignored their questions and grabbed her cell from her desk. She quickly punched in McKittrick's number and waited for the DI—who probably felt as hungover as she did—to pick up. Finally the detective answered, slightly out of breath. It was only at that moment Ingrid remembered McKittrick had an early morning meeting with Internal Investigations. "Can you speak?" Ingrid asked her.

"I'm out of the Spanish Inquisition, if that's what you mean."

Ingrid left the office and quickly explained both her trip to Dulwich on Monday night and what she'd just seen on TV.

"If you think it's her, why are you calling me and not the incident line?"

"I need you to check something for me. The woman I saw had a distinctive tattoo on her throat, in the shape of a crucifix."

"Where was she found? I need to know which murder investigation team to contact."

"In the river, beneath one of the bridges, London Bridge, maybe... I didn't catch it. The body had gotten tangled in some mooring chains of the boats there. According to the report, if it hadn't, it might not have shown up for weeks. Or ever. The body might have washed right out to sea, if the tide was moving in the right direction."

"Leave it with me. I'll see what I can find out."

Ingrid hung up and quickly called Marshall. It was early hours of the morning in D.C., but she figured this was something he should know about as soon as possible. He answered the phone with a mumble.

"It's me."

"Jesus! Honey!"

Ingrid heard the rustling of bedclothes.

"Is everything OK?" he asked.

"I'm fine. Sorry to wake you, but I thought you'd want to know. That address I checked out for you? I'm pretty sure the woman I met there has turned up dead."

There was a pause. Ingrid wondered if she should repeat what she'd just said. Was Marshall even properly awake? Finally he broke the silence. "How did she die?"

"Stabbed—I don't have all the details—I figured you'd want to know right away."

"How many stab wounds?"

"What's that got to do with anything?"

"How many?"

"I don't know, enough to be described as 'vicious'. Why is that important?"

"It's not our guy."

"How can you be so sure?"

"That's not his M.O., is all. He wouldn't kill in that way. It's not his style. He doesn't like to get his hands dirty."

"Maybe he's changed. Who is 'your guy' anyway? You didn't actually give me his name."

"It doesn't matter, because it's not him."

"Why won't you tell me?"

"Because it doesn't concern you." He let out an impatient breath. "Listen, I have to go. I have an important briefing this morning. I can't be late." He hung up.

Ingrid checked her watch and counted back. It was four-thirty a.m. on the East Coast. Any meeting Marshall had would be hours away. He was lying to her. He was notoriously bad at it. The question was, why? Why wouldn't he give her any information about the case? Her desk phone rang.

"Do you want me to get that?" Jennifer started to get up from her chair.

Ingrid held up a hand to stop her. "Agent Skyberg, US Embassy, Criminal Investigation Unit."

"Do you know, I didn't actually realize that's what your little outfit was called." The unmistakable tones of Angela Tate. "So, when are we going to fix up this interview?"

"Don't you have better things to do than harass me?"

"Harass? I haven't even started. It'd be much easier for you to give me what I want, believe me."

"And what is that? You still want to do this damn fool fly-on-the-wall thing?"

"It'll be fantastic, trust me."

"OK! Friday. Ten a.m. I'll meet you at the embassy gate."

"Fine."

"Good."

Ingrid slammed the phone down. It took her a few moments to realize the two clerks were staring at her. "What's the matter with you? Don't you have work to do?" Her cell phone started to buzz. She jumped up from her desk and answered the call outside in the corridor. "Hey, Natasha, that was quick. Does that mean there was a tattoo?"

"No."

"Oh." Ingrid had felt certain the portrait she'd seen on the news report was the cherry soda haired Latvian from Dulwich. "Are you sure?"

"Not at all."

"Wait a minute. Then what are you saying?"

"There was no tattoo on the victim's throat because there was no skin there either."

TWELVE

As soon as Ingrid ended the call from McKittrick, she tried Marshall again. This time her call went straight to voicemail. She cursed him silently and started back toward the office. If she just had the identity of the suspect he was monitoring, she could decide for herself how significant his M.O. was.

Jennifer and Isaac were both looking up at her expectantly when she entered the room.

"What's happened?" she asked them.

"Shouldn't you be leaving about now?" Jennifer said. She pointed to Ingrid's desk. "Kristin Floyd said she had a window between eleven and twelve." It's in my note.

Ingrid glanced down at the indecipherable scrawl and tried to remember who Kristin Floyd was. She wasn't sure it was a name she'd even heard before.

"Matthew Fuller's girlfriend—she's back in London. You wanted to speak to her. I arranged it for you yesterday evening."

"OK—thank you. Can you text me the address? Is it some place I'll be able to park the motorcycle?" She noticed Isaac had grabbed his jacket from the back of his chair.

"We're going on a bike? Awesome!"

What the hell was going on? "Wait a minute. *We* are going nowhere."

"Agent Franklin said I should accompany you the next time you interview someone. To use my victim support skills."

Ingrid vaguely remembered Sol mentioning it the day before. *Dammit.* Isaac's skills better be worth it. "Could you book me a car, Jennifer? I'd really appreciate it."

A half hour later they arrived at an upmarket glass and steel apartment block in Bankside, just a couple hundred yards from the Tate Modern art gallery.

"Do you want me to lead on this?" Isaac innocently asked Ingrid as they ascended the building in an external glass elevator.

"As it's your first case, why don't you just observe on this one? Let me do all the talking."

"But I really want to be able to help."

"Trust me, a sympathetic smile can make all the difference in the circumstances."

His shoulders slumped and he stuck his hands in his pockets. Ingrid wondered if he might sulk his way through the entire interview.

"This isn't about what we want. It's all about Kristin Floyd. We're putting her needs first, OK?"

He nodded his head rapidly and stood a little straighter. If he'd put up any kind of argument, Ingrid would have told him to go wait in the car.

The elevator arrived at the twenty-first floor and Ingrid straightened her jacket. She turned to Isaac. "Ready?"

"Sure."

They walked the length of a thickly carpeted corridor—it seemed more like the hallway of a five star hotel than an apartment block—and Ingrid leaned on the buzzer of apartment 210. The door opened right away, as if Kristin Floyd had been waiting just behind it for their arrival.

"Thank you for fitting in with my schedule," Fuller's girlfriend said. "It's much appreciated." Her accent was pure upstate New York.

Ingrid introduced herself and Isaac as she studied the woman's face. The eyes were red-rimmed, as were her nostrils. She wasn't wearing any make-up and her hair hung loose over her shoulders. It looked slightly damp from the shower.

Isaac stuck out his hand and said, "I'm so sorry for your loss."

Ingrid flinched a little.

"Thank you." Floyd closed the apartment door and led them down a wood-floored hallway to a large, light-filled living room. The room was sparsely furnished, just two couches, a low coffee table sitting on a ten feet by twelve cotton rug, and a large TV mounted on the wall.

"Do you mind if we speak outside?" the woman asked. "I need a little air." She grabbed a pack of cigarettes and a lighter from the coffee table and stepped outside onto a balcony that ran the length of the room.

By the time all three of them had settled themselves around a small circular aluminum café table, Floyd's cigarette was already an inch shorter.

"What is it you want to speak to me about?" Floyd's voice was steady, as was her gaze. She looked first at Ingrid, then glanced in Isaac's direction. Isaac wriggled back in the seat and sat a little taller, the sympathetic smile Ingrid had mentioned earlier plastered across his face.

"I'd like to get a little background on Matthew, if you feel strong enough to talk about him."

"Oh I'm plenty strong enough." Floyd raised an immaculately threaded eyebrow. "Ask me anything you need to. I want to help." She took a long drag on her cigarette. "Although I may not have all the answers."

Ingrid smiled gently at her. "We appreciate any help you can give us." She pulled out a notebook.

"Do you know how the police investigation is going? Have there been any threats toward Fisher Krupps?"

"I'm afraid I can't comment on the investigation. I only have an overview. I believe the police are making progress."

"Who would do a thing like that? Sick bastards."

"That's what the police hope to find out. I'm sure they will." She flicked through her notebook to a fresh page. "How long had you and Matthew been together?"

"Just over..." Floyd stopped and looked up toward the early May sky, fluffy white clouds skudded across the blue. "Eight months."

"So you knew him well?"

"Gosh, no, I wouldn't say that. I barely knew him at all."

Ingrid didn't comment, but leaned in a little closer.

"Matthew was a very private man." Floyd almost whispered the words. "He didn't even really open up to me. It frustrated the hell out of me. We fought about it sometimes." She took a long drag on her cigarette. "I guess I shouldn't say things about him like that. Makes me sound a little callous."

"Not at all." Ingrid tried a sympathetic smile of her own. "Did he speak about his family at all?"

"He doesn't have one."

"He doesn't?"

"Not much of one, anyway. He was an only child. His dad died when he was still at school. I guess he's still pretty close to his mom. Have you spoken to her?"

Ingrid couldn't admit they still hadn't tracked down contact details for the woman. "Not personally, no."

"She must be taking it so hard."

"You haven't spoken to her yourself?"

"I don't have her number. I've never met her. Matthew and I didn't really have a 'meet the folks' relationship."

"You weren't planning to make things more permanent?"

"Gosh no. We both knew it was a temporary thing that would end when one of us went back to the US. Or maybe even before." Her voice caught in her throat. "I guess that's exactly what's happened. Never thought it would be under these circumstances."

Ingrid paused a beat to allow Floyd to regain her composure. "So you hadn't considered moving in together while you were both based in London?"

"No way! I like my own space. Matthew likes…" She wriggled her shoulders as if she were trying to cast off an unwelcome arm. "I mean Matthew *liked* his."

"So you split your time between both apartments?"

Floyd hesitated. "Actually, you know, I don't think Matthew spent a single night here. We always went to his place."

Ingrid jotted down a few notes. "Would you say that Matthew was happy at work?"

"I guess. He was quite driven. You have to be in our business. It's not for the faint-hearted." She stubbed out her cigarette into a dirty saucer on the table. "I'm so sorry—I haven't offered you anything. Would you like tea or coffee?"

"We're fine, thank you."

Floyd lit another cigarette. "What was I saying?"

"You were telling me how driven Matthew was."

"He worked so damn hard. He never really relaxed. He was always twitchy about something. I guess that was all part of his condition."

Ingrid tensed. "His condition?"

"The anxiety and all." She drew on her cigarette and slowly exhaled. "You don't know about it?"

Ingrid said nothing.

"But then, how could you? I only know because I stayed over at his apartment. He kept the whole thing very private. Made me promise I'd never tell anyone. I guess that doesn't matter now."

"What condition did Matthew have?"

"General anxiety disorder. He's had it ever since his dad died. He took it really badly. The OCD was Matthew's coping mechanism."

"He was suffering from obsessive-compulsive disorder?"

Floyd nodded and took another puff on her cigarette. "He was a complete control freak. Everything had to be just the way he liked it. I have to admit—it drove me crazy. My place was way too messy for him. Everything had to be super neat and clean. Like, for example, the towels in his bathroom were always perfectly folded, all facing the same way. Same for the crockery in the kitchen cabinets, all had to point to the left. Or was it the right? Jesus—you'd think I'd remember, he drummed it into me so often." She turned her head and stared toward an oblique view of the Thames. "I'd always get it wrong. And if I ever used any of the special cream he had for his hands…" She shook her head. "Listen to me, bitching about his OCD. What kind of person am I?"

"Tell me about the hand cream."

"It was perfume-free, had extra vitamin E in it. He hands used to get so raw."

"Raw?"

"He washed them over and over. I think maybe he counted how many times. If I ever interrupted him, he'd have to start over. I learned not to interrupt pretty quickly." She let out a shaky breath.

"How did he manage to keep the hand washing thing a secret at work?"

"He learned to be strategic about it."

"But he'd still wash his hands many, many times?"

"He didn't have a choice. Poor bastard."

Ingrid stood up. "Would you excuse me a moment—I need to make phone call."

"What did I say?"

"It's OK. Nothing to worry about." Ingrid shot Isaac an encouraging look before she went back inside the apartment. She hoped he understood now was the time to put his recently acquired victim support skills to good use. He nodded back at her. Ingrid quickly found Mbeke's number in her contact list.

"I don't have any new developments to report. I'd call you straightaway if I did, I hope you know that."

"Sure, sure. Listen, something came up I thought you should know about. I think maybe Matthew Fuller might have been the intended target."

"You've heard from Witness Protection?"

"No—I've just been speaking to Fuller's girlfriend. She told me Fuller had OCD—one of the ways it manifested was in repeated hand washing. We're talking dozens of times every time he visited the bathroom.

"Which is why the toxin affected him so much more than anyone else?"

"It's what I'm thinking. Say he was the intended target. The killer hangs around, watches Fuller die. Then removes the evidence from the restroom, having done what he intended to do."

"Doesn't explain the delay. Fuller died approximately 9.25 a.m. Colin Stewart was taken ill over forty minutes later. Why leave the soap around to do collateral damage once the job was done?"

"Like I said before, maybe the killer doesn't care about collateral damage."

"Like some kind of sadist?"

"I couldn't possibly make that kind of judgement."

"But it's what you're thinking."

"I'm thinking we're dealing with a sick bastard who needs to be tracked down as soon as possible." Another thought occurred to Ingrid. "If Fuller was the target, the killer had to know about Fuller's OCD. According to his girlfriend, no one knew except her."

"So?"

"So Hernandez—let's just agree for the sake of argument right now he's the most likely suspect—must have been observing him closely. He must have been working in the bank planning his move for weeks or maybe even months. This had to be a meticulously prepared attack."

THIRTEEN

The morgue in Westminster wasn't open by the time Ingrid arrived there early the next morning. She'd decided to walk from Marylebone to Horseferry Road through the back streets, feeling a need to clear her head and work through some of the frustration she felt.

After she'd gotten off the phone from Mbeke the day before and wrapped up the interview with Kristin Floyd, Ingrid had returned to the embassy and gone on a hunt for Sol Franklin. She still hadn't managed to have a conversation with him about contacting Witness Protection and forcing them to reveal the details of Matthew Fuller's former identity. In the end she'd had to settle for leaving a longwinded voice message for him, justifying her request as well as she could. He hadn't gotten back to her before she left the embassy for the night. DI Mbeke had, however, and the news he had to share didn't give her much hope they would ever track down Miguel Hernandez. The officers staking out his apartment finally managed to track down one of the property's occupants only to discover that Hernandez didn't live there and never had. At least not for the last five years. The tenant's story was confirmed by the landlord of the property. It seemed Hernandez, or whatever his real name was, had given the cleaning agency a false address.

Ingrid sat down on a wall outside the main entrance of Westminster Public Mortuary and waited, driving herself crazy mulling over the facts of the case and getting nowhere. On the stroke of eight-thirty, she jumped off the wall and banged on the main door until the woman on reception begrudgingly opened up.

"I have an appointment with Jeremy Moorecroft. I spoke to him yesterday. I'm here to see a Jane Doe."

"Jeremy's not in today."

"What?"

"Are you Ingrid?"

Ingrid nodded.

"The pathologist's agreed to see you herself. Take a seat."

Five minutes later, a man emerged from an interior doorway. He was dressed in a dark suit, his tie a little skewed, his top button undone. His face was sweaty and blotchy. He seemed harassed. Ingrid had been expecting to be greeted by a woman in scrubs and rubber boots. "Ingrid Skyberg?" He held out his hand. "I'm Detective Constable Fraser. I'm working on the Jane Doe case."

Ingrid shook his hand.

"I believe you might be able to tell us something about the victim?" he said.

"Only if I can positively ID her. I won't be able to do that until I've seen her."

"No—of course not. Suppose we should get on with it then." He seemed decidedly reluctant to move.

"Shall we?"

She followed Fraser down a series of featureless corridors, each one looking identical to the last, until they finally reached a set of transparent swing doors.

"God, I really hate this part of the job," the detective said. "Never gets any easier, does it?" He screwed up his face as he applied some sort of menthol rub to his nostrils. That approach didn't work for Ingrid. The menthol made her feel more nauseous than the smell of dead flesh and formaldehyde.

He pushed open one of the doors and stood to one side. "After you."

The examining room was like every other she'd ever seen, on the other side of the Atlantic or this. White tile floor, blinding overhead lights, lots of stainless steel. The body was laid on a steel table, uncovered. Even from just inside the door, Ingrid could tell it was the woman she'd met on Monday night. The build was identical, same weight, same height. Plus there was the wild cherry-colored hair. There could be no mistaking that. Ingrid ventured closer to the examining table. A woman appeared from a side door. She was wearing scrubs and rubber boots. She pulled on a pair of nitrile gloves.

"Ruth Freeman. I won't shake your hand." She gave Ingrid a tight little smile. "Would you like to take a closer look?"

Ingrid managed to swallow the saliva that had gathered under her tongue. She joined the pathologist next to the body and saw the cadaver's face for the first time. It was a mess.

"The killer has—rather clumsily, I'm afraid—removed any identifying features. The teeth have been smashed, the pads of her fingers sliced off… and of course, so has the skin around the neck and upper chest. Frankly someone's butchered her to remove any identifying features. Mercifully, post-mortem."

"Is this the woman you met?" The detective constable was staying close to the door, his face had already gone a little green.

"I'm pretty sure it is. Yes."

"How sure?"

Ingrid stared at the halo of red hair, then down the pale arms toward the mutilated hands. "I'd be prepared to testify to it in a court of law. Will that do?"

"But you don't know her name, is that right?" Fraser said from the other side of the room.

"I know where she lived before she died. I guess that's somewhere for you to start."

"It's more than we had five minutes ago. Is there anything else you can tell me? Anything at all?" The detective had retrieved a note book from his pocket.

"She's Latvian. I'm pretty sure. I have a good ear for accents. Especially former Soviet ones." She was transfixed by the synthetic color of the woman's hair. It looked even brighter now under the harsh light of the autopsy room.

"And what's your connection with this woman?"

Ingrid hesitated. She thought it wise to be as vague as possible. Marshall wasn't answering her calls and until she had more information about the watch list and who it was Marshall was actually monitoring, she should tell the local cops as little as possible. "Following up on an unrelated case. An FBI matter."

The pathologist cleared her throat. "If you're finished with me… and her, perhaps you could continue your conversation outside? I do have a lot of bodies to get through."

"About the skin on her neck that was removed," Ingrid said. "She had a tattoo of a crucifix on the left hand side."

"As I said, the killer wanted to remove all identifying marks."

"Sure, I get that. I was just wondering how… professional the work was. You said he butchered her, but do you think it's possible this killer knows how to use a knife?"

"Judging by the untidy nature of the incisions, he's not been medically trained. Or if he has, he was in one hell of a hurry."

"Time of death?"

"Some time between midnight and four on Tuesday morning."

Ingrid took a moment to let that information sink in. The woman was killed just a few hours after she'd seen her.

"That it?" The pathologist looked from Ingrid to Fraser.

"Sure, thank you for your time," Ingrid said.

The pathologist gave Ingrid a nod, one seasoned professional to another, and covered the Latvian's body with a green cotton sheet.

DC Fraser swallowed noisily. "Thanks, Professor Freeman." He was out the door before the pathologist could respond. In the corridor, Ingrid found him leaning up against a wall taking deep breaths.

"Tough, huh?" she said and gave him a sympathetic smile.

"Always." He unwrapped a stick of gum and popped it in his mouth, without offering her any. "So, all I need from you is the deceased's address and I won't take up any more of your time."

Ingrid stared at the cop, his pen poised over his notebook. The green hue had left his face and the red blotchiness had returned. She hesitated. She couldn't help but feel some sense of connection with the woman lying on the cold metal table not twenty feet away. To this cop, she was just another corpse. An immigrant at that. Ingrid suddenly felt the need to protect her. From God only knew what. She couldn't just walk away. Besides, she still wasn't convinced her death wasn't connected to the man Marshall was pursuing. She must have hung up after being transferred to his voicemail over a half dozen times. Why was he ignoring her calls? The more he did, the more curious about the case she became. She was aware the cop had started tapping his pen against his notebook.

"Don't you have it written down somewhere?" he said. "In your phone, maybe?" He was getting visibly frustrated with her—the red blotches had joined up to form an angry flush.

"I want to be there," she said.

"What?"

"When you search the apartment. I want to be there."

"I don't think that's something the boss would go for. I'm sorry."

"Why don't you ask him or her?"

"Are you refusing to give me the address?"

"Not at all—I'm making a friendly request to observe the search—one cop to another."

Ingrid could see the muscles in Fraser's face working overtime as he chewed his gum and considered her request.

"If it's something you can't agree to yourself, maybe I should talk to the SIO myself? Or maybe get my superior at the embassy to do that. It's completely up to you." She smiled sweetly at him.

FOURTEEN

Walking up and down the driveway of the house in Dulwich, phone pressed hard against her ear, Ingrid listened to Marshall's outgoing voicemail message. Again. This time she'd decided not to hang up in frustration, but actually leave him a message.

"Hey… honey, it's me. I have some news on your watch list guy… maybe. Give me a call when you get this." She hung up and shuffled sideways to allow a pair of white suited CSIs to get past. More CSIs were heading in her direction, so she moved to the edge of the police cordon, the blue and white tape fluttering against the brick wall separating the front yard from the sidewalk. The senior investigating officer hadn't said more than a few words to her since he'd arrived. Ingrid had the distinct impression he resented her presence and wasn't afraid to show it. From her marginal position at the edge of the cordon, Ingrid looked up and down the street. Uniformed officers were conducting house to house inquiries. Tedious, but necessary work. She didn't envy them. One cop was standing on the path of the house next door, looking up at the second floor windows.

A car pulled into the curb on the other side of the road. Detective Constable Fraser climbed out. He spent a few moments talking to a uniformed officer then hurried across the street. Ingrid met him at the front gate. "Good morning, detective. Thank you so much for arranging this."

"No worries. We like to help out our American cousins." He gave her an insincere smile. He hadn't been too keen to help her a couple of hours ago.

"That's good to know. What have you managed to find out about the occupants?"

"I'm not sure I can discuss that with you, not before I've okayed it with the boss." He stuck his chin out defiantly.

"Oh come on—you and I are both foot soldiers. We both know what it's like. We do all the legwork while the superior officers get the credit. Surely sharing a little intel wouldn't hurt any."

The detective looked toward the house. Another two CSIs were just emerging from the front door. As far as Ingrid could see, they always moved around in pairs.

Fraser ran his pale tongue over his bottom lip. "I suppose you'll find out anyway," he said, grudgingly. "The property is owned by a private company that's registered overseas. We haven't been able to contact the directors of the company."

"But you have names for them?"

"And we have phone numbers and a P.O. Box. The phones have either been disconnected or they weren't valid numbers to start with."

"You think the owners were living here?"

"No—the property is let via a lettings agency. An online one. There's no local lettings agent to talk to about the flat, unfortunately."

"Have you managed to speak to anyone from the agency yet?"

"They said they never met the tenant. The whole thing was done via the internet."

"Isn't that a little risky? What if tenants didn't pay the rent, or trashed the place?"

"Didn't seem to bother them. But then it's not their flat, is it?"

"So you must have a name for the person the apartment was let to?" Ingrid wondered whether Fraser was telling her the whole truth or keeping something back. Had he really uncovered so little intel?

Fraser peered at a notebook. "Abdul Al-Ala Shehadeh. He's on their books as the tenant. He's been paying the rent regularly, but not always on time." He had a little trouble pronouncing the name. Ingrid repeated it, putting the stresses on the correct syllables.

"Yeah—that's what I said, didn't I?"

"So you think he may have sublet the apartment to our victim? Or maybe they lived there together?"

Fraser glanced toward the house.

"Come on—foot soldiers, remember?"

"I've got absolutely no idea. All I know is, a Latvian name hasn't cropped up on any official documents so far."

"So you're no nearer finding out her identity?"

"It's early days. The name on the tenancy agreement hasn't popped up anywhere else yet either: you know local doctors' surgery, dentist, that kind of thing. But it's not as if we've completed a comprehensive trawl. I do know the registered council tax payer for the property is the same overseas company that owns the flat."

"What about the neighbors? Do they know if there was a man living at the property? Do they know the victim's name? What she did for a living?"

"No one's mentioned a man as yet. And nobody seems to know very much about the victim. But again—we haven't completed our house to house inquiries." He folded his arms across his chest defensively. "You still haven't told me why the FBI is so interested in this case."

"I can't go into the details with you."

"I thought we were both foot soldiers. I've got to tell my DCI something."

"Why don't you leave that with me? The embassy will square everything with your boss. Or, most likely, your boss's boss."

Fraser raised his eyebrows.

"Standard procedure."

"If you say so."

Ingrid watched another CSI lingering just inside the front door of the building. This one was on his own. The man looked exhausted.

"Look—I've got to go," Fraser said. "I need to report back to the DCI."

"Any chance I could take a look inside?"

"I'll ask him, but I wouldn't get your hopes up."

She watched Fraser stride toward the front door. He reached it just as the CSI was coming out. The man in the Tyvek suit snapped off his gloves and shoved them into a large plastic trash can standing on the driveway. Ingrid wandered over to him. "Tough gig, huh?" she said.

"Bloody impossible."

"Really?"

He stepped back and studied her face. "Shit. You're not a reporter are you?"

She showed him her badge.

"You're a long way from home."

"I work out of the American embassy here in London."

"Why are you here? There's no US connection, as far as I know."

"It's a long story—I won't bore you with it." She flashed him a big smile and he seemed to relax a little. "Any signs of a man having lived there?"

"Not as far as I can see, but there's very little of anything. Place is practically empty."

"It is?"

He put his hands on his hips and leaned back, stretching his spine. "Looks like whoever was living there has moved out."

"That must have happened pretty fast. I was here Monday night. I didn't see any packing cases."

The CSI shrugged at her.

"According to the pathologist, the woman died some time in the early hours of Tuesday morning. There's no way she could have packed up all her stuff."

"Maybe the dead woman they dragged out of the Thames didn't live here. Maybe this is all a waste of bloody time."

"No—it was definitely her. I'm certain."

"Well then, I've got another puzzle for you." He leaned his neck one way then the other before he spoke again. "We're getting no samples at all. Not a single one."

"What have you been looking for, specifically?"

"No—I mean no samples *at all*. Of anything. No hairs, no fingerprints, no clothing fibers, nothing."

"How can that be?"

"Exactly what I've been thinking. If this place was where the victim was living, she not only found the time to pack up and remove all her stuff before she copped it, but also managed to arrange for the whole flat to be industrially deep-cleaned."

FIFTEEN

After a rushed sandwich she'd picked up from a Brooklyn-style hipster deli in Dulwich, Ingrid returned to Grosvenor Square. It wasn't until she'd reached her desk and smelled the delicious aroma emanating from Jennifer's desk that she remembered the clerk had told her about the fabulous new menu in the embassy cafeteria.

"What is that?" Ingrid pointed to the steaming bowl.

"I'm sorry—I should have eaten downstairs, but I've got such a lot of stuff to do, I thought I'd work straight through."

"I was admiring it, not criticizing your eating habits."

"It's a vegan pad thai. Organic tofu."

Ingrid screwed up her nose.

"That's not as bad as it sounds. And it tastes as good as it smells." She lifted a spoon toward Ingrid's face. "Wanna try?"

"I'm good—thanks. Is Isaac around? I asked him to do a little research for me."

"I haven't seen him in a while."

"Never mind, I'll catch him later." Her cell started to buzz. Out of area. She hurried out the office and answered the call. "Hey—what the hell happened to you?"

There was a long pause at the other end of the line.

"I've been in the middle of a special operation," Marshall said. "Complete communications blackout."

"Did you even listen to the messages I left you?"

"Just about to. Is something wrong? Are you OK?" His concern sounded sincere. But she could hear the tapping of computer keys in the background. Was he attempting to multi-task?

"I want you to tell me about the guy whose bank account is on the watch list."

"I can't believe you're still talking about that. I told you to drop it." He said something away from the phone. It sounded like he was giving someone his breakfast order.

"Where are you?"

"At the office."

Ingrid distinctly heard the rattle of cutlery and clatter of dishes. "Sounds like you're in a diner."

"Nope. At my desk, working hard." Lying again, badly.

"What's this guy suspected of doing? You still haven't told me."

"It's not important—come on, you said some Latvian woman lived at the address."

"I ID'd her at the morgue."

"You did what? Why are you getting involved?"

"A watch list bank account was accessed from her address, is that reason enough? I don't understand why you're not interested."

Marshall let out a long sigh. "This is strictly between you and me, honey, OK?"

That depended on what he was about to tell her. She made a non-committal 'hmm mmm' sound.

"Lately I've been monitoring a whole heap of watch lists, keeping my eyes and ears open. You never know when you might stumble over something—a quick win. Something to impress the bosses with the minimum amount of effort from yours truly. This was just another example where I got zero results. Happens practically every day. I'm sorry I dragged you into it."

"I wouldn't call a woman's mutilated body a zero result. She went on to describe exactly what she'd seen in the morgue

92

in graphic detail. She pictured Marshall sending his pancake stack and rashers of bacon back to the kitchen.

"But our guy didn't kill her. That's just not his style." It sounded as if he were speaking with his mouth full. "He's not a butcher. I told you—he doesn't like to get his hands dirty."

"Don't you think that the whole thing is way too coincidental? The bank account is accessed by Jane Doe and just forty-eight hours later she's found dead, all identifying marks removed?"

"She must have just been a scammer who stumbled on one of our monitored accounts. You know as well as I do those people keep pretty bad company. I hate to repeat myself, but whoever was responsible for her death, it wasn't our guy." He gulped down some liquid then tried to suppress a belch. "I appreciate your trying to help me, but really, all it's doing is wasting my time."

"Oh really?"

"I'm sorry, honey. That came out all wrong."

"OK—I won't waste another precious second—just tell me his name and I'll do a little digging of my own." Ingrid had marched all the way to the rear of the building and along the main corridor, her pace increasing the madder she got at Marshall. Now she was so pissed at him she wanted to punch something.

"Listen, honey, why don't you just leave the investigation into the Jane Doe's murder to the local cops? It's not FBI business."

"You can't know that for sure. Where's the harm in my pursuing it?" She reached the end of the corridor and started to head back toward the office.

"If you find anything pertinent, you will let me know?"

"Sure—I wouldn't leave you out of the loop, Marsh. We're a team, huh?"

He blew out a noisy breath and mumbled something inaudible. "OK—it's Darryl Wyatt. But don't complain to me when you find out how totally wrong you are."

"What did he do?"

"He murdered a woman in a restaurant in Savannah, Georgia."

"If he doesn't like to get his hands dirty, how did he kill her? What is his M.O.?"

"Our guy's a poisoner."

SIXTEEN

Ingrid pulled up sharply. "Poisoner?"

"Yes—that's what I said—not some knife wielding maniac."

"What kind of poison did he use?"

"I really don't have time for this—check out the details for yourself."

"Please, Marshall, just tell me—"

A fraction of a second later, the disconnected tone bleeped in her ear. He'd hung up on her.

Really?

She was just about to call him back when she thought better of it. Damn Marshall and his 'quick win' watch lists. She'd just have to work this case without any help from him.

A poisoner. What if Darryl Wyatt *was* right here in London? What if the Latvian had gotten too close to discovering his true identity and he'd had to kill her to eradicate the threat. Was it possible he'd had something to do with Matthew Fuller's death?

She started to run.

Ingrid quickly reached the office and hurried to her desk, aware her speed had aroused the interest of both Jennifer and Isaac.

"Is there something wrong?" Jennifer asked.

"Nope. Everything's just fine," Ingrid snapped back at her. She'd been more curt than she'd meant. "Sorry, Jennifer, just really busy right now."

"Can I help at all?"

"I'll be sure to holler when you can."

The clerk shrugged her shoulders a little theatrically and went back to her computer. Ingrid fired up her own desktop PC and waited for long agonizing seconds while the machine went through the slow start-up routine. Then she logged into the main FBI database and tapped Darryl Wyatt's name into the search box. Three records came up for that name, but only one was a murder suspect last seen in Savannah. Ingrid quickly scanned the information for the name and contact details of the investigating detective. She could read plenty of dry facts on the database, but they would constitute just a fraction of the intel gathered by the team on the ground. Only the barest details would have been keyed into the database—Ingrid hadn't met a cop or a Fed yet who enjoyed typing.

A few moments later Ingrid was on hold at Savannah-Chatham Police Department, waiting to be put through to a Detective Trooe. When he finally took the call, Ingrid quickly introduced herself and told the detective what she was calling about.

"The peanut poisoner?" Trooe said as soon as she'd finished. His voice was rich and deep and strangely comforting.

"I'm sorry?"

"Darryl Wyatt, right?"

"I know practically nothing about the case. I was hoping you could enlighten me. Do you have the time right now?"

"Sure. Hang on a second."

Ingrid heard the sound of the receiver clunking down onto a hard surface, then a door close, then the creak of a leather chair. While she was waiting, she scrolled through the records on the database until she found a photograph of Darryl Wyatt.

"That's better," Trooe said, "a little quieter."

"We have a picture of him here," Ingrid said. "It's a little indistinct, but Wyatt is white, thirty-three years of age, dark hair, with a beard. Is that right?"

"I can send you through a better photograph than that. Sounds as though you're looking at his drivers' license picture."

"Just now... you called Wyatt—"

"The peanut poisoner. That's what he did—he killed that poor lady by feeding her peanuts. She had a real bad allergy."

Ingrid felt a sudden sense of disappointment. It seemed Wyatt wasn't quite the 'poisoner' Marshall had suggested. "He hasn't poisoned anyone else?"

"Not as far as we know." The leather chair creaked a little more. "So, you think Wyatt is in London?"

"That's what I'm trying to find out. How well do you remember the case?"

"Oh it's crystal clear. It was only twelve months ago."

With his slow southern drawl, Ingrid wasn't sure whether Detective Trooe was being sarcastic. "I guess you've investigated plenty of other homicides since then?"

"A few, but nothing like this one. This one kinda sticks in the memory."

"Can you go through the highlights for me?"

"I guess you like using the computer about as much as I do, huh?"

"You can give me the background I won't find in the official records."

"I sure can. Where do you want to start?"

"Tell me everything you can about Darryl Wyatt."

She heard the detective sniff. "That particular request won't take real long to answer. He was using a false identity. The ID of a dead man. I can't tell you a whole lot about him. He did have a girlfriend while he was working at the restaurant, he was dating the restaurant manager. I can give you her contact details when we're through, if you want."

"That'd be really helpful." Ingrid wriggled into her chair, it felt like she might be in for a long session. "He worked at the restaurant where the woman died?"

"He was the maitre d', had the job there for a couple months before he made his move." There was a clunk and a buzzing on the line for a few moments. "Tell me your email address, I'll send you the photograph we have of Wyatt that his girlfriend gave us."

Ingrid spelled out the address. "So Wyatt was early thirties, white... dark or fair skinned?"

"Depends how much time he spent in the sun I guess. See for yourself when the picture comes through. He was a little under six feet tall, medium build, maybe even a little athletic, if you're talking tennis player rather than football." He made a sound as if he were sucking his teeth.

"That's it?"

"Real charming with the ladies, by all accounts. He had good dental work, they all seemed to remember."

"Any distinguishing features?"

"He did as a matter of fact. Something only the girlfriend reported—a tattoo on his left forearm."

"Of what?"

"A dark red rose with the word 'MOM' written across it."

Ingrid sketched something similar in her notebook. "Sentimental."

"Not a word I'd use to describe him."

"What was his connection to the victim? Why did he want her dead?"

"We just don't know enough about the guy to work it out. Mind you, Mrs Highsmith musta made plenty of enemies over the years." He sniffed again. "You really haven't looked at the details on file at all, have you?"

"I'm sorry. I guess I was a little eager."

"I'm just joking with you, I'd do exactly the same thing in your position."

"Thanks for being so accommodating. Why did she have so many enemies?"

"Barbara Highsmith was a congresswoman for Georgia. Not when she died, she didn't get re-elected a second time, but before she was elected to the House, she was the District Attorney here. Any number of disgruntled convicts or disappointed voters could have been lining up to take potshots at her."

"Can there be any doubt that Wyatt was responsible for her death?"

"Only three people in the restaurant knew about the allergy: the chef, the restaurant manager and the maitre d'. We interviewed the chef and the manager extensively. We couldn't interview Wyatt because he skipped town right after she was killed."

"Maybe he left for some other reason."

"Highsmith carried around two of those special auto-injectors—just in case she came into contact with peanuts accidentally. She kept both of them in her purse. Her purse never left her side. Except on that day. A number of witnesses confirmed they saw Wyatt remove the purse from under her table. They thought nothing of it at the time. They just assumed he was taking it to the cloakroom. The purse was never found."

"How soon did he leave? Did he stay to watch her die?"

"The sick bastard sure did. While everyone else was screaming for help, looking for the missing purse, calling 9-1-1, he just stood there and watched while she gasped her last breath."

"What did you find at his address when you searched it?"

"The address he gave the restaurant was fake. Just like every other piece of information they had about him. We couldn't track down an address for him hard as we tried. It was as if he didn't really exist. The whole thing musta taken some careful planning." The creaking leather noise sounded again, louder than before. "Listen, I've got a briefing I got to be at in precisely two minutes."

"Thanks for your time, detective. Would it be OK if we spoke again later?"

"Sure. And the name's Carl. I'll send over the girlfriend's details."

Ingrid put down the phone and sank back in her seat, thinking about what she'd just learned. Wyatt was a poisoner who was aware of a weakness in his victim that wasn't widely known. He used that vulnerability to kill her. Matthew Fuller had kept his OCD and excessive hand washing secret. Very few people knew about his vulnerability.

The similarity between the Highsmith and Fuller cases might be slight, but too significant to ignore. Now more than ever she had to know who had wanted Matthew Fuller dead. And the best place to start was Witness Protection. For any hope of success she'd have to bring in the big guns.

She grabbed her cell from the desk and ran out of the office.

SEVENTEEN

Ingrid reached Sol's office to discover it was empty. There was no sign of his cigarettes on the desk, so she guessed he was out back in the embassy compound getting his nicotine fix. She headed back downstairs.

Sure enough, she found Sol standing on his own, keeping his distance from a nearby group of kitchen and janitorial staff. It wasn't like Sol to act so aloof, he could talk to anyone about pretty much anything. Then she saw the reason for his enforced isolation. He had a wire trailing from his ear to his cell phone. He obviously didn't want anyone to overhear his conversation. As Ingrid approached, she noticed he was nodding every few seconds, but not saying anything. She supposed it was another conference call. He seemed to be spending more and more time on trans-Atlantic calls and less and less managing his agents. Ingrid wondered idly why the big cheeses in D.C. were so interested in the Bureau's International Program and whether it might have any impact on her own work. She sure as hell hoped it wouldn't.

When he saw her, Sol held up a finger, then hit a button on his cell.

"Bureaucratic bullshit," he said, and smiled at her. "Hey, I hope you're getting excited about dinner at chez moi?"

"What?"

"I thought it'd be a chance for Isaac to get to know you a little, outside the office environment. I get the impression he looks up to you."

Ingrid had been forced to endure Mrs Franklin's cooking shortly after she'd started working at the embassy. She wasn't keen to repeat the experience. "I think I'm busy that night."

"I haven't even finalized a date yet. Tell me when you're free and we'll work around your... commitments." Sol knew very well that her social engagements were few and far between. She was more likely to be at her desk than anywhere else most nights. He had her. There was no way she could politely back out now.

"This week is completely full. What about next month?"

"It's a welcome to the embassy dinner for Isaac, don't you think next month may be a little late?" Before she could answer, Sol held up his finger again. He un-muted the phone, said, "I couldn't agree more, Jason." Then hit the mute button again.

"You're listening to them and me at the same time?"

"Incredible, isn't it? Multitasking, huh? Meanwhile you still haven't come up with an excuse to wriggle out of your dinner date."

"Monday!" she said without thinking.

"Good. I'll tell Maddy. She'll make us a feast."

That was exactly what Ingrid was afraid of.

"What can I do for you?" Sol asked.

"You listened to the message I left you about my new case?"

"The dead trader?"

"I need you to try again with Witness Protection."

Sol pulled a pained face then shook his head. "I'm sorry—I just can't. They're acting completely within their remit. If they responded to every request for information, they wouldn't be doing a real good job of protecting their witnesses, now would they? The system works—let's not screw with it."

"Did you even speak to them yet?"

"I didn't think it was appropriate."

"You might have let me know."

"I'm telling you now."

"But Fuller is already dead. His dad's dead. He didn't have any siblings. There's no one to protect except his mother."

"Doesn't she deserve protecting?"

"Oh come on, Sol. You know what I mean."

"I'd look for a motive for his murder a little closer to home if I were you. Dig a little into Matthew Fuller's life here. Something that happened to his family when he was a small child isn't likely to have come back to haunt him so many years later."

"But he's been here less than a year. How likely do you think it is he's crossed someone so badly they'd want him dead?"

"Hey—he's a City trader. They can't go anywhere without crossing somebody. And according to your message, the local cops still haven't ruled out the possibility that the attack was on the bank rather than specific employees."

"Only officially—that's just a political exercise to make Fisher Krupps feel as if they're taking a potential threat seriously. There's been absolutely no intel on possible extremists targeting the bank. It seems the toxic substance was removed shortly after Fuller's death. How does that square with doing as much damage as possible to Fisher Krupps?"

"But isn't that scenario still much more likely than someone from Matthew Fuller's dim and distant past coming all the way to London to kill him?"

For a moment Ingrid considered mentioning a possible link between Fuller's death and the murder of the ex-congresswoman in Georgia. But she knew the similarities between the two cases weren't strong enough to convince Sol of any connection. He'd just tell her to dig up more intel.

A first few drops of rain started to fall, fat and heavy. Sol pulled up his collar and sucked on his cigarette.

"You'll catch pneumonia," Ingrid told him, and realized she must have sounded just like his wife.

"Don't worry about me—I've located myself a quiet little closet inside the building that's warm and dry. No smoke detectors, no nicotine police. This turns into a downpour, I can still carry on smoking."

"Maybe the rain is a sign you should stop."

"Oh sure. If I didn't smoke, I'd never be able to get through these interminable conference calls."

"Fine, you carry on." Ingrid held up both hands in surrender, said goodbye and returned to the office.

Back at her desk, she punched the number for the Savannah-Chatham Metropolitan Police Department into her phone. She got through to Carl Trooe a lot faster this time.

"Detective Trooe, S-C-M-P-D." There was that rich tone again. Ingrid hadn't realized before just how much he sounded like her father. The accent was all wrong, but the honeyed tones were just the same.

"Good morning, Detective Trooe, I'm Special Agent Ingrid Skyberg, we spoke earlier."

"Now I'm not likely to forget your lovely voice, am I?" He chuckled a little. "Did that photograph come through OK? And the contact details for Wyatt's girlfriend?"

Ingrid quickly scanned her inbox. "They did—thank you so much for that. Now you're out of your briefing, can you spare me a little more of your precious time?"

"As you ask so nicely…"

"I appreciate that—thank you… Carl."

"The pleasure is all mine. What do you need to know?"

"I have a case I'm investigating here at the moment, also a poisoning, very different circumstances to the Barbara Highsmith murder, but—"

"Similar enough to make you want to dig a little deeper, huh?"

"That's right, I figure, if Wyatt was responsible for both murders, and it's a really big stretch, no more than a dumb hunch at this stage—"

"Hey, no hunch is so dumb it doesn't deserve a little attention."

"If he did murder this guy in London, I need to know as much as I can about him. I need to know why he targeted an ex-congresswoman and a City trader. What did he have against them both to want them dead? Do you know if Wyatt had any connection to high finance or big business?"

"Like I told you before, we know very little about the guy. He covered his tracks too damn well. We did recover some DNA samples from the girlfriend's apartment. But the DNA didn't match anything on record, so that didn't help us any. You got DNA from your crime scene over there?"

Ingrid remembered the Latvian's apartment in Dulwich that had been industrially deep-cleaned. She supposed it was just possible Miguel Hernandez had left some trace of his DNA behind at the bank. She'd have to speak to Mbeke about it. Was it really possible the same man was responsible for killing an ex-congresswoman, a City Trader and an internet-scamming Latvian? "I'd need to talk to the local cops about any DNA evidence. Wyatt's girlfriend… earlier you said you interviewed her intensively."

"We did. She was real pissed at Wyatt for duping her the way he did. She was happy to cooperate."

"But still she couldn't tell you anything about his history?"

"Nothing he'd told her about himself turned out to be true."

"Can you tell me anything about her?"

"She was seriously freaked out by what happened. I think she was a little scared of what Darryl Wyatt might do to her. I tried to reassure her he was long gone. But then she told us about his temper. He'd hit her a few times. Never where it'd show, he was real clever about it."

"Why did she stay with him?"

"Too scared to end it. I think she was mighty relieved when he skipped town."

"How long had they been together?"

"Not long—she got him the job at the restaurant."

"She did?"

"She blames herself for the whole thing. Like I say, you're better off speaking to her directly. She might remember something relevant she didn't even tell us."

"I'll do just that, thank you, Carl."

"Anytime."

Ingrid exchanged direct dial numbers with Trooe then and immediately called Darryl Wyatt's ex-girlfriend. Her call transferred straight to voicemail. At least the woman was using the same cell phone number. Ingrid left a short message and spelled out her email address—she didn't want the cost of a trans-Atlantic call to deter the woman from getting back to her. As soon as she put the phone down, her cell started to buzz.

It was Patrick Mbeke.

"Can you spare an hour or so?" he asked.

"You've got a lead?"

"Not exactly. Just an appointment with the pathologist. He wants to show me something. Thought you might like to take a look too."

EIGHTEEN

Before she left the embassy, Ingrid emailed a copy of Darryl Wyatt's photograph to DC Fraser, together with strict instructions for him to ask the Latvian's neighbors if they'd seen Wyatt at the property. It was a long shot—Wyatt had probably altered his appearance since his time in Savannah, but it was just possible the picture might jog somebody's memory. She also told Fraser about the rose tattoo on Wyatt's left arm.

Detective Inspector Mbeke met her at the main entrance of St Pancras Public Mortuary and escorted her to the autopsy room. "I haven't been in one of these places since I was in uniform," he said.

At that moment Ingrid realized it was her second morgue of the day. God it had been a long one. "Will you be OK?"

"Don't really have much choice." He managed a smile. It was possibly the first time Ingrid had seen him properly smile. Even though it flashed across his face for a matter of moments, it brightened his whole expression so much she felt she was looking at a completely different man.

"Thanks for bringing me in on this," she said.

"You make it sound like a visit to the mortuary is a pleasant afternoon excursion."

"Some of the local cops I've worked with here in London find it a little hard to be... inclusive."

"You're referring to my SIO?"

"Not specifically." She was actually thinking more of Detective Constable Fraser.

When they reached a set of double doors, Mbeke stopped and stepped to one side. "I was about to say, 'after you', but I suppose that would be a very *un*gentlemanly thing to do."

"Don't worry about me." Ingrid pushed through the doors and saw Matthew Fuller's naked body laid out on a steel examining table. His chest was open, the ribs pulled apart on each side and the skin clamped down, away from the gaping hole. She pulled up quickly. A man in scrubs on the other side of the room turned to look at her. In his hands he was holding a bloody organ. From the shape and size, Ingrid guessed it was a heart.

"Ah good, you've arrived," the pathologist said. "I'm Colm Anderson." He carefully laid the heart in a steel dish. "Sorry to get you down here, but I thought it made sense to show you, rather than try to explain it over the phone."

"What are we looking at, exactly?" Ingrid stepped closer to the examining table and forced herself to peer into the corpse's thoracic cavity. It was just that—a hole where his organs should have been.

"It's easier to demonstrate." The pathologist held up the steel dish containing Fuller's heart. "Look at this."

Patrick Mbeke shuffled a little closer. He seemed even more reluctant to be in an autopsy room than DC Fraser had been earlier. He screwed up his eyes and nose and glanced toward the dish, all the while angling his head away from it.

Anderson prodded the heart with a gloved finger. "I've rarely seen a healthier example." He pulled a green cloth from another dish with a flourish, as if he were a conjuror snapping a table cloth beneath a full set of dinnerware. In the dish was a large liver, deep maroon in color and smooth in texture. "Same with this. In fact all his organs are in perfect working order."

"And you wanted us to see this for ourselves because…" Mbeke swallowed repeatedly. Ingrid wondered whether he might be forced to excuse himself from the room altogether.

"The healthy nature of the deceased's organs got me thinking. We're looking for a toxin that left no visible trace.

Mbeke swallowed again. "OK. But would you mind saying whatever else it is you have to say in your office?"

"I have something else to show you first." The pathologist strode toward the body. He lifted Fuller's left hand and gently laid the fingers over his, more like a lover than a medical examiner. With the little finger of his left hand he traced around the edges of Fuller's fingernails. "See how red they are? And the skin on the knuckles too?" If I didn't know this man was a City trader I would have sworn he worked in an old-fashioned laundry, his hands immersed in strong detergent all day long."

"And?" Mbeke was edging back toward the door.

"The broken skin on the hands is key. Even with repeated washing, if a poison is absorbed through the subcutaneous layer of skin, one wouldn't normally expect its effects to have quite the impact it had on this chap. But the broken skin meant that he absorbed much more of the poison than the other victim and at a much faster rate." He pressed a fingertip against one of the corpse's knuckles as if to reinforce his point. "The skin on the hands signifies something else too. There's no blistering or ulceration. That means we can rule out the obvious substances—sulfuric or hydrochloric acid. Which prompted me to do a little research of my own. Having dismissed the possibility of harsh chemicals, I decided to look for something a little more… natural. And I think I've hit on the culprit. It's consistent with the symptoms and the ultimate fatal outcome."

Mbeke had made it half way to the door by now. "Fascinating. Would you mind sharing that information with us?"

"Aconite."

Mbeke shrugged and looked at Ingrid. She shrugged back at him.

"I've requested it's fast-tracked, ahead of any other tests, I'm so sure. As soon as it's confirmed, the doctors can set about helping that poor chap in the hospital."

"Aconite?" Mbeke said.

"You might know it by another name: monkshood or wolf's bane?"

"Still not ringing any bells. Is it easy to get hold of?" Ingrid said.

"Common as anything. In fact I think I may have some in my garden. Tall stems with bell-shaped purple flowers. Beautiful... but rather deadly. As this unfortunate gentleman can testify." He snapped off his gloves and marched toward the doors, pushing one open with his behind. "Now, I rather think you may need a cup of hot, sweet tea, inspector."

Ten minutes later, Patrick Mbeke seemed to have completely recovered. He thanked Anderson for his time, even though, Ingrid thought, it should have been the other way around, and they made swiftly for the exit.

All the while the detective had been drinking his tea, Ingrid had been wondering whether or not to mention the poisoning case in Savannah. Like Detective Trooe had said, no hunch was so dumb it should be ignored. So when they reached the front entrance and stepped out into the fresh air, Ingrid launched into an abridged version of the Barbara Highsmith investigation not forgetting to mention the fact that the perpetrator had given his employers a false address. She spoke so rapidly she barely paused for breath. When she was done she stared at Mbeke expectantly.

"And you think your... what do you call them... your *unsub* is here in London?"

Ingrid supposed Mbeke was basing his information on some American cop show he'd seen. "He's not strictly speaking an *un*sub, as we have identified him."

"But you don't know his real name."

"True. But we do know what he looks like. We have a pretty good photograph of him."

"Even if it is a long shot, I suppose we should at least rule it out." He pointed his key fob toward a black BMW parked in the lot outside the morgue. The alarm chirruped and the doors unlocked. "You need a lift down there or do you have your own transport?"

"Why, where're we going?"

"Fisher Krupps. See if your unsub looks like our missing suspect."

NINETEEN

Ingrid had Jennifer send the best quality photo of Darryl Wyatt to both her cell and Mbeke's. First stop was the cleaning supervisor's office. Even if the woman wasn't that familiar with Hernandez's features herself, she could point them in the direction of Patience Toure, who had to know what he looked like. Hopefully Toure was on duty today.

"Nope, don't know him," the supervisor said after glancing at Ingrid's phone for barely two seconds.

"Please take a closer look, madam," Mbeke asked, and shoved his phone under her nose. She stared at the image for a little while.

The picture of Darryl Wyatt showed a youngish man with short cropped dark brown hair and a tightly shaved beard. His faced was slightly turned away, from the camera, as if he hadn't been aware his photo was being taken. His skin was tanned, but hardly lined at all.

After a few more moments studying the picture, the supervisor's answer was exactly the same. "Sorry—that's not a face I've seen before."

"How well do you know the cleaners who work here, in general?" Ingrid asked.

"We don't go to bingo together, if that's what you mean."

"But it's possible you're not that familiar with his face?" Mbeke gave her an encouraging smile.

"S'pose not. You'd be better off speaking to Patience."

"She's in the building?"

The supervisor grabbed her rota from beneath a half-empty cup of coffee and studied it carefully. She sniffed. "You're in luck. Kind of."

Mbeke raised an eyebrow.

"She's here, but she's on toilet duty today. She could be anywhere in the building. I've got a mobile number for her, I can give her a call." She reached toward the phone on her desk.

"That won't be necessary, I have it too." Ingrid didn't want the cleaner to get spooked and decide to flee. "Thank you for your time, ma'am."

"Do we really have to trawl through all the lavatories in this building?" Mbeke said when they emerged from the elevator onto the main reception area.

"Hey, come on—it's only sixteen stories. The exercise will do us good."

He looked her up and down. "I think neither of us particularly need it." He folded his arms across his chest, his biceps straining against the material of his jacket. Ingrid felt her face warming.

"So, how about I take the ladies' restrooms and you take the men's?"

Mbeke started to move away then stopped. "What if we miss her? What if she's in the lift while we're in the toilet?"

"Maybe we'll get lucky." Ingrid let out a breath. It was a stupid idea. "OK, rather than call in a whole army of cops to do this—"

"Believe me, the SIO is not going to approve that much manpower."

"Why don't I call her cell while you wait at the rear exit, just in case she decides to leave the building. The guy on the front desk can watch the main doors."

"Give me five minutes to get down there," he said, but made no attempt to move. "Unless we do this the other way

113

round. It is my investigation, after all." He planted his feet more firmly on the marble floor of the lobby.

"I think she's more likely to speak to me. You represent authority here. I'm just some schmuck from the US embassy with no ax to grind and no powers of arrest. And anyway, I'll be showing her a picture of *my* unsub." She pulled her phone from a pocket. "Before you go, you should call the personnel department to circulate this photograph to all members of staff. I'm guessing they all have smart phones. The traders at least. See if they recognize the guy."

"Any more orders?"

"You know I really appreciate your help."

He raised an eyebrow before swiftly turning around and heading toward the security guy sitting on the reception desk. "I'll text you when I'm in position," he called over his shoulder.

Less than ten minutes later, Ingrid's phone bleeped with Mbeke's message. She called Patience Toure. To Ingrid's surprise, the woman didn't hesitate in telling her where she was. Ingrid headed for the fifth floor ladies' restroom.

When she found Toure waiting for her in the corridor outside the bathroom, leaning heavily on her cleaning cart, Ingrid texted Mbeke.

"You still looking for Miguel?" Toure said as Ingrid approached. "He's a good man. You are wasting your time."

"We only want to speak to him, ma'am. If he hadn't just disappeared, we'd have found out for ourselves whether he's good or bad."

Toure shook her head and muttered, "Wasting your time."

Ingrid found the photo of Darryl Wyatt on her phone and showed it to the cleaner.

"What's this?"

"Please take a good look, ma'am."

Toure squinted down at the image. "One second." She produced a pair of glasses from a pocket and stared at the photograph good and hard.

114

"You recognize him?"

"Never seen him before."

Ingrid studied the cleaner's face carefully. Her expression remained blank. Too blank. As if she were struggling to keep it that way. "You're saying this isn't Hernandez... this isn't Miguel?"

Toure shook her head.

"Please take another look. Try to imagine him without the beard and maybe with darker hair. Or paler skin."

"It's not him."

"Is there any way you could be mistaken?"

"I may need glasses, but I'm not blind." Toure shoved the cell back at Ingrid and muttered to herself in French. "You are wasting your time looking for Miguel. He's a good man. I have met plenty of bad ones. Miguel is not one of them."

"I look forward to discovering that for myself."

"When you find Miguel. What will you do to him?"

"We just want to talk. He may know something important. Can you think of anywhere he might have taken himself?"

The cleaner blinked her disgust at the question and turned her head away, as if answering was the last thing she would dream of doing. "He's not a bad man. That is all you need to know."

Out of the corner of her eye, Ingrid noticed Mbeke appear at the end of the corridor. He'd taken his time. Maybe he was keeping his distance so that he didn't freak Toure so much she'd stop talking altogether. But Ingrid doubted anything the detective could throw at this woman would scare her. She was made of sterner stuff. Ingrid saw him shrug his shoulders. "I appreciate your help, Madame Toure, I really do." She said goodbye and jogged toward the detective inspector.

"Make any progress?"

Ingrid shook her head.

"It was worth a try."

"I'm not convinced she's telling me the truth. Seems she thinks a lot of the guy. Maybe she's protecting him."

"Got any ideas?"

"If she does know something about Hernandez, she's decided not to talk, and I don't think anything I can say would persuade her to." She looked down at the picture of Darryl Wyatt then shoved the phone in her pocket. "You'll let me know if Fuller's tissue tests come back positive for aconite?"

"I'm surprised you even need to ask." He gave her a smile.

Ingrid stopped at the exit and turned to the inspector. "What's your next move?"

"We're still in the process of interviewing everyone Fuller knew here in the UK. He doesn't seem to have been the most popular of blokes—he pretty much kept himself to himself—but so far we haven't found any evidence that he made any enemies either."

"So we're no closer to discovering a motive?"

"Not by a long way. You will let me know if you tip up any evidence that connects my case with the one in the US?"

"Of course," Ingrid said.

All she had to do now was find some.

TWENTY

Ingrid returned to the embassy to do a little more digging. Even if the two poisoning cases weren't linked, in theory it was still possible the man on Marshall's watch list was right here in the UK and was responsible for the murder of the cherry-headed Latvian.

She reached her desk to discover another note from Jennifer. This one had to have been written in less of a hurry. It clearly informed her she had an appointment in Kilburn at ten-thirty a.m. the next morning. A woman had reported her husband missing to the local cops, but was frustrated they hadn't taken her seriously. She wanted the embassy to do something about it.

Ingrid slammed a hand down onto her desk and cursed under her breath.

Angela Tate was due to arrive at ten to conduct her 'fly-on-the-wall' interview. Ingrid had been hoping it'd be a really slow day and the journalist would get so bored watching her sitting at her desk, maybe helping Jennifer a little with her filing, that she'd give up on the idea and leave of her own accord. An actual missing persons interview might be just a little too interesting. Then there was the whole issue of client confidentiality.

Screw it.

Keeping the hack away from the embassy could only be a good thing. She decided to leave both arrangements just the way they were. If Tate misbehaved, Ingrid would have the perfect excuse to terminate their little 'arrangement' and hopefully the debt she owed the journalist could be written off.

She tapped the woman's details into her phone and screwed up Jennifer's note. For some reason Jennifer liked communicating on paper when Ingrid wasn't at her desk. Maybe she thought an actual physical message was less likely to be ignored.

Maybe she was right.

Judging by the lack of coats and bags on and around Jennifer and Isaac's desks, Ingrid figured they'd both left for the night. Which meant she had all the time she needed to investigate the Barbara Highsmith case without interruption. She dialed Detective Trooe's number.

"Detective Trooe, how can I help?"

"Detective, hi. This is Special Agent Skyberg, I wonder, do you have time to speak to me about the Highsmith case?"

"I just finished my shift."

"Oh, I see." She couldn't mask her disappointment. "I can call back tomorrow."

"No—I meant you got as much time as you need. Nothing to rush home for except a leftover pizza and a couple cans of beer. They sure ain't going anywhere. You spoken to the girlfriend yet?"

"I left her a message."

"Keep trying. She'll get back to you eventually, I'm sure."

Ingrid settled back into her seat. "I'm guessing, given the high profile nature of the victim, you investigated who she might have crossed so badly they wanted her dead?"

"Sure. I looked into who she put away when she was a District Attorney. Then narrowed it down to anyone who had been released from jail. Then reduced the list again, to those matching even a vague description of Wyatt."

"And?"

"No one of interest fitted the bill. Just when I thought I'd gotten a little closer, I'd discover the ex-con had died, or was built like a quarterback, or couldn't string two sentences together. You gotta remember, Wyatt was civilized and charming enough to get himself a job as a maitre d'."

"So you found no likely candidates at all from Highsmith's past?"

"No one she put away. So then I moved on to her new profession as a congresswoman. Again—lots of potential enemies in politics. I just wasn't prepared for how many. She had a lot of fights during her time in Congress. Just a little too outspoken to stay the course. It's incredible she ever got re-elected. Folk are real conservative here in Georgia, even the Democrats."

"She was elected for the first time in November 2006, is that right?"

"Re-elected 2008, then lost in November 2010."

"And the people she fought with? Did she make any of them mad enough to want to plan her murder?"

"Plenty mighta wanted to strangle her right there in the House, but nobody who'd bear a grudge so strong they'd actually do anything about it."

"So pretty much all your leads came to nothing?"

"It's heartbreaking. We put in so many man-hours. And came up with diddly."

It didn't give Ingrid much hope she'd find a potential enemy lurking in Highsmith's past. She let out a sigh. Trooe must have heard her.

"It ain't all bad. There's one little thing you might find interesting." He paused. "I'm sorry, I got another call coming in, give me a second to get rid of them."

Ingrid had been doodling thoughtlessly on a notepad as she listened to the detective. She glanced down at the page to discover she'd drawn a cube with lots of arrows pointing toward it. The inside of the cube was empty. It reflected the conversation she was having pretty accurately. She tore out the page and threw it in the trash.

"Sorry about that. My ex-wife," Trooe said. "Doesn't do to ignore her." He sucked in a breath. "Where were we?"

"Something I might find interesting."

"Sure. Well, maybe not that interesting. But anyhow, back in 2008, the congresswoman had a pretty close call with the Grim Reaper. Same deal—she ate something she shouldn't."

"Peanuts?"

"Yep—but she had one of those pen whatchamacallits she stuck into her leg and came back from the brink."

"You think she was deliberately poisoned then too?"

"Who knows? Her people hushed it right up at the time— Georgia being the peanut state and all. Didn't want the voters finding out she was violently allergic to one of the state's biggest exports. I only know about it because I got talking to an agent who was on her security detail at the time. You know how it is—one cop to another—strictly off the record."

"But if an attempt was made on her life at the time, shouldn't it have been investigated? The Bureau should have gotten involved."

"They did. Your people were very discreet about it. They just put it down to an unfortunate accident. Someone at the restaurant got fired. And before you ask, yes I did follow up on that. It was an assistant chef. Who was a woman."

"Must have been very frustrating for you."

"The case is still open. I go back to it once in a while, on my own time. Occasionally the ex-congresswoman's family kicks up a stink and then I'll get permission from the boss to dedicate some proper resources to it. But I guess if our man doesn't wanna be found he's just gonna stay hidden."

TWENTY-ONE

Ingrid hung up and looked down at the pad on her desk. This time the arrows were inside the cube pointing out. She tore off the page of scribblings and wrote a note on a fresh page to remind herself to follow up what Barbara Highsmith's legal specialism had been before she became District Attorney. But right now she had a restaurant manager to track down.

It was easier than she expected. Darryl Wyatt's ex-girlfriend picked up almost immediately. Ingrid quickly introduced herself.

And the woman hung up.

Ingrid called back and the voicemail kicked in right away. She left another message, imploring the woman to call her back. Without more information about Darryl Wyatt, Ingrid felt her investigation would go nowhere at all.

As she sat at her desk, staring at her phone, willing it to ring, Ingrid felt the first pang of hunger. She checked the time—it was ten minutes after eight. She wondered if the kitchen would still be open. There were plenty of personnel in the building, and would be right through the night. Surely someone on duty would be able to fix her a sandwich? She quickly made her way to the cafeteria, her hunger growing with every step, her cell phone gripped tightly in her hand. If Wyatt's ex-girlfriend did call back, Ingrid sure as hell didn't want to miss her.

When she arrived, Ingrid discovered the cafeteria in darkness. She'd half expected to see a group of drivers or counter-terror agents huddling around a corner table discussing the latest ballgame over a cup of drip. Or maybe playing a came of cards. The lights flickered on as she stepped over the threshold. She called toward the kitchen, on the other side of the counter. "Hey! Anyone home? Hello?"

No welcoming greeting called back to her. As she approached the counter she could see the coffee machine was lifeless, the glass jug that seemed permanently full during the day, empty and upside down. For a moment she thought she heard movement from within the kitchen. She called out again. Again there was no reply. Maybe she could fix herself a sandwich. She slipped behind the counter and pushed at the door that led into the kitchen. It was locked. Her fantasy of freshly-seared tuna salad on wholewheat dissolved in an instant. Instead, she headed for the vending machine and got herself a Snickers bar. Just as she was tucking it into a pocket, her phone started to vibrate. It was an out of area number. She answered and gave her name.

"Sorry I hung up before," the woman on the other end told her. "I guess I panicked."

"That's quite all right, Miss Townsend. This call must be costing you a fortune, shall I call you back?"

"It's OK—has he killed again?" She swallowed. "Only if he has, I'm not sure I want to know about it."

"What makes you think that?" Ingrid would have expected the woman's first question to have been, "have you found him?"

"I... I guess... I wasn't totally surprised when it happened the first time."

Ingrid hurried around the tables and out of the cafeteria. She took the stairs back to her office. Now she had Bella Townsend on the line, she didn't want to risk losing the connection due to bad reception in the elevator.

"It'd be really helpful for me if you could explain why you felt that way."

"Where do I begin?"

"How about we start when you first met Mr Wyatt?"

"Or whatever his goddamn name is." Townsend took a noisy breath. "You know he only got that job because of me?"

"There's absolutely no way you should blame yourself."

"I'm just so mad I let myself be sucked in like that."

"How did you meet him?"

"You want the whole, drawn out story?"

"I'd like to know everything I can about Wyatt, you're the only person who knew him well."

"I'm not sure I really knew him at all. But I can certainly tell you how we met. He was a customer at the restaurant. I helped him get to his table—his leg was in a splint, he was on crutches. I felt sorry for the guy. Not only had he busted his leg, but his date didn't turn up." There was the noisy breath again. "There he was all dejected and stoic, trying to make a joke out of a bad situation. He told me it was a blind date. 'She must have taken one look at me and run!' he said. He was kinda cute. Handsome even. I guess he charmed me. When he spoke to me it was as if I was the only person in the room. That never happens to me." She fell silent. Ingrid could hear her breathing at the other end of the echoey line. "With hindsight I realize that the whole thing was an act. He wanted me to feel sorry for him. His ankle probably wasn't even sprained, he probably never even had a date. What a pushover I must have seemed."

"You were just in the wrong place at the wrong time." Ingrid got back to the office, she threw the slightly melted Snickers bar onto her desk and sank down onto her chair.

"Tell me about it. So, anyway, long story a little shorter, we started dating."

"How long before he got the job as maitre d'?"

"Clifford, the previous maitre d', left unexpectedly just a couple weeks after I first met Darryl."

"Can you give me Clifford's last name?" Ingrid grabbed her notebook.

"Sure, it's... Quigley. Why?"

"Do you know what happened to make him leave so suddenly?"

"He just upped and left."

"Without an explanation?"

"We got a postcard from him from Hawaii, saying he needed a break."

"Was he a postcard kinda guy?"

"Actually no—it wasn't Cliff's style at all. I was surprised when we received it... Wait a minute... are you investigating Cliff's disappearance or something?"

"The detectives who investigated the case at the time didn't talk to you about Mr Quigley?"

"They never even asked me about Clifford. Jesus, you don't really think—"

"I'm sure Clifford's just fine. I'm just covering all the bases." Ingrid made a note to follow up. A name like Clifford Quigley had to be pretty straightforward to track down. "Was Darryl Wyatt good at his job?"

"He was a complete professional. When we first started dating, I thought his charm was dedicated to me. What a joke! He could turn it on like a kitchen faucet. The female patrons loved him. Some of the male ones too. Barbara Highsmith was particularly enamored."

"How did that make you feel?"

"Is this relevant to your investigation?"

"Humor me, if it's not too intrusive."

There was a long pause. "I was jealous as hell at first. But he still came home with me at the end of a shift. So I got over myself."

"You don't think he was seeing anyone else?"

"Thanks a lot."

"I'm sorry to be so blunt, but we are talking about a murderer."

"It's kinda hard reliving my own stupidity."

"You weren't stupid. He was manipulative. In a sense, there was nothing you could do. He's an expert at getting what he wants."

"Well he didn't get everything he asked for."

"He didn't?"

"He wanted keys to my apartment. I told him no way. I wasn't going down that road again."

"Did you visit him in his apartment?"

"No—I thought at the time that he was ashamed of it, like maybe it was in a bad neighborhood. I felt for the guy. Now I realize he just didn't want anyone to know his address."

"Do you think he was seeing anyone else?"

"I don't know. I guess now I know what he was capable of, I suppose it's possible. Why do you want to know?"

"Just trying to build up a picture of the guy. Detective Trooe has sent me the photograph you took of Wyatt. Is it a good likeness?"

"I guess. He didn't always have the beard. He could grow one real fast. I preferred it when he shaved. He was a good looking guy. Well-groomed too. Always spent a lot of time on his appearance. Which is why he never stayed over, I guess—didn't want me to see what he looked like first thing in the morning. How vain is that? I used to tease him about it."

"Did he share the joke with you?"

"He hated me even mentioning it. I soon learned not to."

"What do you mean?"

"Darryl had... an underdeveloped sense of humor. He wasn't very good at laughing at himself. Whenever I tried to tease him about it, he'd get really angry with me."

"Violent?"

"You've spoken to Detective Trooe?"

"He said Wyatt hit you a few times."

"More than a few. But he always said it was my fault. Like I'd driven him to it. After a while, I started to believe him."

She let out a sigh. "I know what you're thinking… if it was so bad, why not end it?"

"I'm thinking nothing of the sort. Wyatt was manipulating you. He knew exactly what he was doing." She flipped over to a fresh page in her notebook. "While you were together, did Wyatt ever talk about his family?"

"He didn't like to. Every time I tried, he'd change the subject. I just supposed he'd had a big fight with them at some point and lost contact."

"And what about his friends?"

"He wasn't local. His friends were all back home."

"And where was that?"

There was another long pause. "Some place out west. But now I think about it, he never actually told me where. He told me only what he wanted me to know. Looking back I can't trust a single goddamn word he said." She sucked in a noisy breath. "Look, if he has done something like that again, can you make sure you catch the bastard this time?"

"I'm working on it."

"Good. You need anything else from me, just call. I hate the thought of him being out there some place. Still makes me feel uneasy."

"Thanks for your time." Ingrid hung up and spent a moment staring at her phone. She was no expert—the sum total of her knowledge wouldn't even fill a single lecture in Psychology 101—but from the way Bella Townsend had just described Darryl Wyatt's character traits, he had exhibited some of the hallmarks of a narcissistic sociopath.

She knew an agent working at the Behavioral Analysis Unit at Quantico, a guy she did her training with. She should run through Wyatt's profile with him, get a professional opinion.

But right now she wanted to track down Clifford Quigley. If her assessment of Wyatt's psychological profile was even halfway accurate, Barbara Highsmith wouldn't have been his first victim. And she sure as hell wouldn't be his last.

TWENTY-TWO

The two a.m. security check of the third floor finally pried Ingrid from her desk. She hadn't managed to track down Clifford Quigley, but she had discovered a John Doe who'd turned up dead just a few days after Darryl Wyatt's first visit to the restaurant. The unidentified male was found over the state border in South Carolina and ended up in a morgue over a hundred miles away. It was possible the man lying in the chiller drawer wasn't Clifford Quigley, but Ingrid knew she'd feel a lot easier once she'd found out one way or the other. She tried calling the local cops in South Carolina, but discovered the officer she needed to speak to wasn't available. She made a note to try him again the next day.

Before she left the building, Ingrid put in a call to Mike Stiller, her one remaining contact at Bureau headquarters, to ask him to delve as deeply as he could into the history of ex-congresswoman Highsmith, especially the FBI investigation of the earlier poisoning attempt. Stiller had higher security clearance than Ingrid and he might just uncover something she couldn't. By the time Ingrid returned to her hotel, it was already three in the morning. Less than five hours before she needed to head back to Grosvenor Square.

Early the next morning, when she shoved her hastily purchased breakfast on her desk, Ingrid couldn't help wondering if a fold-up bed tucked away some place in the building might be a good idea. She kept a sleeping bag in a drawer just in case she had to stay over, a bed might make things a little more comfortable.

Isaac arrived before Jennifer, presumably still eager to impress.

"You want another crack at using those victim support skills of yours?" Ingrid asked.

"Absolutely. Yes please."

"Great—we have a missing person case to investigate."

"The one in Kilburn?"

"Jennifer told you about it?"

"Not exactly." He looked down at his feet. "I overheard her taking down the details."

"Nothing wrong with paying attention. Don't worry about it."

Ingrid actually felt a little sorry for him. He didn't know Angela Tate would be accompanying them to the interview. He had no idea what was in store for him. If he could handle whatever awkward questions Tate might throw at him, he'd be able to cope with anything else that might come up in the course of his embassy work. After a dealing with an investigative reporter with a fearsome reputation of getting to the truth, however deeply it was buried, anything else would be child's play.

Ingrid steeled herself for Tate's arrival. She'd already decided to meet the journalist at the gate—it was too dangerous to have her setting foot inside the office. God only knew what precious nugget of information Tate might manage to glean from somebody's desk. Or their trash can. The landline rang at a quarter before ten. Sure enough, Tate had arrived. She was certainly keen. Ingrid puffed out a breath and grabbed her jacket and purse.

"Ready, Isaac?"

They reached the lobby and found Angela Tate sitting in the main reception area. Her hair was a little wilder than usual and she'd chosen a particularly deep shade of red lipstick. It looked a little like dried blood. Tate must have wrangled her way inside the building, despite Ingrid's strict instructions to the Marine manning the desk. Tate was obviously in a combative mood. It didn't bode well for Isaac. Like a lamb to the slaughter.

"Agent Skyberg. I'm so glad you finally found me a window." Tate's gaze shifted to Isaac. "And who's this charming young man?"

Isaac opened his mouth, but no words came.

"This is Isaac Coleman. He'll be accompanying us today." Ingrid smiled first at Tate then at Isaac. He still seemed completely lost for words.

Tate reached out her hand toward him. "I'm DCI Jane Tennyson—Special Branch. Here in an observational capacity only."

Ingrid glared at her. What the hell did she think she was doing? It was bad enough having to include the reporter in an investigation, but introducing herself to Isaac as a cop? She'd better not try that with their interviewee. "Shall we?" Ingrid tore her admonishing stare from Tate's face and ushered them outside onto the sidewalk. Less than a minute later the embassy car arrived to dispatch them to Kilburn.

Once they were settled in the car—Isaac had insisted he sit up front with the driver—Tate pulled out a notebook. "So what case are we starting with today? Unexplained death perhaps? Is that possible, statistically? Would you expect to get two in a single week? I do hope a visit to Fisher Krupps is on our itinerary."

Ingrid lowered her voice. "What kind of stunt was that?"

"Stunt?"

"Introducing yourself as a cop?"

"A purely fictional one."

"Makes no difference."

"What possible harm can it do? It was only a bit of fun." She dragged a hand through her hair and tilted her head back.

"My little joke was totally wasted on you anyway." She glanced out the window. "So, is the first stop Fisher Krupps?"

"Let's just see how we get on with our initial interview, shall we?"

"Initial interview?"

"A missing persons case."

Tate turned in her seat to face Ingrid. "Tell me you're joking. Do you mean I've schlepped all the way to Grosvenor Square for a missing person? I presume a child's disappeared." She stared into Ingrid's face. "Something serious."

Ingrid said nothing.

"Oh please."

"I don't have much detail yet. I do know it's a male aged thirty-seven who's gone missing. Besides, you said you wanted 'warts-and-all' access. That's just what you've got. Welcome to my world."

"But your world also contains a City trader who died in suspicious circumstances. Why can't I observe you on that investigation? Maybe we should rearrange for another day."

"One time offer."

"Need I remind you just how indebted to me you are?" Tate didn't bother to lower her voice.

Ingrid glanced toward Isaac. Thankfully he was too busy talking to the driver to eavesdrop on her conversation. "You're making this really difficult for me."

"Them's the breaks. Perhaps you should never have come to me asking for help. Perhaps I should have refused to have anything to do with your highly dubious scheme. No wait, I don't mean dubious do I? I mean illegal."

Two weeks ago Ingrid had thought long and hard before asking Tate for help, she was well aware of the journalist's reputation for ruthlessness. At the time she'd had little choice but to get her involved. Right now she was deeply regretting the decision. The way things were going, she wasn't entirely sure her debt would ever be repaid. "We'll speak to the wife of the missing man. I'm already breaking the rules letting you come along."

"Don't worry—I'll behave myself."

Ingrid wasn't sure Tate even knew how.

They arrived at the house a couple of blocks south of Kilburn High Road just ten minutes later. Before they got out the car, Ingrid held on to Tate's arm. "You are here in an observational capacity only—we are clear on that? I'll be doing the talking."

"Don't fret. Do as much talking as you like. Quiet as a mouse, that's me.

TWENTY-THREE

After a half hour of quietly observing the interview, barely making a note in her reporter's pad, Angela Tate stood up. "Would you excuse us for a moment, madam?" She put a hand under Ingrid's elbow and dragged her to her feet and all the way to the front door. "My God—what are we all doing here wasting our time? If I didn't know better, I'd think you set this whole thing up. A little crumb to throw to the annoying journalist."

Isaac hurried down the hallway toward them, his face crumpled in confusion.

"Don't say a word," Tate warned him. "You might look decorative, but my God you're as useless as a sunhat in a monsoon." She stared at Ingrid. "Is this really how you spend an average day? Doing something this… mind-bogglingly boring?"

"Most of my work is mundane, procedural. I'm sorry to disappoint."

"Oh sure. You're not telling me this investigation isn't something that pretty boy couldn't handle on his own?"

"Wait a minute!" Isaac said. Tate had obviously hit a nerve.

"You're right. Isaac can handle this one from here." Ingrid turned to her eager apprentice. "Are you OK with that?"

"Absolutely!" He eyed Tate defiantly.

Brave boy, Ingrid thought.

"Get as many details as you can about where her husband might have taken himself off to. Be as sympathetic as you can."

"Don't worry—I won't let you down."

"Good. You OK to get back to embassy on public transportation?"

"Sure."

Ingrid and Tate quickly exited the property. Once outside, Tate lit a cigarette.

"I can't believe that's the sort of thing you'd normally investigate." She shook her head and took a long drag on her cigarette as they walked back to the car.

"Where can I drop you?" Ingrid asked as she opened a rear passenger door.

"What?"

"Back at the *Evening News* building?"

"You're not getting rid of me that easily. Let's just agree that performance in there was the rather tedious short before the main feature. You want to know where to drop me? How about Fisher Krupps, EC3?"

Ingrid's phone started buzzing in her pocket. She checked the screen: an "out of area" number. She really didn't want to speak to Marshall right now, not with Tate breathing down her neck. "Excuse me, would you? Feel free to wait in the car."

Tate stood her ground, staring at Ingrid through a cloud of cigarette smoke. Ingrid answered her phone and marched up the street.

"This really isn't a good time."

There was a pause at the other end of the line, then, "In that case, I'll keep the information to myself."

"Mike?"

"Expecting somebody else?"

"What time is it there?"

"Do you want to know what I found out about Barbara Highsmith or not?"

"Please, I do—but I'm not at my desk. Could you also email the details?"

"You do know I'm not your personal Stateside secretary, huh? You only ever check in with me when you've got a problem."

Although Ingrid accepted that was true, she also knew that Special Agent Mike Stiller loved a challenge. "You know how much I appreciate any help you can give me." She turned to see what mischief Tate was getting up to. The reporter was leaning against the hood of the embassy sedan, staring at her cell phone.

"OK—as long as we're clear how much you owe me. There's a lot of stuff here, so I'll just give you the edited highlights." He took a deep breath. "Barbara Highsmith, born Barbara Jane Reese, grew up in a nice middle class home, attended Wellesley College for her first degree—she majored in English—and then went on to study law at Harvard. Didn't graduate top of the class, but she was in the top third. After law school she went to work for a law firm in Boston, lasted there four years before switching sides to go work in the District Attorney's office. In Philadelphia." Finally Stiller took a breath.

In the brief lull, Ingrid took the opportunity to interrupt. "Anything interesting in her medical records?" The medical records of an ex-congresswomen were highly classified—only an agent with Stiller's security clearance could access them.

"Are you referring to the peanut allergy?"

"Dig up anything interesting about the earlier allergic reaction that nearly killed her?"

"The investigation was snuffed out pretty much before it began. Foul play was dismissed as a possibility right away."

"It was? Why?"

"The agents were directed to drop it. By people close to the congresswoman herself. I can't find out any more than that. There's nothing on file. And I had to call in a couple favors from the D.C. field office to find out that much."

"It happened in Washington?"

"You didn't know that?"

"My information is as sketchy as yours."

"Thanks for the vote of confidence in my intel gathering skills."

"I know you're the best agent there is for intel—why do you think I keep hassling you for information?"

"Because you got nobody else?"

"There must be something more about it you can find out."

"The general consensus is it was hushed up because she didn't want to jeopardize her re-election prospects. Doesn't do to have a secret peanut allergy leak out if you want to retain your seat representing the peanut capital of the USA."

"I guess not." She glanced up at Tate again. The journalist seemed to be behaving herself. "Did you find any link between Wall Street and Highsmith? Any Wall Street traders in her past?"

"Not that I've been able to find."

"Oh."

"The legal firm she worked for specialized in tax law, I think that's the closest she got to the world of high finance. Helping corporations pay as little tax as possible. What angle are you working, anyway?"

"It's not so much an angle as a wild stab in the dark." It didn't look like she was going to be able to establish a direct link between Matthew Fuller and Barbara Highsmith. Maybe the poisoning thing was a just a coincidence. But coincidences made Ingrid feel uncomfortable. She glanced toward Tate, who was mid-yawn. When Tate saw her, the reporter tapped a finger against her wrist. Ingrid held up her hand. "So apart from the tax attorneys, nothing else financial?"

"I said there was no link to Wall Street. If you'd read her file on the database a little more carefully, you would have discovered she worked as an Assistant US Attorney."

"I thought she was at the District Attorney's office."

"She was. Then she moved on to the US Attorney's office in Washington state.

Dammit. Ingrid had conflated the ex-congresswoman's sojourn at the district attorney's with the time she'd devoted to the US Attorney's Office. How had she missed that? "So she was dealing with federal cases?"

"For seven years in total. Started out in Spokane then transferred to Seattle two years later. Could be she dealt with plenty of finance-related cases. But it would have been small beer. Nothing newsworthy."

"Equally it could be just what I'm looking for. Can you get me a list of all her cases during her time at the US Attorney's Office?"

"Oh come on, Skyberg. I got my own work to do, you know."

"I promise this is the last request I'll make."

"Oh sure."

"Is that a yes?"

The line went very quiet.

"OK."

"Great—call me when you have the list." She hung up before Stiller had a chance to say goodbye, or complain, and started wandering back toward Tate, trying to work out how the hell she was going to get rid of her.

Tate ground the stub of her second cigarette under a boot. "What was that all about?"

"I can't say."

"Off the record."

Ingrid raised her eyebrows.

"Truly. Cross my heart."

Ingrid doubted Tate had one. "I can't go into the details. I was just checking some information with a colleague of mine back at Bureau HQ."

"Something to do with the Fisher Krupps trader?"

"Not at all," she lied.

"So—what was it then?"

"Another case—I told you, I can't give you the details." Her phone, still in her hand, started to buzz again.

"You are popular." Tate eyed the phone.

"Maybe we should forget all about this."

"I've cleared my diary for the day. I'm an optimist. I'm sure I'll pick up something of interest during our time together. But right now I could murder a bacon sandwich."

Ingrid turned away again and glanced at the screen. It was a call she couldn't ignore.

TWENTY-FOUR

"Detective Fraser, thank you so much for getting back to me."
Ingrid tried to keep her voice controlled and even, but she was
inwardly cursing him for previously ignoring her calls. "What
can you tell me?"

"Nothing. There have been no new developments."

"You haven't even identified the victim?" Ingrid walked
down the street, further away from Tate.

"It's proving more difficult than we thought."

"Still nothing back from Latvian police about the tattoo?"

"You're assuming she had a record."

"What about the media over there—have the police been
liaising with the newspapers and TV?"

"I haven't seen any evidence of it. She's not a priority for
them. We don't even know for sure that she was Latvian."

I know. "Extend your inquiries to include Lithuania and
Estonia then."

"I'll have a word with the SIO." From the noncommittal
tone of Fraser's voice, Ingrid doubted he'd do anything of the
sort.

"Maybe I should speak to him." She'd actually already tried
that approach. The senior officer running the case was
ignoring her calls too. It was possible Fraser knew that. "Are
you in the incident room? Is the SIO there with you now?"

"He… er…"

Ingrid could hear mumbling in the background.

"He's just had to step out. Important meeting."

"I don't understand, if you have nothing new to tell me, why are you even calling?"

"To be honest... to stop you calling me. You have to believe I'll get in touch if something of interest comes up."

"How about the house-to-house inquiries? Do any of the neighbors remember seeing a man at the address?"

"Nope."

"And none of them recognize the man in the photograph I sent you?"

Fraser drew in a noisy breath.

"What is it?"

"When no one confirmed a sighting of a man, we wound down the house-to-house interviews. We're concentrating our efforts elsewhere."

"Are you saying that the woman's neighbors haven't even *seen* the photograph?"

Another rasping inhale.

Goddammit.

"Why aren't you treating her murder as a priority? Is it because she's an immigrant?"

"Of course not! We take all homicides very seriously. It's not like America. We don't have this sort of thing happening every day of the week. Thank God."

"Where are you concentrating your efforts?"

"The boss is due to fly out to Latvia on Sunday morning. He's liaising with the police force in Riga."

"That's it?" It sounded like an excuse for a weekend away to Ingrid.

"We're still looking at the CCTV footage from the area around her flat. Nothing of interest has come up so far." He let out a long sigh. "Look, we're all as frustrated as you are with the lack of progress on this case. But it doesn't mean we've given up on finding out who killed her.

Ingrid hoped he meant what he said. She hung up and opened the search app on her cell. Tate was striding toward her.

"And what was that call about?"

"Another ongoing case."

"That you can't share."

Ingrid looked up from her phone. "Actually, I can. But I need some help first."

"From me?" Tate threw what was left of her third cigarette into the gutter. Ingrid nodded back at her. "Fire away!" The reporter rubbed her hands together.

"Do you have a chain of copy shops here in the UK? I need to find one—fast."

Forty minutes later, Ingrid and Tate were walking out of a Kall Kwik copy shop on Wembley High Road, laden down with a box each of 250 color copies of Darryl Wyatt's photograph.

"Where to now?" Tate said as they shoved the boxes onto the front seat of the car.

Ingrid leaned in and punched an address into the sat nav. The driver shifted uncomfortably in his seat a little but offered no word of protest.

"Actually—before we go anywhere," Tate said, "I need to find some lunch." She slammed shut the door and grabbed Ingrid's arm around the elbow. "My God you need feeding up. Let's get you something substantial to eat, shall we?"

Lunch took a lot longer than Ingrid would have liked, and mostly consisted of her deflecting Tate's intrusive questions about her life in London and her work in the FBI. By the time they were back in the car and turning off Lordship Lane, the traffic was starting to get heavy—mainly moms picking up their kids from kindergarten and the first signs of the evening rush hour—it was Friday afternoon after all—and the embassy driver seemed a little irritated.

"You know, you still haven't told me where we're going," Tate said as she wriggled to get comfortable in the plushly upholstered rear seat of the sedan. "Though I've got to admit, I could get used to having my own personal driver. What a treat!"

The car pulled into the curb a few minutes later and Tate peered out the window. "What are we doing in Dulwich?"

"Something I guess you've done plenty of over the years."

Tate arched a single eyebrow.

"A little doorstepping."

"Really? Let me at 'em. I thought I might die of boredom."

Ingrid reached into the front seat, pulled a sheaf of color copies from one of the boxes and handed them to Tate, who was practically limbering up on the sidewalk like a marathon runner, she was so keen to start. She looked at the photograph of Darryl Wyatt. "I'm already sick of this bloke's face. What's the score—asking people if they recognize him, if so when did they last see him, etcetera etcetera... Does he have a name?"

"I doubt he'd be using the one I have on record for him."

"So, if they happen to put a name to the face, I get bonus points."

"You only get those if they give you an address for him."

"I'm glad you're not my boss."

Ingrid pointed to the Latvian's building. A little blue and white police tape had gotten caught in the branches of a nearby tree and was fluttering in the breeze. "We'll start there. With the other apartments in the building, then work outwards."

Tate was already halfway up the path leading to the front door before Ingrid finished speaking. She rang all five buzzers, leaning her hand against them until she got a response. An intercom crackled and a distant voice hollered at her. Ingrid decided to give the reporter some space and tried the neighboring property. She knocked on the door and a dog started barking almost immediately. A deep, menacing bark. She heard an internal door open and close. The barking got louder for a moment then faded. A few seconds later the front door opened a few inches.

"Where's the bloody fire?" The woman holding onto the door was dressed in training pants and a sweatshirt, she had bright white sneakers on her feet.

Ingrid flashed her badge at her and held up one of the copied sheets.

"Not more bloody coppers. I've already told you, I don't know anything and I haven't seen anything. I mind my own business." She started to close the door.

"Please ma'am, just a take a quick look."

"You're a Yank."

"FBI, from the American embassy, ma'am."

"So who's this then?" She pointed to the sheet. "One of your Most Wanted?" She let out a little snort of laughter.

"He is, as a matter of fact. The sooner we track him down the safer we'll all sleep in our beds." Ingrid had grown sick of the subtle, softly, softly approach. She decided to try scaring the crap out of this woman. See if that made her pay attention. So far it seemed it might just be working.

"What's he supposed to have done?" The woman jabbed a finger at the photograph.

"Murder."

"Of her next door?"

"You know the deceased?"

"No—but I've seen her around. Said hello a couple of times." She scrutinized Ingrid's face. "Why's the American embassy getting involved? She wasn't American. Not with that accent."

"This man is the prime suspect in a murder investigation in Georgia."

"And you think he's come all the way over here?"

"It's one line of inquiry we're pursuing."

"God you sound just like the policewoman I spoke to yesterday. Do you all get the same training?"

"Please, ma'am, take a good look at his face. It's possible he's clean shaven now, maybe his hair's a different color. He could be wearing glasses."

The woman stared a little longer at the color copy, then started shaking her head. "I've not seen him."

"Is there anyone else in the house who might have?"

"My husband. But he doesn't pay attention to anything outside work and football. I'm lucky if he even notices me."

"Please keep the photo and ask him, would you?" Ingrid handed her a card too. "Call me anytime if you think of something."

The woman closed the door just as Tate approached from the next door property.

"Any luck?" Ingrid asked her.

"The only person to answer their buzzer was half deaf. I popped a few photocopies through the main letter box anyway. I scribbled my phone number and 'have you seen this man' on the back of each one."

"Don't you think asking them to contact the embassy would have been more appropriate?"

Tate shrugged. "Didn't occur to me." She reached into her purse and pulled out her pack of cigarettes. "I heard most of what you told that woman."

"So?"

"Who did this one kill in Georgia? I'm guessing it's got to be quite a high profile case for the FBI to get involved."

"We take every homicide just as seriously as any other. High profile doesn't come into it."

"Sure, sure. So who was it?"

"Just some woman in a restaurant." She'd already revealed too much.

"Another stabbing?"

Ingrid wondered if she should lie. It wouldn't help her investigation to have Tate sniffing around the ex-congresswoman's death. She decided to be as vague as possible. "That's right. I haven't received the case file yet—I don't know all the details."

"Maybe when you do, we can have a follow-up interview?"

"Sure, why not?" As if that would ever happen.

Tate looked down at the cigarettes and shoved them back in her purse. Then she quickly moved on to the next house. "We'd better get stuck in, or we'll be here all night."

Ninety minutes, and at least three dozen properties later, Ingrid met Tate back at the car. "Anything to report?" Ingrid asked her.

"Most people were either out or chose not to answer. I shoved the picture through their letterboxes anyway. You never know, someone might get in touch. What about you?"

"Same story. It was worth a try."

"Yes—and it kept me out of your hair for a while. But I'm not that easily deterred. We've done everything we can here. You can tell me all about the dead trader while we drive to Fisher Krupps."

Ingrid pursed her lips and shook her head. She pointed at her watch. "Five-thirty. End of my working day. You've had all the access you're going to get."

TWENTY-FIVE

Ingrid had only managed to get rid of Angela Tate after promising to update her with any progress on the City trader case, just as soon as it happened.

"Be warned—I will hold you to that. If I don't hear from you, I shall make your life absolute hell," she'd said.

Ingrid didn't doubt that for a second. She knew well enough not to cross Tate. If she were being entirely honest with herself, she would have to admit she was a little in awe of the journalist's single-mindedness. And maybe even a little intimidated.

When she returned to the embassy, after dropping Tate at the *Evening News* building on Blackfriars Road, Ingrid decided to check in with DI Mbeke.

"Have I caught you still on duty?" Ingrid asked him after she'd almost hung up—the call rang out for what seemed like ages.

"Actually I was just heading out of the building." He sounded slightly out of breath.

"Any news?"

"I was going to leave it until Monday."

Ingrid sat up in her chair.

"It's not earth shattering. We still haven't located Hernandez. But we have confirmed that aconite was used to kill Fuller. The lab found traces of it in his liver and kidneys."

"What about the washroom?"

"Nothing. Which presumably means the poison was in the soap dispensers."

"Which the killer removed. Right under our noses."

"Wait a minute—I hadn't arrived at that point."

"OK—I admit it—I was the law enforcement officer he made a fool of."

"I didn't mean—"

"No offense taken. I'm just still so mad at myself about it."

"But why would he take that risk?"

"Maybe it was his only opportunity to remove the evidence."

"He could have just left the poison there. Wreaked more havoc."

"He did what he came to do."

"You're still certain Fuller was the intended victim?"

"It's the explanation that makes the most sense."

"Then why not leave as soon as Fuller was dead? We still have that hour and a quarter to account for between Fuller's death and the footage of Hernandez making his escape. Why did he hang around for so long?"

"Maybe he enjoys the thrill." Ingrid tried to recall her Psychology 101: narcissistic sociopaths take great pleasure in watching the drama they've created unfold. Especially when it makes them feel so much smarter than the investigating officers. He must have been there, silently mocking them. Mocking her. Ingrid thought of Darryl Wyatt standing in the restaurant, watching Barbara Highsmith gasping her last breaths. "During your interviews of Fuller's colleagues, did anyone mention seeing a cleaner hanging around the area while Fuller was actually dying?"

"Don't forget, no one discovered Fuller for a little while. He was lying in the corridor outside the main trading area. It wasn't until someone visited the toilet that anyone even knew he was in trouble."

"Where the hell is Hernandez? You really have to put all your efforts into finding him."

"You think?"

"Sorry. I'm really not telling you how to do your job."

There was a silence at the other end of the line. Had she really offended him so much?

"Listen, I'll be working right through the weekend," Mbeke eventually said. "I'm just popping out of the station now to get a bite to eat. Would you like to join me?"

Ingrid paused. It didn't *sound* like he was asking her out on a date.

"We could discuss the case in... slightly more pleasant surroundings."

"The case? Sure, why not? I can be with you in less than thirty minutes."

"Good, great. I'll text you the address of the restaurant."

By the time Ingrid and Mbeke had ordered their meal, they'd already raked over pretty much everything about the investigation that they'd discovered so far. Ingrid updated Mbeke on the Savannah poisoning case and he ran through how the City of London Police were liaising with other forces up and down the country to try to track Hernandez down.

"Without a photograph, or any consistent description of the man, we're not holding out much hope," Mbeke told her.

"Nobody on staff recognized the photograph I sent you?"

"Don't you think you would have been the first to know if they had? No one notices the cleaners."

"Apart from the other cleaners."

"None of them is comfortable speaking to us. I think the cleaning agency might be running some sort of immigration scam. I've got some colleagues looking into it. But whatever they find, it isn't exactly going to encourage any of the employees to tell us anything." Mbeke was leaning his chin in his hands, his elbows planted on the table. He stared into Ingrid's eyes, his gaze almost uncomfortably intense.

Ingrid started playing with the corner of her napkin, just for something else to focus on. "I guess it's possible Hernandez has left the country already."

"It's impossible to say. Hernandez probably isn't his real name. If he has left, I would imagine he's got alternative paperwork for a different identity. Border control can't help us."

Ingrid wondered if maybe the suspect *was* smarter than the law enforcement agents investigating the case. She was certainly feeling decidedly dumb right now.

Mbeke sniffed loudly and sat up straight. "This is my first murder case, and I'm completely lost. I don't have a single promising lead to follow up. I feel useless. I can't help thinking there's something blindingly obvious that I'm missing."

"If there is, then I'm missing it too."

A waiter approached their table holding a steaming bowl of pasta in each hand. Following the ritual of the black pepper grinding and the parmesan shaving, Ingrid and Mbeke ate in silence for a few minutes. They'd pretty much exhausted all case-related avenues of conversation. Then they both awkwardly started to speak at the same time.

"You first," Ingrid insisted.

"I was just going to ask you about your life back in the US. A pathetic attempt at small talk." He smiled at her.

Ingrid sensed this was the time to bring her fiancé into the conversation. But the thought of even mentioning Marshall's name right now reminded her she was still mad at him. "Oh there's not much to talk about, really. I pretty much live for the job. Sad, I know."

"Not at all. I'm guilty of the same thing myself. You can ask my ex-wife!"

"Oh—I'm sorry."

"It was all my fault. In the end it came down to choosing between the job and my marriage."

"Do you ever regret choosing your career ahead of your love life?" Ingrid was aware just how career-focused she and Marshall were.

Mbeke raised his eyebrows.

"I'm sorry—that was too personal."

"Not at all, I just wasn't expecting it. When it came down to it, I couldn't imagine doing anything else for a living. But I could see myself single again. I guess I'm just too selfish to be in a relationship."

This was all getting a little too intense. Ingrid attacked the bowl of linguine with her fork as if she were trying to harpoon the prawns in their sea of cream sauce.

"What about you?" Mbeke asked.

Ingrid was afraid he might ask that. "Oh I love the job too. It's in my DNA."

"Literally? Your dad was a policeman?"

She laughed. "My dad was a hog farmer."

"Some people might say those two professions are closely related."

Ingrid laughed again, more out of embarrassment than amusement. Time to bring in the cavalry, much as it pained her to do so. "But my fiancé's dad was a cop. A sheriff, as a matter of fact."

"Your fiancé?"

She nodded and shoved another forkful of pasta in her mouth to avoid the need to speak. She couldn't help but notice Mbeke's shoulders sag a little. He stared down at his meal and chased a button mushroom around the bowl.

"Marshall and I are both married to the job, I guess," she said, attempting to fill the awkward silence. "Maybe dating a fellow cop is the answer. We understand the issues. The missed dates, the forgotten birthdays."

"How long have you been engaged?"

"Just over a year. But we started dating two years before that. And we've known one another forever—since Academy training at Quantico."

"You joined the FBI at the same time?"

Ingrid nodded, regretting having brought the subject up. She tried to remember what Marshall had been like eight years ago. Her one abiding memory of him then was his old fashioned Southern charm. He was popular with all the female trainees. When he asked her out five years later, he not only impressed her with his charm, but with his tireless hard work and ambition. They had both wanted to make a difference back then. She wasn't sure either of them had achieved anything close.

"I can see you're a bit uncomfortable talking about it. Now it's my turn to apologize for being too personal."

"Oh, not at all. I was just lost in a little reminiscence."

"And the long distance thing is working out OK for you?"

Ingrid thought about why she'd agreed to take on the embassy job in the first place. She'd needed time to work out what she wanted in her life. She'd hoped a little space and distance from her old job, and from Marshall, would help her in the decision making process. But she still hadn't worked out what it was she wanted. Thinking about it now, she hadn't really missed Marshall in the five months she'd been away. "Oh it's working out fine."

Mbeke frowned at her, making it quite clear he didn't believe her.

Ingrid wondered just how much she and Marshall truly needed one another. What they continued to get out of their relationship. As she smiled blandly across the table at Mbeke, she knew she had some serious thinking to do.

TWENTY-SIX

"And what happened after that?" Natasha McKittrick had agreed to come apartment hunting with Ingrid. She should never have mentioned her brief supper with Mbeke to the detective inspector. Now McKittrick just wouldn't let it go.

"We pretty much agreed on a strategy to implement going forward. All resources are now focused on finding Hernandez."

She grabbed Ingrid's shoulder. "You do realize Mills can never find out about your date. He'll be devastated."

"For crying out loud! How many more times? It wasn't a date. I don't go on dates. Ingrid turned back toward the real estate agent's window. "I've got a new home to find." She glanced at the details of the two or three rentals that were both in the right price range and more or less a fifteen minute motorcycle ride from the embassy. None of them screamed 'pick me!' at her. Maybe this was a mistake. Perhaps staying at the hotel made more sense.

"I can't understand why you'd voluntarily walk away from four star luxury and twenty-four-hour room service," McKittrick said, somehow reading Ingrid's mind. "Not to mention having someone else wash and iron your clothes for you."

"The novelty wears off after a while."

"Does this mean you're planning on staying in the UK? Only you've never actually said how permanent your posting is."

"The Bureau will pay rent for the first six months, so maybe I'm here that long."

"And what does Marshall think about that?"

Ingrid turned away and marched to the door of the realtor's. "Are you helping me find an apartment or not?"

"Oh my God—you haven't told him yet, have you?"

"I haven't had the chance—every time I call he's busy."

"Time to take the bull by the horns—why not call him right now?"

Ingrid ignored her and stepped through the door, leaving McKittrick stranded on the sidewalk. After a few moments the detective slunk into the office, her head angled toward the floor.

"I'm sorry—I genuinely didn't realize this was an issue for you."

"It isn't—I'll call Marshall when I'm good and ready. I may not even find an apartment." She headed toward the desk beneath the 'lettings' sign and waited for the agent to get off the phone. He smiled up at her.

"How can I help you two ladies today?"

Behind her, McKittrick let out a little groan and mumbled 'Ladies' in a sarcastic tone.

"In the window—you have details of a couple of apartments I'd be interested in seeing."

"Sure, no problem." He got up. "Care to show me which ones?"

After an extended, and clearly, as far as McKittrick was concerned, tedious few minutes of small talk, the agent took Ingrid's details and they headed off in his logo-emblazoned Mini to the first apartment in Maida Vale. Ingrid had selected the area because it was a straight run from there to the embassy along Edgware Road. She'd be door to door in ten minutes most days. The small talk continued in the car until

McKittrick put a stop to it when the agent asked them if it was their first home together.

"I'm not her partner," the detective told him firmly. "I'm just here to make sure she doesn't get ripped off."

Ingrid was more than capable of ensuring that for herself, but she let McKittrick continue to harangue the guy for the rest of the ten minute car ride and throughout the viewing of the first apartment. It was actually quite entertaining to watch McKittrick ask the agent a series of awkward questions about both the property and the lease that he struggled to answer.

They finally exited the two-bedroom duplex on Elgin Avenue and the detective let rip. "Do you really think anyone would be desperate enough to live in a place like that? It's barely fit for human habitation."

"The rental market in this area is highly competitive," the agent said. "Properties are snapped up before we can even print out the details."

"OK—show us one of those," Ingrid chimed in.

"I'm sorry?"

"One of the highly-sought after residences that everyone is clamoring for."

"It's not quite as simple as that. We've got people on waiting lists. I can't just let you jump the queue."

"Oh, come on. I bet you've got something so new it hasn't even made it onto your books yet." Ingrid treated him to her most fulsome smile. Then she pulled her badge from her purse. "I'll be a very reliable tenant."

He wrinkled his nose while he considered her request. "Oh, what the hell." He reached into a pocket and pulled out a set of keys. "I only got the instruction yesterday. Haven't see the property myself yet. It won't have been cleaned or anything."

"I think I have the imagination to see beyond a little dirt."

"It's in a mansion block—all services included in the rent. Fully furnished. About five minutes away. On the Maida

Vale—St John's Wood borders." He said it like it was meant to impress her.

"Sounds perfect."

It was a little more than five minutes, the property was on the far eastern edge of the area Ingrid had identified, but as soon as she walked through the apartment door she knew she had to have it. It was on the top floor, which meant it was light and airy and had fantastic views right across Regent's Park. Leading off the square lobby area were five doors. The one right opposite the apartment door led into a large, high-ceilinged living area, sparsely furnished, white walled and wooden floored. Just the way she liked her apartments. She stood at the southern-facing of the two windows and gazed toward the park. Between the two windows was a door. Ingrid tried the handle—it was locked.

"Do you have the key?"

The real estate agent produced a key from a pocket and opened the door. It led out onto a small roof terrace. Ingrid stepped outside and inhaled. This was why she had to get out of the hotel: she needed to see the sky when she woke in the morning—to get a sense of space. She turned back toward the agent, he was barely inches away, literally breathing down her neck. "Can I have a little time to think about it?"

He looked at his watch. "I have another appointment at one."

"Plenty of time then." Ingrid waited for him to go back inside. She could stay up here all day.

McKittrick joined her. "I'm guessing you're sold on it?"

"Is it that obvious?"

"Might want to lose the big sloppy grin that's been on your face since we set foot over the threshold, if you're going to stand any chance of negotiating a good deal."

"Don't worry—my dad taught me how to haggle."

"I look forward to seeing you in action."

Ingrid walked to the rail at the edge of the roof terrace and surveyed the horizon through one-eighty degrees. Already her head felt clearer than it had in weeks.

"What's next for you today? Going back to work?" McKittrick asked.

"How did you guess?"

"You are in the middle of two investigations with so many loose ends you could crochet them together and make a hat. What else are you going to do on a glorious Saturday afternoon?"

"You know me so well."

"What can you usefully do on the weekend anyway?"

"Go through the files again, read up a little more on Darryl Wyatt, the ex-congresswoman, the City trader. Maybe find something I've missed."

"You're still convinced there's a connection between the dead Latvian and the trader?"

Ingrid closed her eyes and enjoyed the warmth of the sun on her face for a moment. "Convinced is too strong a word. I'm keeping an open mind."

"Have you worked out what his motive might have been for killing the Latvian woman?"

"She was accessing his bank account back in the US. Getting a little too close to his former identity. She was a security risk, I guess."

"But if he's... what did you tell me earlier... a narcissistic sociopath?"

Ingrid nodded.

"And that means he's a meticulous planner..."

Ingrid nodded again.

"Then why leave his bank details lying around for the Latvian to discover?"

"I don't have that worked out yet. Which is why I need to go back to base and do some more digging."

"All work and no play."

"I'll fit in a little parkour before the end of the day. A few easy moves."

"And that's your idea of fun?"

"Closest I'll ever get to flying. Maybe you should give it a try."

"I'll stick to taking the stairs and getting off the tube a couple of stops early for my exercise, thanks very much. I don't know how you fit it all in. Oh no, wait, I remember— you don't have a social life."

"Gee thanks."

The real estate agent was knocking on the glass and pointing at his wristwatch.

"Time for some deal making." Ingrid rubbed her hands together.

"This I've got to see." McKittrick grabbed Ingrid's arm as she started to head back to the roof terrace door. "I really think you should take a break from work. Maybe it'd give you a fresh perspective. A new look at everything on Monday might really help you crack the case."

Ingrid wondered what might be coming next. Hopefully not another invite to a goddamn awful flea market. She'd tried it once and vowed never to do it again. "What do you suggest?"

"Funny you should say that."

The realtor banged on the glass again.

"All right!" McKittrick hollered at him. "A few colleagues have arranged an unofficial team building exercise for tomorrow—it's an excuse to let off a bit of steam, really. I wouldn't mind having you come along for moral support."

"You think you'll need it?"

"Even off the job, they still think of me as their boss, they can be a bit guarded around me."

"You could just not go."

"They've gone to the trouble of inviting me. I can't say no. I'd appreciate a little company." She started walking toward the door. "God—I'm not going to beg."

"OK. I'll come."

"Fantastic! I owe you one."

Having a detective inspector of the Metropolitan Police in your debt had to be a good thing. Ingrid stopped before they went inside. "Wait a minute. Will Ralph Mills be there?"

"Don't worry—I'll make sure he doesn't get anywhere near you. I know what trouble you have keeping your hands off him."

TWENTY-SEVEN

Ingrid's digging into the case files on the FBI database all Saturday afternoon and most of the evening produced no new leads. She was still waiting for Mike Stiller to get back to her about Barbara Highsmith's cases from her Assistant US Attorney days. Mike worked long hours, but she couldn't ask him to give up his weekend for her. So—reluctantly—she left the embassy with as many loose ends as she had before she embarked on her marathon trawl of the records.

After a light thirty-minute parkour session on the south bank of the Thames near Waterloo railway station—it was pretty much a playground for free-runners—she headed back to her hotel for another boring room service dinner and a night in front of the TV. She really did need to get something else to do outside of work: there were only so many walls a girl could scramble over for entertainment.

More than once she pulled her phone from her purse and considered calling Marshall. But what was there to say? "Hey, honey, I've just found myself a great new apartment. Oh and I've decided to stay on in London for a little while longer." She could hear his whine of complaint clearly enough in her head without having to suffer the real thing.

With a little time to think, she was also beginning to regret accepting McKittrick's invitation to attend her 'bonding day'. The thought of spending that much time with Detective

Constable Ralph Mills made her feel more uncomfortable than she knew it should.

So he was a nice guy.

So he made her laugh.

So he reminded her of her very first junior high school crush. She stopped the thought right there, switched channels on the TV and distracted herself with some dark Danish cop show. She struggled to concentrate on the subtitles until sleep finally got the better of her. Investigating two murders in one week had taken its toll.

The next day she skipped her five-mile morning run and spent the time fueling up on a healthy breakfast before embarking on whatever it was McKittrick had planned for her. She had arranged to meet the detective at Kentish Town Tube station in north London and arrived there a little after ten.

"*Now* will you tell me what we're going to be doing?" Ingrid asked McKittrick when the detective finally turned up fifteen minutes later than planned.

"First of all—we're getting on a train." She strode away, toward the entrance of the overground station. "We, my dear, are going to the country."

"Wouldn't it be better if we drove?" Ingrid followed her in.

"Might not feel up to getting behind a wheel afterwards." She strode away.

"After what?" Ingrid joined McKittrick on a bench. The platform was empty apart from a mom and dad struggling to keep two toddlers under control at one end, and a guy in sweats who appeared from the entrance and immediately started some weird T'ai Chi routine, fixing his gaze on the opposite platform.

"I don't want to spoil the surprise." McKittrick looked first at the boisterous young family then the man, who was now balancing on one leg. "Let's make sure we don't get in the same carriage as the Munsters or the weirdo, all right?"

"Can you at least tell me if I'm dressed suitably for the occasion?"

McKittrick looked at the leather biker jacket, the jeans and the biker boots. "I suppose you'll do. But I'm not sure you needed the back pack. What's in there, anyway?"

"Just a flask of water. Some fruit. Something to read. First aid kit."

"My God, you do like to come prepared." McKittrick glanced down at the small purse slung over her shoulder. "Must be your FBI training." She smiled, a twinkle in her eye.

The train came quickly and their journey lasted less than forty minutes. Four people were waiting for them outside the station when they arrived: Detective Constable Ralph Mills, a detective named Cath Murray from the London Crime Squad Ingrid had met for the first time a couple of weeks ago, a smiling petite Indian woman, and a scowling, pink-faced blonde woman who seemed to be a little self-conscious about the few extra pounds she was carrying. Mills looked surprisingly muscular dressed in track pants and tight tee shirt. It was the first time Ingrid had seen him not wearing his trademark brown suit.

"Ingrid, hi!" Mills called out to her. He nodded toward McKittrick. "Boss." His smile was wide and generous, Ingrid couldn't help but beam back at him. "Now, you've met Cath, I know... but this is Manisha Kapoor..."

"Please, call me Nisha. It's a pleasure—we've heard so much about you," the Indian woman said as she shook Ingrid's hand. Her comment was rewarded with a sharp dig in the ribs from Mills.

"And this is Jane O'Brien," he said, gesturing toward the self-conscious woman, "who I used to work with at Catford Borough Command a few years back. My first job in CID, as a matter of fact."

"And you've come such a long way, pet," Jane O'Brien said. "All the way to the H-S-C-C." This remark, for some reason, was met with guffaws of laughter from Murray and Kapoor.

"What did I miss?" Ingrid asked.

"Nothing at all. They're all a bit over-excited." He glared at them. "They were like this all the way here. They don't get out much." He smiled at her and turned away. "I've booked a cab. Should be here any minute."

Right on cue, a few moments later, a mini-van pulled into the quiet station's small forecourt and Mills opened the side door. "All aboard the Skylark," he said, inexplicably.

Ingrid feared the day ahead might turn out to be long and arduous. No wonder McKittrick wanted a little support. Ingrid already felt like she was missing all the in-jokes. Judging by the glowering look on the detective inspector's face, she supposed McKittrick was too.

"We were talking on the train," Murray said, when they had all settled into the taxi. "We think you should maybe compete with one arm tied behind your back. You'll have an unfair advantage otherwise."

"I will?" Ingrid looked at McKittrick for guidance. "I still don't know what we're doing today."

"Paintballing!" they all said in unison.

Swell. Ingrid forced a smile. "Sounds like fun."

After five minutes on the road from the station, the mini-van turned off onto a muddy track and pulled through a ranch-style, wide wooden archway. It then bumped along a rough unmade road for about a half mile before depositing them at the opening of a long narrow marquee. Ingrid watched the taxi leave wishing she were still on board. *Paintballing* for God's sake. Definitely *not* her idea of fun. A man dressed in army fatigues stepped out of the marquee to greet them.

"Hello! You're a bit late. Your opposition have already gone into the forest. Not to worry. Let's start off by grouping you into pairs."

Mills glanced at Ingrid but made no move.

"Nisha!" McKittrick said. "How's your aim?" She marched over to the Indian woman and threw a mischievous smile back at Ingrid.

Cath Murray had looped her arm through Jane O'Brien's.

Mills cleared his throat. "A fait accompli."

Ingrid was feeling decidedly set up. What did McKittrick think she was doing?

A sudden throaty wail sounded from somewhere in the distance.

"What the hell was that?" Murray asked.

"Primal Scream. We have a men's warrior course on at the moment. Like a boot camp for your emotions," the man in fatigues explained.

"Stupid bastards," McKittrick said. "Haven't they got better things to do on a Sunday?"

Ingrid was thinking just that about this whole excursion. She could have been enjoying a ten mile run right now. She reached across to a long table at the entrance of the marquee and picked up a glossy brochure. Flicking through it, she discovered the establishment also offered a wild food foraging course, basket weaving and whittling, and archery using traditional Navajo bows and arrows. As if anyone in England would know the first thing about it. The paintballing arm of the operation seemed incongruous to say the least.

"Right, first of all you need to sign a health and safety form indemnifying Nature's Playground against any claims for injuries." The group leader handed them all a clipboard with a sheet of paper attached that contained such tiny small print it was impossible to decipher in the gloom of the forest.

Ingrid signed her form using a false name and quickly handed it back. The man in the fatigues gave her a bright orange bib and a half-inch diameter length of bamboo. Ingrid inspected what she supposed was a weapon. A small trigger was attached to one end of the stick, next to the trigger was a circular chamber. "What is this?" She inspected the trigger more closely. The whole contraption looked lethal. No wonder they had to sign a form.

"It's based on an Cherokee blowpipe. Originally we used a completely authentic design, but discovered that most punters don't have the necessary puff to send the paint pellets much further than a couple of feet. With the pneumatic pump," he said, pointing at the chamber, "everyone can achieve a range of twenty-five to thirty feet. It levels the playing field."

Ingrid slipped the orange vest over her head. It was so bright, they might as well have painted a target on her chest.

"A blowpipe? You're not serious," Cath Murray said. "Where are the unfeasibly large bazookas?" For some reason that comment elicited hearty guffaws from her teammate, Jane. "I wore my Ellen Ripley white vest especially for the occasion. Jesus, Ralph what have you got us into?"

Everyone turned to glare at Mills. He held his hands up in surrender. "Let's make the best of it, shall we? You never know—we might actually enjoy ourselves."

The organizer ran them through an all too brief demonstration on how to fire and reload the blowpipe, and told them their prey were three other couples, dressed in bright green vests.

"One clean shot to a member of the opposition's back or chest retires them from the game. Last person standing wins for the team."

"What's the prize?" Murray asked.

"The satisfaction of a job well done."

Murray, Kapoor and O'Brien groaned.

"Let's make it a bit more interesting then, shall we?" Murray said. "The couple with the most 'kills' gets to… enjoy an intimate Sunday lunch at a venue of their choice."

Mills glared at her.

Ingrid made eye contact with McKittrick, who quickly looked away. McKittrick was so going to pay for this.

TWENTY-EIGHT

The three teams split up and fanned out across the forest. After fifteen minutes or so, Ingrid and Mills had covered a lot of ground. The unnerving sound of grown men howling at the sky had even subsided a little. So far they hadn't spotted a member of the opposition.

"We should maybe slow down. Start to circle back a little." Ingrid pulled the vest over her head and shoved it in a pocket. "No point in advertising our presence."

"Isn't that cheating?" Mills said. He seemed genuinely alarmed at the idea.

"Do you want to win?"

"Not especially."

"What?"

"I just want to have a bit of fun."

"Nothing wrong with doing both."

They doubled-back and stopped in a small clearing. Ingrid held a finger to her lips. They listened. After a few moments Mills shrugged at her.

"What do we do now? Just wait for someone to stumble past? That doesn't seem very sporting."

"How are your tree climbing skills?"

"Wait in ambush for them? Shouldn't we be using our highly tuned detective tracking skills?"

"I left my eyeglass and deerstalker at home."

Mills looked around the clearing. "None of these trees look particularly climbable. I suppose… I mean, we could use the opportunity to get to know one another a bit better."

"Tell me you weren't part of this whole goddamn set up."

"No!" His hand shot up to his mouth, the word had come out a little loud. "No, not at all," he whispered. "But as we are both here… where's the harm in being friendly?"

Ingrid was just about to remind him how inappropriate that would be, given she was an engaged woman and all, when a sharp crack echoed around the forest: the sound of a tinder dry branch snapping. She pointed in the direction of the sound and Mills nodded back at her. They crept to the side of the clearing and slipped behind the thick gnarled trunk of an oak tree.

They waited.

After a couple of minutes Mills started to get restless. Ingrid laid a hand on his arm and looked up into his eyes. She felt the muscles in his forearm flex. He held on to her gaze for a moment longer than she was expecting. But, never one to look away first, Ingrid continued to stare back at him. An unexpected and unwanted thrill ran up her spine.

Another crack sounded. Much louder this time. Coming from directly ahead of them. Ingrid lifted the strange blowpipe contraption to eye-level and steadied herself. She saw a figure dash between two trees. Too fast to get a shot. The figure wasn't wearing a vest either. Without the hi-vis marker it was impossible to identify their opponent. Could it be one of their own team? The individual was too tall to be McKittrick, too fast to be Jane and too broad-shouldered to be Kapoor or Murray. From this distance, Ingrid couldn't even work out if it were a man or a woman. She continued to stare hard in the direction of the movement until her eyes started to water. She pointed behind where the figure was standing, away from the clearing and raised her eyebrows at Mills. He shrugged back at her.

She leaned in close and lowered her voice. "We should try to circle around and come at them from behind—use the element of surprise."

Mills nodded.

They started to move further into the forest, using the trees for cover, both taking extra care to step over twigs and fallen branches as quietly as possible. Continuing this way for two hundred yards or so, Mills stopped, forcing Ingrid to pull up sharply. Her forward momentum sent her crashing into him. For a moment she felt the intense heat coming off his body like steam. She quickly withdrew. They both stood there, staring at one another. Motionless. Listening. Ingrid's heart was pounding. She wasn't entirely sure why.

Another sharp noise sounded out, not the same as before. This was more like a splintering, creaking sound. Then it came again. Emanating from some place above their heads. Ingrid looked up to see an arrow sticking out of the trunk of the tree right next to them, fifteen or so feet up.

"What the fu—"

Another arrow whizzed past them. The quill close enough to brush Ingrid's cheek before it slammed into a tree trunk not two feet from her head. She dropped to the ground, dragging Mills down with her. They half crawled, half snaked along the ground, scrambling onto the other side of the tree that had been hit. Now Ingrid's heart was banging so hard and so fast she thought it might stop. She drew in a deep, slow breath. She listened. Heard footsteps crashing over the undergrowth. She couldn't tell if they were heading toward them or retreating. She tried to speak, but her mouth was so dry her tongue had stuck to the roof of her mouth. She swallowed.

"Hey! I don't know what you think you're playing at, but this isn't a game. Put the bow and arrows down and your hands above your head. You picked on the wrong people to have a little fun with."

"Police!" Mills shouted. "Stop pissing about now and this doesn't have to go any further. Step into the clearing and make yourself known."

The footsteps had slowed, but they were louder now.

Ingrid whispered to Mills, "How fast can you run?"

"As fast as I have to."

"If he doesn't cooperate, we need to head back to base, just as fast as possible. Don't run in a straight line, zig-zag and change direction as often as you can." She pulled herself up into a crouch. "OK, this is your last chance," she hollered, "make yourself visible and put down your weapon."

The footsteps stopped.

Ingrid and Mills looked at one another.

Moments later, another arrow hit the tree right next to them.

Dammit. "Ready?"

Mills nodded back at her.

They both sprinted away from their temporary refuge, Mills heading left, Ingrid going right, creating so much noise herself, it was impossible to tell if the shooter was in pursuit.

Until another arrow flew past her head.

This one was so close it nicked the skin of her right temple. Now she knew two things: he *was* following and for the moment at least, she was his target. Some crazy sky-howler had gone berserk with a lethal weapon in his hands.

She carried on crashing through the forest, trying her damnedest to keep her pace up while zigging and zagging her way around trees, sticking to the most densely wooded areas. She leaped over a fallen trunk and landed heavily on the other side on a mulch of leaves and moss, the surface too slippery to keep her footing. She thumped onto the ground, her right hip and shoulder taking the worst of the impact. She lay there for a moment, just listening for footsteps behind her. When she didn't hear any, she scrambled to her feet.

Big mistake.

An arrow hit her shoulder, skidding off the thick leather strap of her backpack, and deflecting upward, narrowly missing her face. She ran, faster than she'd ever run before. Pumping her arms, willing her weary thigh muscles to carry her further. On and on, she went, forcing her numb brain to remember to adjust her direction every few strides.

Her lungs were screaming at her to stop, but she blundered blindly on. Hoping she was still headed in the right direction, disoriented by the number of times she'd adjusted her course. Her limbs started to feel loose and weak. Still she managed to maintain her speed.

At last she reached the marquee. Mills was already there, a cell phone stuck to his ear, a grim expression on his face. When he saw her his mouth fell open.

"Jesus Christ! You're bleeding!"

She collapsed at his feet.

TWENTY-NINE

Although Ingrid was unable to persuade Mills not to phone for emergency medical assistance, she at least managed to convince the two EMTs that arrived thirty minutes later that their time would be better spent elsewhere, attending real emergencies. They took a look at the wound on her temple, decided it didn't need stitches and stuck on a dressing. Before they left they examined her shoulder and told her it was badly bruised, but nothing was broken.

After she'd made it back to the marquee, Mills had refused to leave her side, like some kind of loyal rescue dog, when all she wanted was a little time alone to properly get her breath back. To gather her thoughts. To try and work out how some crazy guy had managed to get his hands on a bow and a seemingly endless supply of arrows.

As far as she could tell—no one was telling her very much of anything—the local cops had tried, in vain, to secure the area. The adventure facility was just too big to cordon off. Given that the lunatic with the lethal weapon hadn't hung around to take pot shots at anyone else, she had to presume he had made his escape long before the police arrived. But did that mean he was still out there, lying in wait for some other innocent member of the public to cross his path?

The staff at Nature's Playground had confirmed that one of their Navajo bows was missing, together with around a dozen arrows. All the customers who had been on the archery shooting range had been accounted for. So they were certain the person responsible had nothing to do with their organization.

"Shame they didn't keep their weapons better secured," Mills had complained to no one in particular.

Forty yards or so away, a uniformed officer from the local Hertfordshire force was speaking earnestly with a plain clothes colleague, glancing in Ingrid's direction every now and then. They were keeping her out of their conversations, like some kind of frail invalid. But she was suffering from no more than a superficial head wound and extreme fatigue. Mills had been fielding any approach by the local officers and sending them away again, acting like a one man human shield. He couldn't protect her from their interview forever. Everyone else in their party had been interviewed and made statements. Not that they would have seen anything.

With some effort, Ingrid struggled to her feet. Immediately Ralph Mills hurried to put a supportive hand under her elbow. His concern would have been touching if it hadn't been irritating the hell out of her for the past half hour.

"It's OK, Ralph—I think I've got this." She pulled away her arm, but maintained a fixed grin as she did so—she didn't want to hurt his feelings. Her legs were very weak, but she managed to limp over to the plain clothes detective from the Hertfordshire force. "I guess you need to speak to me."

The detective scrutinized her through narrowed eyes then glanced in Mills' direction. "You sure you're up to it? Wouldn't want to overtax you."

"I'll survive. I'd prefer to get through your questions sooner rather than later—I wouldn't mind getting myself into a hot bath."

"Of course. Shall we talk in the car? You can take the weight off."

"I'd like to stand. Sitting down for so long doesn't work well for me." She smiled and took a closer look at the detective. He was in his fifties at least, had a tired face, thinning gray hair and his back was stooped as if a great burden were bearing down on him.

"Can you give me a description of your attacker?"

"I didn't see him. I didn't stick around to find out what he looked like."

"You're sure it was a man?"

"An assumption on my part. He or she was pretty damn fast. And not a bad shot. Thankfully not quite good enough though." She paused for a moment, reliving the moment the fourth arrow struck her shoulder. Immediately the area just below her shoulder blade felt a little more tender. "I did see a figure between the trees shortly before the shooting started. He was just a blur. I think that was a man, just from the way he moved. He was pretty well camouflaged against the trees. So I guess he was wearing green, or gray, or maybe light brown clothes."

"Height? Build?"

Ingrid closed her eyes and imagined herself back in the thicket of trees just south of the clearing. "I only saw him for a split second. Average height and build, I guess—not what you want to hear, I realize."

"And you think this may have been your attacker?"

"I have no idea."

The detective let out a weary sigh.

"I'm sorry I can't be more definite. It all happened so fast."

"Is there anything else you remember about the attack that might be relevant?"

Ingrid tried hard to think of something, some nugget of information she could give the guy. In the heat of pursuit her mind was focused on nothing more than survival. Her observational skills pretty much deserted her. She felt a little ashamed she couldn't be more helpful.

The cop handed her his card. "Anything else occurs to you, however unlikely... I don't need to tell you that... just call me, anytime." He turned away and trudged back toward his uniformed colleague.

"Detective!" Ingrid called after him. "Am I free to go?"

He turned slowly back. "Do we have your contact details?"

Ingrid nodded.

"We'll be in touch." He dismissed her with a cursory wave of his hand.

McKittrick and Mills, who had been keeping their distance while Ingrid was talking to the cop, both approached her.

"I've just been talking to one of the PCs," McKittrick said. "They've done a quick search of the area and found no arrows."

"Well they need to do a slower one." It wasn't possible a crazy man wielding a bow and arrow would tidy up after himself. "They just haven't looked hard enough."

"Forensics will be a nightmare," Mills added. "Too many pairs of feet trampling through the area. I don't envy them."

"Do you want someone to stay with you tonight?" McKittrick said and glanced in Mills' direction.

"What, you think someone should sleep on the floor of my hotel room like a guard dog?"

"I was more thinking along the lines of the futon in my spare room." McKittrick raised her eyebrows.

"Thanks for the offer. But I'll be just fine by myself. I don't know why you're assuming he was targeting me in particular."

"No one else was shot at."

"He probably saw Mills and me and decided I'd be the easier prey to hunt down. Slower and weaker."

"Had no idea who he was taking on, did he?" Mills smiled at her.

Ingrid was mad she'd gotten hit at all. If she'd been in optimum shape the guy wouldn't have come close. And if she'd really been in form, she would have outrun him, circled back, climbed a tree and ambushed the bastard.

"I'll order us a cab to the station," Mills said.

"Sod that. I'll get one of the uniforms to drive us back. It's the least they can do," McKittrick said and marched off toward the nearest cop car.

"I feel like I abandoned you," Mills said. "I should have come with you."

"And give him twice the target to aim at? Forget about it. In the circumstances, we did the only thing we could."

"Even so." Mills sniffed and looked down at the ground.

"Stop beating yourself up. It doesn't help." She touched him lightly on the arm. "Believe me, I've had plenty of experience."

He smiled at her and nodded, then, seemingly instinctively, he craned his neck down and planted a kiss on the top of her head. Taken completely off guard, Ingrid reared away from him and stumbled backward. Mills' expression suddenly turned from sympathy to something approaching horror.

"God. I'm so sorry," he blurted, "I don't know what I was thinking. I just… You looked so… I wasn't thinking."

Ingrid didn't know what to say. So she said nothing. She turned her head to see McKittrick waving at her from a patrol car twenty or so yards away. Ingrid hurried toward her without risking a backward glance at Mills.

THIRTY

"My God—what the hell happened to you?" Sol Franklin stood at his front door and stared at Ingrid open-mouthed.

Without thinking, Ingrid raised a hand to her head. "It's nothing. Someone got a little out of control with a bow and arrow."

"They did what?"

"Are you going to invite me inside, or should I tell you all about it in your front yard?"

Sol pulled the door wide open and ushered her inside. "Isaac's here already, tucking into the hors d'oeuvres."

Poor bastard. Ingrid remembered her initiation dinner at the Franklins like it was yesterday. Sol took enormous pleasure in torturing new recruits with his wife's cooking. If Isaac managed to get through to dessert, he'd pass the assistant deputy chief's test with honors. Unfortunately, Ingrid would be forced to endure the same menu. She hoped she could blame her injury for her lack of appetite and Madeleine Franklin would accept the excuse.

By the end of the first course of mushroom pulp on carbonized toast—not the way Mrs Franklin had described it—Ingrid had told the little gathering all about her outdoor adventure.

"And the local cops don't have any leads?" Sol asked.

"Short of the guy handing himself in, I don't think they stand a chance of getting anywhere. They have closed down the facility for the time being. They were breaking every health and safety code in the book, apparently."

"Do you think he was targeting you specifically?" Isaac asked as he placed his fork deliberately in the middle of his plate, signaling he was done. To his credit, he'd managed to ingest the whole of his mushroom mush.

"How could he be? I didn't even know where I was headed until I arrived there."

"Maybe he was following you." Isaac dabbed at his mouth with a linen napkin and leaned a little closer toward Ingrid, who was sitting opposite him.

"I think that's a little fanciful."

"But not impossible?"

"As good as." The thought had crossed Ingrid's mind. But since she'd been in the UK, only a half dozen cases had resulted in the arrests of suspects. Ingrid knew for a fact four of those were back in the US and the other two were both in custody here in London. She'd dismissed the idea that someone was targeting her specifically almost as soon as it had occurred to her. "It's not like I've made any enemies."

"Oh I don't know, I can get pretty pissed at you from time to time." Sol smiled broadly at her.

"You look so pale," Madeleine Franklin said. "Do you think maybe you should be in the hospital?"

"No, ma'am, really, I'm just fine. I'm just so sorry I don't have much of an appetite." She offered a weak smile while Sol shot her an admonishing glare.

Uncomfortable with so much attention focused on her, Ingrid was keen to change the subject. "Say, Isaac, did you get a chance to follow up on the missing person case on Friday?"

Before he could answer, Madeleine Franklin got to her feet and announced that the main course would follow imminently. Ingrid saw Isaac stiffen slightly. "I suggest you stop talking about work by the time I come back in."

"Need a hand, my love?" Sol said it with the demeanor of a man who is permanently banned from the kitchen. He hadn't moved a muscle—he knew before he asked what his wife's answer would be.

"Did you manage to pull up the phone records?" Ingrid asked Isaac.

"He hasn't used his cell phone for three straight days. Or his bank cards."

"You think it's time to call in the local cops?" Ingrid asked him.

"Can I do that?" Isaac glanced at Sol for guidance.

"Sure you can," Ingrid answered. "This is your case now."

Isaac straightened his back and sat a little taller. "OK—I will."

"Just keep me posted."

"Of course. I'll get onto the local Borough Command first thing in the morning."

"If he survives the next two courses," Sol mumbled to Ingrid. "In the lull before the oncoming storm, I'm going to smoke a cigarette very slowly. I'll see you good people later."

"You OK here on your own for a while?" Ingrid asked Isaac. "I need to speak to Sol about something."

"Sure—just come back before the food arrives."

Ingrid smiled at him and squeezed his shoulder as she walked past. Isaac Coleman was shaping up OK, especially if he graciously made his way through the main and dessert. Ingrid headed for the kitchen and Madeleine pointed to an open back door. Through the gap Ingrid saw Sol leaning on a wooden rail at the far end of his deck.

"Don't be long," Madeleine said, and dabbed at her brow with a napkin. She peered into the oven and sighed.

Ingrid hurried to join Sol and stood at the rail with him— staring out into a darkening backyard.

"Has he passed the test?" she asked him.

"Too early to call. He didn't play with his first course like you did. So he gets some Brownie points for that." He turned and peered into her face. "Does it hurt?"

"I'll survive."

"That's not what I asked."

"You know me, takes more than a lunatic playing cowboys and injuns to keep me down."

"How's the City trader case coming along?"

"Still waiting for the cops to locate the missing cleaner. I don't hold out much hope."

"You don't think the cops are up to the job?"

"They don't really stand a chance. Hernandez could be anywhere. I'm still trying to figure out why Matthew Fuller was targeted. I'm sure if we could just persuade Witness Protection to reveal his former identity—"

"We've been through this already. You know what I think about it. He was a kid when his name changed and the family moved house. Too young to make any enemies. Especially the kind who would spend the next twenty or so years hunting him down. You're chasing your tail on that one. It's not a percentage shot."

"But we've played all the percentage shots already. And we're losing the game."

"Maybe I'll run it past the deputy chief. Let her make the decision."

"Thanks, Sol," Ingrid said begrudgingly. She knew there was as much chance of Amy Louden agreeing her request as Isaac asking for a second helping of his main course.

Sol took an extra long drag on his cigarette, then stubbed it out in an old champagne bucket filled with sand. "We'd better get back in there, give the poor kid some moral support."

"Hey," Ingrid said, "I forgot to tell you… I found myself a perfect apartment."

"I didn't even know you were looking."

"It was a spur of the moment thing, I guess."

"Sick of hotel gourmet cooking, huh?"

"Something like that."

"I'm glad to hear it."

"You are?"

"It means you're planning to stay on at the embassy. And that makes me very happy."

THIRTY-ONE

The next morning Ingrid felt remarkably good, considering what she'd been through the day before. She was at her desk by eight. Isaac didn't show up until well after nine.

"You survived the night," Ingrid declared when he shuffled to his desk. "For moments at dinner it was pretty much touch and go."

"I've got a strong constitution." He laid a hand gently on his stomach.

"You certainly have. I've got to admit, I was impressed."

He gave her an uncertain smile and lowered himself gingerly to his seat.

Ingrid then spent the next three hours chasing Mbeke, Fraser and the detective from the paintballing place for updates. When she eventually tracked them all down, she discovered they had nothing new to report.

At midday she received the call she'd been hoping for.

"Mike—you got something?"

"You wanted a list, I got you a list."

"And so fast too." Ingrid knew Mike Stiller wouldn't just put the information she'd requested in an email. He needed praise far too much for that. She just needed to remember to heap some on him at every given opportunity. "You are a miracle worker, Agent Stiller."

"You know me, I try to squeeze in three miracles before breakfast."

Ingrid had to remind herself that it was still only seven a.m. in D.C. He must have been working on her request over the weekend. Things had to be difficult at home, with Mary or the kids, for him to need to escape to the office quite so much. "What can I say—I owe you majorly." She waited for him to continue in his own good time.

He cleared his throat then made a gulping sound. Knowing Mike it was probably his fourth latte of the morning. "So... Barbara Highsmith." He swallowed another gulp of coffee. "The ex-congresswoman handled thirty-two financial cases in total while she was working as an Assistant US Attorney. That's an average of just under five a year. Seems she specialized."

Great.

"Any stand-out cases I should pay closer attention to?"

"You haven't exactly been clear what I was supposed to be looking for."

"A defendant who had some reason to want to finish her off."

"I guess at the time, any one of them might have wanted to wreak revenge. But bearing a grudge over twenty years later? You'd think the rage would have subsided after all that time."

"Unless it was festering while he was inside."

"I don't have time to analyze all thirty-two cases for you."

"No, of course not. And I don't expect you to. Email over the files and I'll start on the analysis myself."

"Oh... OK." He'd managed to convey a whole world of disappointment with just two words.

"Did any of the cases involve Witness Protection?" Ingrid asked.

"Wait a minute, I'll check." Less than thirty seconds later he had an answer for her. "We have a grand total of three witnesses who traded key evidence for immunity from prosecution and a new identity."

"Can you give me their names?" She grabbed a pen and pad from her desk drawer.

Mike spelled out each one for her. "But wouldn't it help to know their new identities too?"

"In a perfect world. The guy who's death I'm investigating here in London was in Witness Protection, but the Marshals Office are refusing to let me know anything about his former life."

"You want me to speak to them?"

"Would you?"

"I have a buddy in the Marshals Service. He owes me a couple favors. What's the guy's new name?"

Ingrid gave him Matthew Fuller's details, cursing herself for not thinking of asking Mike for help before. He'd been a Fed so long, he had contacts in pretty much every law enforcement agency there was.

"Leave it with me."

"Thanks, Mike." Ingrid was trying very hard to contain her excitement. Knowing Matthew Fuller's former identity might crack the whole case wide open.

"Is that it?"

"Before you go, can you tell me the names of the convicted defendants in the Witness Protection cases?"

Again, Stiller spelled out the names for her. Then made his excuses and hung up.

Ingrid set to work, searching the database for information about the three defendants. By the time she'd discovered the fate of the third, she felt like banging her head against the desk. If she didn't already have a throbbing headache, she would have done just that.

All three defendants were dead. Two had died after they'd completed their sentences, the third had died in custody, shot dead by a prison guard after attempting to attack the deputy governor. The prisoner went down only after the third bullet was pumped into his chest. Ingrid stared at the screen as she tried to picture the incident. The prisoner must have known his act was suicide, plain and simple. There was a phrase the Behavioral Analysis Unit was fond of using in those circumstances: suicide by cop.

Ingrid continued to stare at her computer monitor. Her last behavioral training session had taken place almost twelve months ago at Quantico. She tried to recall any details that might be relevant. The subject of 'suicide by cop' had come up more than once. She was pretty sure, that according to the Behavioral Analysis guys, sociopaths were much more likely to choose that option of suicide than any other. They were still determined to make their mark, to bend law enforcement officers to their will, right up until the end. She looked at the details of the inmate: Henry Ellis.

If he'd still been alive he would be sixty years old by now. Too old to fit the description they had for Darryl Wyatt in any case. But possibly the right profile in terms of his psychology. And sociopathy often ran in families.

She continued to study the details of the case and discovered that Henry Ellis' crime involved a Ponzi-style scheme that swindled dozens of innocent investors out of millions of dollars. He used the money from each tranche of new investors to pay out to the existing ones at fabulous rates of return, generating an investment frenzy and an endless supply of greedy, if decidedly gullible, investors. The original investor gave evidence against Ellis in return for immunity from prosecution. Then, with his family, he disappeared, courtesy of the Witness Protection Program.

It was way too early to expect Mike Stiller to have contacted his buddy in the US Marshals Office, but Ingrid had to at least try him. She tapped his number into her cell. He answered after the first ring. "Mike, you got any news for me?"

"Hey, I just got off the phone. I'm feeling a little harassed here."

"I'm just eager to get some place with this goddamn case."

"Take it easy, you're sounding a little... stressed."

"Stressed? No way. Just enthusiastic."

"Answer me one question."

"Anything."

"How much do you owe your successful career in the Bureau to yours truly?"

"You know I owe you everything, Mike. It goes without saying."

"Sometimes it's nice to hear it."

"So… your buddy in Witness Protection?"

"Matthew Fuller's name, aged seven, was Matthew Brite. His dad testified against a Henry Ellis, some Ponzi investment scam."

A chill ran across Ingrid's shoulders.

It was the information she had been hoping for. Finally she had a connection between Barbara Highsmith and Matthew Fuller: Highsmith the highly successful, career-focused prosecuting attorney, Fuller the son of the man whose testimony the whole case depended on.

"David Brite is dead, you know that?" Mike said.

"Matthew's dad? Yes—he died in an accident."

"You make it sound straightforward."

"Are you going to tell me that it wasn't?"

"He died while water-skiing, if you can believe it."

"Is that relevant?"

"Did you know the reason for death was asphyxiation?"

"He drowned, I guess."

"No—his asthma inhaler was empty when he tried to use it. He died of an asthma attack."

"Are you suggesting his inhaler was tampered with?"

"I'm just putting two and two together and making plenty. Think about it: the prosecuting attorney in the Ellis case is dead, the star witness is dead, the witness' son is dead. Seems a pretty comprehensive wipeout to me."

"But Henry Ellis is dead too. He didn't kill those people."

"I'm looking at his details right here." Mike's tone sounded decidedly smug.

"What is it?"

"How much do you owe me?"

"Give me a break, Mike." Ingrid's head was pounding.

"Ellis had a son, Cory, born 1979."

Ingrid did the math. "He'd be thirty-four now."

"Don't tell me, that just happens to be the same age as your suspect."

"Mike! You are a genius."

"I know."

"Thank you so much." Ingrid looked up to discover Jennifer looming over her desk, a panicked expression on her face. "Listen Mike, something's come up. I'll call you back." She slammed down the phone. "What is it?"

"You've got blood running all down your face."

THIRTY-TWO

"How many more times will I have to patch you up, huh?" The embassy doctor was standing in the doorway of the office, wagging a finger at Ingrid.

As far as she could recall, she'd never even asked for his assistance. She threw an accusatory glance at Jennifer, who quickly looked away.

Ingrid then managed to force herself to sit still through the doctor's examination, an endless list of questions and finally the application of a fresh dressing. All in all, she was incapacitated for well over an hour.

Eventually he snapped off his latex gloves. "Now please—take it easy, will you? How's the shoulder?"

"A little sore, but fine. It's nothing more than a big ugly purple bruise."

"I've a mind to sign you off active duty."

"That really won't be necessary."

"There's nothing wrong with admitting you're hurt, you know."

"I'm just sitting at my desk—what possible harm can I come to?"

The doctor turned to Jennifer. "Can I rely on you to make sure she does exactly that?"

Jennifer nodded meekly at him, but avoided Ingrid's gaze. When finally he exited the office, the clerk said, "I only did what was right. I'm not going to apologize for that. You need somebody looking out for you."

Ingrid immediately got back on the phone to Mike Stiller.

"What was the problem?"

"Just an open head wound."

"Yours?"

"Yep."

"You OK?"

"Right as rain. Couple Tylenol and I'll be fully restored."

"Something else you want to discuss?"

"I've been thinking… if you were Ellis' son, why wait so long to avenge your dad's death? Henry Ellis died in 1992, David Brite was killed in 2003."

"Cory Ellis was only thirteen when his dad died. What did you expect him to do? Quit school and go on the rampage?"

"But the ex-congresswoman was murdered just last May, *twenty* years after Henry Ellis committed suicide. Cory Ellis must be an exceptionally patient man."

"Maybe we could describe him as goal-oriented and extremely focused. Determined, single-minded."

Mike Stiller had just set out more character traits for a narcissistic sociopath. Ingrid got a little fidgety. She had a link connecting Highsmith and Fuller and a profile that fit the one she'd sketched of Darryl Wyatt. Cory Ellis had to be her man.

"Wait a minute," Mike said.

"What is it?"

"What a tragedy."

"What have you found out?"

"Mary Ellis, Henry's widow, Cory's mom, also committed suicide, May 15th 2001."

The date was significant, Ingrid was sure. If her head had been a little clearer, she might have remembered why before Mike Stiller chimed in.

"The ninth anniversary of Henry Ellis' death," he said, a note of smugness creeping into his voice.

Ingrid sat very still. She tried to concentrate. The date of Henry Ellis' death wasn't the one she was thinking of. Then, despite the anvil pounding in her head, it came to her. "That's the day Barbara Highsmith was killed."

"It was?"

"When did David Brite have his fatal accident?"

Mike tapped in something to his keyboard. Ingrid waited. "Same date," he told her after a few moments.

"That's one way to mark the anniversary of your parents' deaths."

At the other end of the line Mike Stiller let out a breathy whistle.

"Can you send me everything you have from the Marshals Office?"

"Sure. Who knew a stupid Ponzi scheme could cause so much havoc?"

"It wouldn't have been the first time. Or the last."

"Listen, I'll send you everything I've got. But you should take it easy, you hear? Open head wounds don't heal without a little help."

"No need to worry about me." She hung up and stared for a little while at the phone. Something was niggling at her, but the harder she tried to pin it down, the more elusive it became. She waited for Mike's email to arrive, and tried to get a little more comfortable at her desk.

Just a couple of minutes later, a cascade of emails and attachments arrived courtesy of Agent Stiller. Ingrid set to work. After an hour or so of going through both Matthew 'Brite' Fuller's records and those of his mother and father, her eyes started to swim a little. She closed them and relaxed back in her seat. Maybe it was time for another couple Tylenol.

Ingrid snapped open her eyes. The stabbing pain in her temple was so intense that she saw black dots in front of her eyes. It took her a few moments longer to realize her head was resting on her arms and her arms were leaning flat on her desk. She blinked. Someone had thoughtfully draped her jacket over her shoulders. Her mouth was connected to her sleeve by a trail of drool. She managed to lick her lips.

Slowly, painfully slowly, she pushed up off the desk and sat up straight. The room spun a little. She waited for it to stop before trying to move again.

Both Jennifer's and Isaac's desks were empty. They'd obviously left silently, not wanting to disturb her. Given how stiff her limbs felt and how sharp the pain in her temple, she might have welcomed a little gentle prodding. Then she noticed an old-fashioned alarm clock sitting on the corner of her desk. It was set to go off in five minutes. Next to the clock was a bottle of Evian, two white, oval-shaped pills and a note telling her to take it easy. Jennifer Rocharde had thought of everything.

Ingrid's cell started to buzz. She watched it creep a little further across her desk with every vibration. She peered at the screen before picking it up.

Crap.

It was the real estate agent. She was supposed to be moving into her apartment today. She grabbed the phone.

"Hi." The word came out as a croak.

"Ms Skyberg?"

She was so used to having her name prefaced with "Agent" she was momentarily at a loss how to respond.

"I'm here outside the property. Have been since six-thirty." His voice sounded weird, a little higher pitched than she remembered it. He was obviously very pissed at her.

"I'll be there in ten minutes, I swear."

She shrugged into her jacket, grabbed her purse and headed for the women's restroom. A splash of cold water turned out to be even more restorative than she'd hoped.

She headed for the basement parking lot, her stiff legs getting a little looser with every stride.

THIRTY-THREE

Getting out onto Park Lane and then around Marble Arch at the north-east corner of Hyde Park was no problem at all. Ingrid maneuvered the bike around stationary buses and black taxis, and quickly turned left into Edgware Road, made it fifty yards north, then stopped. Suddenly nothing seemed to be moving up or down the street. There was barely enough space for pedal cycles to squeeze through the gaps. Most of the cyclists had taken to the sidewalk. All she could do was sit and wait. She pulled her phone from a pocket and sent an apologetic text to the realtor. He responded with a text back: *no worries*.

The bike crept forward by tiny increments for the next twenty minutes. More than once, Ingrid considered abandoning it at the side of the road. But she was still faster on two wheels than two legs—especially given the soreness in her shoulder and the throbbing pain in her head. Frustrated as hell, she continued to make very slow progress for another ten minutes, until she passed under the Marylebone expressway. Then, as if by magic, the gridlock ceased. Glancing across the street, Ingrid noticed an ambulance and two smashed up cars. The snarl-up had been caused by an accident on the southbound carriageway and rubberneckers on the northbound side, curious to see what was happening. Ingrid had slowed down herself to take a good look at the wreckage at the side of the road. She quickly chastised herself and accelerated toward Maida Vale.

Five minutes later she was climbing off the bike in the forecourt of the apartment block. She took off her helmet and gloves, stored them in the box on the bike and surveyed the parked vehicles for a red, white and blue Mini. There wasn't one. She jogged out onto the street. No Mini there either. And no sign of the realtor on the sidewalk.

Dammit.

He must have gotten tired of waiting for her. So much for his laid back response to her text. She checked her phone. She definitely hadn't missed a call. She returned to the bike and glanced at the main entrance of the building. An envelope was wedged inside one of the long brass door handles. Ingrid pulled it free and discovered her name was scribbled on the front. She tore it open and shook out a set of keys, three in total. Two for the apartment itself and one for the main entrance. She peered inside the envelope expecting to see a note, but there wasn't one.

She thought about going straight up to remind herself just how great the view was, but it was already after eight p.m., so she decided to return to her hotel to check out.

The journey to Marylebone was much easier than the one to Maida Vale. No sign of the road traffic accident at all. Less than a half hour after leaving the apartment block, she was stuffing her handful of possessions into a small suitcase.

She opened the safe inside the closet and removed her Glock 23. She didn't really have any safe place to store it at the apartment—she'd need to invest in a strong box. Meanwhile she'd just have to leave it at the embassy, which meant an unwelcome detour on the way back to her new home. She shoved the gun in a daypack and pulled out the remaining items from the safe: her passport, a little under $1000 in cash, and her engagement ring. She slipped the ring onto her finger. It felt cold. And a little loose. She must have lost weight since she last wore it. Staring down at the cluster of diamonds set in white gold, she pictured Marshall on one knee—in the middle of his favorite restaurant—reciting a little speech he'd obviously rehearsed. It had to be one of the few times she'd actually detected a flicker of vulnerability in his expression. He'd looked so earnest, so serious, so needy. And the most handsome she'd ever seen him. She wasn't sure how long it had taken her to say yes, but long enough for all the other diners to stop eating and stare at them. With that kind of audience anticipation, she couldn't really say no.

They had been engaged for over a year now. She'd have to agree to a date for the wedding soon. But she couldn't think about that right now. She took off the ring and slipped it into her purse. Immediately she felt a little lighter.

She sank onto the bed. What was she doing? She hadn't even told Marshall about the apartment yet. And here she was, getting excited about her first night there. Thinking about waking up in the morning to glorious views. She wondered if she should call him right then. Tell him she was planning to stay on in London—at least for the next little while. She pulled her cell from her purse, then just stared at the screen.

Tomorrow. She'd tell Marshall tomorrow.

With her daypack on her back and the suitcase strapped to the back of the bike, Ingrid rode the short distance to the embassy, deposited the Glock with security, picked up the sleeping bag she kept in the large drawer beneath her desk, then headed north to her new home.

When she finally got inside the building she discovered the elevators were out of order. She struggled over to the stairway with her suitcase and stood looking up at the first flight. A sudden and overwhelming fatigue enveloped her. The eight-story trek to the top floor felt like an attempt on Everest. She took a deep breath and started to climb. By the time she'd reached the halfway point she texted McKittrick, suggesting a little company and a large bottle of tequila seemed like a nice way to welcome her into her new home.

The final flights seemed to go on forever, but she finally made it to the apartment door, fumbled a little with the keys, and practically fell into the hallway.

The apartment was way too hot. It felt like a tropical plant house in there. Or maybe she had overheated because of the eight-story climb. Immediately, her head pounded a little harder. The heating had to be on. The realtor had promised her all the appliances would be checked before she moved in. Presumably, whoever checked the gas heater had forgotten to turn it off. She dumped her bags in the hall and headed for the bathroom, where she remembered seeing the heater on her earlier visit.

Sure enough, the heater was busy distributing heat to all the chunky white radiators in every room. She searched for an off switch, but couldn't find anything that looked right. She did find a red dial, which she gave a good hard yank counter-clockwise. Half the dial came off in her hand, the plastic fracturing in a jagged diagonal line.

Her head throbbed a little harder. Her breathing quickened. She needed to get some cool evening air into the apartment. As she turned toward the window, she noticed something shiny lying in the bath. She bent down and reached out a hand. In an instant her head started to spin. She straightened up and leaned against the wall, wondering if the dizziness was a result of her head injury or the lack of air. She took a couple of deep, steadying breaths and turned again toward the window. She unscrewed the latch and tried to push the top sash upward. It wouldn't budge. It looked painted shut.

Goddammit.

Maybe she could open the door onto the roof terrace. She spun around and started to head for the hall, but the sudden movement made her dizziness worse. She grabbed onto the doorframe with both hands, but her head started to buzz. She took a deep breath and stepped out into the hall.

Her sense of balance abandoned her completely. Her legs buckled and she sprawled across the floor. She tried to get up again, but her limbs felt so weak. Her eyes started to close and there was nothing she could do to keep them open. She laid her head on the floor—her flushed cheek found some relief against the cold floorboards—and drifted into unconsciousness.

THIRTY-FOUR

An intense pressure squeezed Ingrid's arms. Her head lolled from side to side. She couldn't seem to stop it. There was more pressure across her chest, as if something were pressing down on her. She tried to open her eyes.

She saw her dad, his arms open wide, just waiting for her to run into them. But how could she run when she couldn't move her legs? In the distance she heard a voice she recognized. A woman's voice, far, far away.

Natasha? What was Natasha McKittrick doing here in Minnesota? Was she on vacation?

"Ingrid! Wake up!"

Ingrid's head lolled again, faster than before. She was shaking. No—being shaken. Why couldn't Natasha just let her sleep? She was so tired. The pressure on her arms subsided. It started up again around her wrists. Then the floorboards started to slide beneath her. Who was moving the floor? She heard a door slam behind her. The floor felt wonderfully cold. Colder than it had before.

She didn't know this place. Where did her dad go? This wasn't Minnesota.

Cold liquid splashed across her face. What was that smell? Tequila? She heard Natasha's voice again, urgent and loud. What was she saying? Ingrid opened her eyes. Even though she could have sworn they were already open.

This time she didn't see her dad. Where was she? "Natasha?"

"Oh thank God. Stay with me, Ingrid."

Ingrid managed to prop herself up on an elbow. She had seen this place before, but couldn't recall when.

"The ambulance is on its way."

"I'm so hot."

McKittrick helped Ingrid to her feet and they limped out through a set of doors and into a stairwell. They sank down onto the first step. "That's it," McKittrick said, "big deep breaths."

Moment by moment, Ingrid's head cleared a fraction more. Her apartment. *That's* where she was. "What happened?"

"I'm not sure. How're you feeling?"

"Like crap." She tried to swallow. "Thirsty."

McKittrick fished around in her purse and pulled out a half full bottle of mineral water. Ingrid gulped down the lot. Then threw it all back up again two seconds later. All over her friend's shoes.

"I'm sorry."

"In the circumstances, I don't think that really matters."

Ingrid grabbed the banister rail and managed to haul herself up to her feet. She blinked hard a few times and dragged a sleeve across her mouth. She swayed left then right.

"Sit down, for God's sake." McKittrick put a hand under Ingrid's elbow to support her.

"I don't understand. What happened?"

"Let's not worry about that for now, shall we?"

A siren sounded in the distance. "You called the police?"

"No—I'm hoping that's the ambulance."

Ingrid pulled her arm away from McKittrick's. "I don't need an ambulance. I feel better already." She lurched to one side and reached out a hand for the banister rail.

"Tough. You're going to hospital even if I have to arrest you first." McKittrick punched a number in her phone. "This is Detective Inspector Natasha McKittrick, HSCC, area team four. I'm going to need police and fire brigade. I think there might be a gas leak." She pulled the phone from her ear. "Ingrid—could you smell gas when you arrived?"

"What? No—there's no leak. What are you saying?"

"Did you hear that?" McKittrick said into the phone. "I'd hazard a guess at carbon monoxide." She listened for a moment to the person on the phone. "I might not be here when they arrive, I've got to take my friend to the hospital. But if anyone needs to speak to me, you can give them this mobile number." She hung up.

"Carbon monoxide?" Ingrid's words continued to slur, no matter how hard she tried to speak normally.

A loud bang echoed up the stairwell. Then a door slammed. A minute or so later the door into the stairwell opened and an EMT ran through. He took one look at Ingrid and called out to his colleague, who was still in the lobby. A gurney appeared in the doorway.

"I'm not getting on that thing. I can walk." Ingrid stumbled forward a couple of steps and her legs gave way.

The next thing she was aware of was a torch shining in her eyes. "You're going to be just fine," a soothing female voice told her. Then sleep overcame her again.

When she woke up Ingrid could feel something digging into her nostrils. She raised her hand to her nose, but another hand stopped her before she reached it.

"Leave that just where it is."

Ingrid fought to focus on the face that the voice was coming from. Natasha McKittrick. She blinked and took in her surroundings. A hospital room. The blanket felt heavy against her legs. Light was coming in from a large window to her left. She had a gray plastic clip on one of her fingers and a tube of clear liquid feeding into her left arm.

"What day is it?" She struggled to get the words out, her mouth was so dry.

"Here." McKittrick lifted a plastic beaker to her lips and Ingrid took a sip of water. "It's Tuesday, you've been in overnight."

Ingrid tried to sit up. "My apartment." Memories of the night before were drifting in and out of her mind in a muddled mess.

McKittrick helped raise the pillows behind her and Ingrid pulled herself up. "Do you need the nurse or anything?"

"Not right now. Tell me what happened." She was having trouble focusing, so she closed her eyes. When she opened them again, the chair McKittrick had been sitting in was empty. She glanced toward the door. Through the porthole window she saw the detective speaking to a uniformed cop. A moment later the door opened and McKittrick came back in carrying a Pret A Manger plastic bag.

"Hey—you're with us again." She dumped the bag on a tall bedside cabinet and pulled out a cardboard cup. "I went for decaf—hope you don't mind. I didn't want your heart rate setting off any alarms. There's a pot of muesli and yogurt there for you when you're ready."

Ingrid smiled up at her. "Thank you."

"Don't mention it."

"I fell asleep earlier. I didn't mean to."

"Go right ahead and drift off again, if you need to."

Ingrid blinked a few times and wriggled upwards in the bed. She puffed out a breath.

"The color's come back into your face. You look a bloody sight better than you did earlier."

"What time is it?"

"Two in the afternoon."

"Why is there a cop outside the room?"

"Protection."

"What?"

"You really don't remember what happened?"

"It's a little hazy." She gave her friend a weak smile.

McKittrick sat down on the edge of the bed. "You may want to get comfortable. It could take a while." She handed Ingrid the coffee. "The fire brigade have done some analysis, and it was definitely carbon monoxide poisoning. The flue leading out of the boiler in your bathroom had come loose, and instead of the waste gases going straight outside, they all leaked into the flat."

"That doesn't explain the cop."

"I'll make allowances for your slowness, given you've only just come round. But I'm warning you now, my patience might wear a bit thin—I've been up most of the night." She pulled another cup from the Pret bag and took a sip. "The friendly neighborhood bobby is outside because three of the four screws that were meant to fix the flue in place had been removed." She stared into Ingrid's eyes. "Not come loose with general wear and tear, not rusted away... removed deliberately."

A sudden memory of the shiny objects she had seen in the bathtub popped into Ingrid's head. "Someone tried to..."

"Kill you... bump you off... do you in... yes." McKittrick put her coffee on the bedside cabinet. "Second attempt on your life in as many days. Even the Met aren't going to ignore that."

"Contact Sol Franklin—he can send someone from the embassy."

"You saying our boys can't handle it?"

"Only thinking of your budgets."

"Sod that! Besides, I've already spoken to Sol, he was in earlier with a huge bunch of inappropriate flowers. The nurses weren't at all happy with him."

Ingrid drank a little of her caffeine-free, and frankly, pointless black coffee while she considered who the hell might want to kill her. "I've got to get out of here." Pulling the blanket from her legs she noticed the tube that had been anchoring her to a drip was gone. All that remained was a cannula leading into a vein in her arm with transparent adhesive tape. She wondered how bad the bleeding would be if she just yanked it out.

"Stay exactly where you are."

"I need to find out who did this." She sat very still for a moment, the sudden movement had made her head spin. "How did they know about the apartment? Or the paintballing thing on Sunday? I didn't even know where I was going until we arrived."

"As it happens, I've been giving it some thought. I've had a bit of time on my hands, sitting here, listening to you snore."

"I don't snore."

"Well all last night you did. Thank God you're in a private room."

"And what did you come up with?"

"He must have followed you. To the paintballing place on Sunday and to your apartment yesterday evening."

Ingrid screwed up her face as a wave of nausea swept over her then gradually subsided.

"Jesus—should I fetch someone?"

"Oh God—I just remembered—I threw up on your shoes last night."

"It's OK—I wasn't that fond of them anyway."

"Sorry." Ingrid sniffed. "Whoever sabotaged the boiler would have needed to reach the apartment way ahead of me, just to have enough time to do what they did. They couldn't have followed me."

"Glad to see the gray cells have started firing. I suppose he must have already known about the flat."

"He?"

McKittrick raised her eyebrows. "You said it was a bloke who fired arrows at you."

"You should speak to the real estate agent."

"Tried that. He didn't show up for work today."

"He didn't?"

McKittrick shrugged. "Gone AWOL. I don't think he's our man, though."

"I really do need to get out of here."

"The registrar's doing his rounds later this afternoon. If he says you're good to go, fine. Otherwise you're here for another night."

"Better make sure I pass the test. I'll have that yogurt now."

"I should warn you, you might get a call from Marshall at some point." McKittrick couldn't look her in the eye.

"You told him?"

"I didn't—but someone at the embassy must have. I called your colleagues to find out who your next of kin was—I guessed, as he's only your fiancé, it wouldn't be Marshall. The hospital insisted on having a name."

Ingrid shuddered slightly.

"You cold? Want another blanket?"

"It's my mom."

"I know that now. Svetlana Skyberg. Now that's got a good old American ring to it."

"It's a Russian name."

"I would never have guessed."

"Should I expect a call from her too?" Ingrid shuddered again.

McKittrick shrugged back at her. "Judging by the look on your face, I'm guessing you don't want to speak to her?"

Ingrid shook her head.

"If she calls," McKittrick said, "I'll take it."

A half hour later Detective Constable Ralph Mills arrived with a bunch of magazines shoved under one arm. He hesitated at the door, too awkward to come straight in.

In a rush, Ingrid remembered the way she'd recoiled from the kiss he'd planted on the top of her head on Sunday. Thinking about it now, the kiss was as chaste as a grandson pecking his grandmother's cheek. She had completely overreacted. She needed somehow to make amends.

"I was expecting the doctor," she told him as he closed the door. The words came out like a criticism, not as she'd intended at all.

"Sorry to disappoint." He handed her the magazines. "I wasn't sure what you'd like, so I bought a range." He offered her the merest hint of a smile.

"That was very thoughtful of you. Thank you."

Ingrid fanned the glossy monthlies out across the bedclothes. *Parkour and Free Running, Motorcycle Monthly*, and *Rolling Stone*. Not a bad selection. She wasn't even sure she'd have chosen as well for herself. His insight into her personality unnerved her.

"And if you don't like any of these, you can read the paper." He laid the late afternoon edition of the *Evening News* on top of the magazines.

As Ingrid stared at the paper, she couldn't stop her mouth dropping open.

"What's wrong? Are you OK?" Mills asked her.

Two portraits dominated the front page of the paper. The one on the left was the photograph of Darryl Wyatt taken by his girlfriend, sent to Ingrid by Detective Trooe in Savannah. The one she and Angela Tate had distributed to dozens of properties surrounding the dead Latvian's apartment. The picture on the right was some sort of artist's impression of the same face, but this one had much darker hair and clean-shaven chin and cheeks. Ingrid checked the byline, even though she didn't really need to: Angela Tate.

The headline: *Have you seen this man?* was followed by a brief reminder of how the cherry-headed Latvian woman was murdered. Ingrid continued to read, fighting hard to keep her head clear, and discovered a witness living in the same apartment block had confirmed seeing a man fitting the description of Wyatt visiting the Latvian's apartment regularly for the last few months. He even occasionally stayed over.

"What is it?" Mills asked again.

The clincher came in the next paragraph. A fact that Ingrid had not revealed to Tate: the witness had also confirmed he'd seen a distinctive rose tattoo on the man's left forearm.

"He's definitely here." Ingrid swung her legs over the side of the bed. "There's no doubt now." The facts about Cory Ellis and his connection to both Matthew Fuller and Barbara Highsmith swam up through layers of murky memories and finally surfaced in her mind. "Darryl Wyatt. Cory Ellis. Whatever he's calling himself now."

"Who?"

"Help me find my clothes. I've got to get out of this place."

THIRTY-FIVE

Mills finally located Ingrid's clothes in a large green plastic sack shoved into the bottom of the bedside cabinet. Just as he was handing them over to her, the door opened. McKittrick marched in. A man in smart suit pants and a short sleeved shirt trailed after her. The man raised both eyebrows in an exaggerated expression of surprise.

"I do hope you weren't thinking of going anywhere, Ms Skyberg," he said.

"First of all, it's *Agent* Skyberg, and I am thinking of getting the hell out of here."

"I'll be the judge of that."

The registrar—McKittrick had apparently dragged him all the way from the Emergency Room—spent the next five minutes running through tests: checking her blood pressure, temperature, oxygen absorption and reflexes, before finally giving her the OK to be discharged.

"A nurse will be along in a while to remove the cannula," he explained.

"Can't you take it out for me?" Ingrid lifted her arm toward his face.

"I'm afraid matron wouldn't allow that."

"All right—I'll rip it out myself." Ingrid tugged on the adhesive transparent tape and managed to loosen a corner. "I've got to get back to work."

"Stop that! Good grief." The registrar quickly washed his hands, grabbed a pair of disposable gloves from a dispenser above the bed and carefully unpeeled the adhesive tape. When the cannula was out he told Ingrid to apply pressure to a folded dressing on the needle site for a minute or so.

"*Now* you can get the hell out of my hospital. But there is absolutely no way you're returning to work. I'm discharging you into the care of a responsible adult on the clear understanding that you rest for the remainder of the day." He looked from Ingrid to McKittrick and back again.

"He means you, Natasha. How responsible are you feeling?" Ingrid peered at the needle puncture. It oozed a little more blood. She pressed the dressing again.

"Well I'm definitely an adult—that'll have to be good enough. We'll get you fixed up at mine, in the spare room."

"I'd be perfectly fine on my own."

"I didn't hear that," the registrar said, and left the room.

Ingrid and McKittrick were sitting in a taxi stuck in traffic, just a few hundred yards from the hospital when Ingrid decided to make her escape. She reached for the door handle.

McKittrick grabbed her arm. "What the bloody hell do you think you're doing?"

"I need to get to work. I'll pick up another cab."

"You've been released into my care."

"Jennifer's perfectly capable of looking out for me in the office. I've already taken up far too much of your time. You need to get back to work too."

"No way. I'm not letting you out of my sight."

"But I need access to the Bureau database. I know who killed Matthew Fuller. And the Latvian woman. I need to put together a profile of the perp to try and work out where he might be now."

"Fine. But not today."

"Tomorrow might be too late."

"Tough. Call someone. Get your boss to handle it for you."

"It's my case. I've worked damn hard on it."

"You're in no fit state. You're coming home with me and resting. You can watch a bit of television maybe. But mostly, you're going to be lying down and dozing. Carbon monoxide poisoning isn't something you can just shrug off."

"I've had a night in hospital. I'm fine now."

"Are you still talking? I'm not listening anymore."

"At least let me make a couple of phone calls."

"OK—but make them quick."

Ingrid found her cell phone buried deep in the bottom of her purse and scrolled through the contacts list until she found the name she was looking for. She hit call and waited. And waited. The call was finally answered just as she was about to give up.

"Agent Skyberg, so good of you to get back to me." The sarcasm in Angela Tate's tone was unmistakable. "I've been leaving you messages all morning."

Ingrid glanced at McKittrick, who was staring out of the window. "I've been a little... tied up."

"Seems those flyers worked a treat."

"Have you reported all the information to the investigating team?"

"Of course I have. The witness is probably giving his official statement as we speak."

"Who is this witness?"

"Bloke who lives in the upstairs flat in the same block as the Latvian woman. He'd been away for a few days. Couldn't believe what had been going on in his absence. I got the impression he was rather fond of the woman."

"He gave you the description of the man?"

"He noticed him coming and going. He'd asked Mary about her new boyfriend a couple of times, but she never wanted to talk about him."

"This neighbor knew her name?"

"Only her first name."

"And the name of the boyfriend?"

"Nope."

"How was he so sure the man he'd seen was the same as the one in the photograph?"

"He wasn't one hundred per cent. But the likeness was close enough for him to call me."

McKittrick cleared her throat nosily. Ingrid turned to her.

"I'll take that bloody thing away from you. Hurry up and finish the call."

"Who's that?" Tate asked.

"Don't worry about it."

"So—is he your man? You never mentioned a tattoo to me."

"Maybe. I need to do a little more research to be sure."

McKittrick cleared her throat again. Ingrid held up a finger and mouthed "one minute" at her.

"When was the last time the neighbor saw the man?"

There was a pause at the other end of the line. "Last Tuesday evening. That's when he left for his holidays."

"Can you give me the neighbor's details? I'd like to speak to him myself."

Tate told Ingrid his name and flat number. "Though you might want to wait a while. He's rather tied up with the police at the moment. Perhaps you should liaise with them." Tate hung up.

As Ingrid stared down at her cell phone, trying to work out the significance of the timing of the Darryl Wyatt's last visit to the property, McKittrick snatched it from her hands.

"That's enough. You already look paler. No work. And that's final."

"I have another call to make."

"It can wait."

"I don't think it can."

"What was that all about anyway?" McKittrick waved Ingrid's phone in the air.

"According to the witness, my suspect returned to the property hours and hours after he killed her. I don't understand why."

"To clean up after himself, I expect. Didn't you say no forensic evidence was found at the flat?"

"It's more fundamental than that. If I'm right and the man responsible for the Latvian's death also killed Matthew Fuller…" Ingrid's head was just too fuzzy to figure everything out.

"Yes?"

"Bear with me here—"

"Wait a minute… how is this any different from you sitting at your desk working through things? I shouldn't even be talking to you about it."

"Matthew Fuller is on his hit list, he comes all the way to London to kill him. He watches him die a terrifying, painful death. Why not leave the country straight after? You've achieved your goal. Why stick around long enough to discover that your Latvian girlfriend is trying to screw money out of your old bank account in the US?"

McKittrick shrugged. "Maybe he had another reason to stick around."

"Like what?"

"I don't know. I really shouldn't be encouraging you. Let's talk about it later, once you've settled into the spare room."

"For God's sake! I'm not an invalid."

"Actually, right now that's exactly what you are."

"What possible reason could he have to stay in the UK?"

McKittrick shook her head. "Maybe he's not finished yet."

"What?"

"Is it possible there's someone else on his hit list?"

"Huh?" The fuzziness in Ingrid's head was starting to feel a little worse.

"Maybe he's planning to kill someone else here."

The thought hadn't even occurred to Ingrid. "Someone else?"

"Isn't that possible?"

"I guess. But it'd have to be someone connected to the original trial of his father. All the other deaths were." Ingrid blinked hard, trying to recall all the details of the killings. "In each case, the method of killing was connected to the victim's weakness, a vulnerability."

"Any other similarities?"

"We've spoken about the cases. I'm having a little trouble recalling—" Ingrid hated to admit that her injuries were affecting her ability to do her job.

"Right that's it—let's talk about something else. This is too taxing."

"No, wait." Ingrid struggled hard to remember something she'd discovered that linked David Brite's murder to Barbara Highsmith's. After a few moments it came to her. "The date. Two of the victims were killed on the anniversary of the suspect's parents' deaths. May 15th."

"That's tomorrow. So Matthew Fuller's murder broke the pattern."

Did two kills constitute a pattern? "You think maybe he's planning to kill someone else on the 15th?"

"You're the one who can't work out why he hung around after the City trader's death. I'm just brainstorming with you."

"I need my phone."

"Later. All this talking has already made you a bit sweaty. You really are supposed to be taking it easy."

"Please. It won't take long, I promise. I need to find out who else was involved in Henry Ellis' trial. Whether it's possible they're here in the UK."

Reluctantly, McKittrick handed Ingrid her cell. Ingrid found Mike Stiller in her contacts list and waited for him to pick up.

"Hey, what happened to you?" he said as soon as she'd managed a 'hello'. "You haven't hassled me for more information for over eighteen hours. I was beginning to feel a little unloved."

"I've been in the hospital."

"Jeez—that open head wound of yours?"

"No… something else. It doesn't matter. I'm feeling much better now." She threw McKittrick a look.

"Is this going to take long? Only I've got a meeting to get to ten minutes ago."

"No time at all. I won't have access to the Bureau database for a while—I'm supposed to be convalescing—could you send me everything you can on the Henry Ellis investigation? I'm certain now his son is my suspect. And I know he's right here in London."

"What?"

"Come on, Mike, just this one favor for today."

"How long have you been in the hospital?"

"I don't understand."

"I guess you didn't get a chance to finish your research into Ellis, huh?"

"I didn't. That's why I'm asking for this favor now. Please, Mike."

"I really gotta get going."

"OK—send me the information after your meeting."

"You're wrong."

"What?"

"About Cory Ellis being your suspect. And he certainly isn't in London right now."

"Quit kidding around, Mike. Just send me the information, will you?"

"There's no point. Cory Ellis died in 2002."

THIRTY-SIX

Ingrid woke up in the middle of the night with a desert-dry mouth. In the half-light, she managed to make out the glass of water sitting on the floor beside the bed. She grabbed it and downed the lot, but it did nothing to quench her thirst.

She wandered to McKittrick's kitchen, her head full of questions she couldn't answer. She'd been so sure about Cory Ellis, and his connection to Matthew Fuller and Barbara Highsmith. It had all fitted together so perfectly. Maybe a little too perfectly. At least she knew that a man fitting Darryl Wyatt's description had been seen at the Latvian's apartment. The Fuller and Highsmith murders may not be linked, but Highsmith's killer seemed to be in London. McKittrick had called the team investigating the Latvian's death on Ingrid's behalf, giving them all the information Ingrid had managed to piece together with Mike Stiller's help.

Just before she'd retired for the night, McKittrick had given Ingrid back her phone. Ingrid thought about calling Mike Stiller again. But all she could have done was whine to him about how certain she'd been and how disappointed she was her theory hadn't panned out.

She refilled her glass from the faucet, and stood at the sink for a moment, enjoying how good the coolness of the tile floor felt beneath her feet. She thought about the kitchen in her own apartment and wondered when she'd be able to set foot in it again. Whether she ever would. She made a mental note to try calling the realtor in the morning.

The morning seemed an eternity away. She hoped she'd be able to get back to sleep, but she knew she'd be endlessly reliving events and running through the hasty plan she'd put together a few hours ago to apprehend her attacker. Under McKittrick's strict supervision, she'd arranged for a security contact of hers, Nick Angelis, who worked for what was effectively a private MI5 and MI6 combined, to follow whoever might still be following her. Angelis had been trailing marks for the past two decades. If there was a mark to spot, Angelis would spot him. In the meantime, there were two cops sitting in an unmarked car parked up outside McKittrick's building. It felt like overkill, but Sol and McKittrick had made it quite clear they weren't prepared to take any chances.

Ingrid padded back to bed and discovered that her cell phone was buzzing on the floor. It would be Marshall again. He'd tried her at least a half-dozen times already. She almost felt a little sorry for him. In her sleepy daze, she found herself scooping the cell from the floor and answering the call.

"Hey, Marsh."

"Honey… I've been worried about you."

"I texted you back."

"I needed to hear your voice."

"Well here I am."

"How are you?"

"Fine."

"Come on, honey—you can tell me how it really is."

"I'm a little tired maybe. But it is three in the morning here."

"I'm sorry—I've been trying you for hours. I just had to speak to you. Satisfy myself you were OK. I feel better now."

Well good for you. Ingrid regretted picking up the call.

"I think you should come home," he said, his voice a little whiny. "I miss you. I want to protect you. You must have been so scared."

Scared? Fear hadn't really come into it. Maybe when she had time to sit back and consider just how close she'd come to death, she might get a little terrified. But right now she was too goddamn frustrated that her theory about Cory Ellis had come to nothing. Marshall was wasting his time if he thought he could *scare* her into returning to the US.

"Do the police have any leads?" Marshall asked.

"They're working on several lines of inquiry. No one's really telling me very much of anything—I'm the frail victim in this scenario."

"What do you think? You must have a hunch."

"I really haven't been in London long enough to make any enemies. I'm no threat to anyone." Her head had started pounding again. She let out an exaggerated yawn. "Listen, Marsh, I'm really exhausted—I've got to get some rest. It's what the doctor ordered."

"Sure, sure. I feel so much better for hearing your voice. Goodnight, baby."

Ingrid hung up and tossed her cell into her purse that was sitting on her neatly folded clothes on a chair in the corner of the room. It wasn't until she got back under the quilt that she realized she didn't remember seeing her engagement ring since she'd slipped it into her purse at the hotel.

Showering and dressing early the next morning, Ingrid was eager to start her day. When she emerged from the spare room she was surprised to see McKittrick already perched at the breakfast bar in the kitchen, nibbling at a slice of toast.

"There's coffee in the cafetière. I can make you a fresh pot if you'd rather."

"This is fine—thank you."

"That shirt really suits you. I never wear it—you can keep it if you like." McKittrick popped the final corner of toast into

211

her mouth. "Have you spoken to your spook man yet this morning?"

"I don't have to—Angelis knows exactly what to do."

Twenty minutes later Ingrid was standing outside McKittrick's building waiting for an embassy car to convey her to work. She looked up at the tall, white stucco Victorian house. There had to be at least six apartments inside. McKittrick's was on the second floor. Ingrid saw her looking out of the living room window, like an anxious mother waiting for the school bus to arrive to take her child to its first day at school. Ingrid waved and smiled at her, giving her the thumbs up. Her head still hurt like hell, and her brain was fuzzy if she tried to concentrate too hard, but she was playing down the symptoms in order to be freed from what felt like house arrest.

The thirty minute journey from Kentish Town to Grosvenor Square was without incident, much to Ingrid's dismay. She'd been hoping for a little action. She wanted to flush out her attacker and be done with it. When she disembarked from the black sedan in the parking lot beneath the embassy, she phoned Nick Angelis to find out what he'd seen.

"Anything?" she asked.

"Not a sign."

"Is it possible you missed him?"

"If he's good enough to be able to follow you across London without me spotting him then we are dealing with a very talented individual indeed. Better than anyone currently working for the CIA, Mossad or MI6. Trust me—no one followed you this morning. Give me a call as soon as you want to leave the embassy and I'll do the same again."

"Thanks, Nick."

"You really don't have to thank me. I'm not having anyone hurt you again."

Ingrid hung up. She was a little surprised to hear Angelis sound quite so paternalistic. She didn't like it one bit.

She took the elevator to the third floor—her one concession to her impaired fitness—and tried to slip into the office and behind her desk without anyone noticing.

She failed.

"Ingrid!" Jennifer jumped up and hurried toward her. "How're you feeling? Can I get you anything?"

Ingrid waved her away. "I'm fine. Really."

Isaac hurried from his desk too. "Did you like the flowers? Agent Franklin let Jennifer and I choose them."

"They were just beautiful—thank you." Ingrid hadn't even laid eyes on the flowers Sol delivered to her hospital room. Hopefully somebody some place was enjoying them on her behalf.

"Do you know who tried to kill you?" Isaac said.

Jennifer shot him a look.

"I mean, you must have some idea, right?"

"I don't think it's anything you need to concern yourself with," Ingrid told him.

"Maybe we could help—look into the cases you've handled since you've been here. Work out who might be targeting you."

"That won't be necessary, Isaac. I'd appreciate it if you both got back to work. It's what I'm trying to do."

Jennifer grabbed Isaac's arm and forcibly marched him back toward his own desk. Although Ingrid was grateful for Jennifer's intervention, she did feel a little like an invalid. It wasn't a feeling she planned on getting used to.

THIRTY-SEVEN

For the next two hours, Ingrid laboriously researched the cases Barbara Highsmith worked while she was an Assistant US Attorney. If Cory Ellis hadn't murdered the ex-congresswoman, it was just possible that the answer to who had was right here in the files, waiting to be discovered. If Ingrid dug deep enough, she might just find it. But as she struggled to concentrate, fighting the fuzziness in her head, she felt she was making no progress at all. She switched databases and brought up Barbara Highsmith's details again. Maybe it was time to get back to basics. She was just starting to jot down a few notes about Highsmith's early life when her cell phone rang. She answered hesitantly, not wanting to have another awkward conversation with Marshall.

"Hey it's Mike."

Ingrid let out a sigh.

"Are you sitting down? You need to be when you hear this. How's that head wound of yours?"

"It's the least of my worries. What is it, Mike?"

"You know how I like to be thorough? How good I am at my job? How I can't leave something I'm investigating half-assed and incomplete?"

Ingrid really wished she could dispense with the 'boosting Mike Stiller's ego' section of the conversation just this once. Nevertheless, she played along. "You Mike, as has been well established, are something of an investigative genius. A god among men. A professional in a world of amateurs. A—"

"OK! You coulda stopped at the 'god' part. I've been looking into your suspect's file a little more closely. I wondered if he'd kept the family tradition of suicide going. I was curious, I guess."

Ingrid presumed he must also be very, very bored with whatever he was supposed to be working on. "And did he? Was it pills? Hanging? Or maybe he jumped in front of a subway train?"

"You sound a little pissed."

"I just got out of the hospital yesterday, give me a break."

"All right—take it easy."

"So how did he die?"

"According to eye witnesses, in September 2002, Cory Ellis paddled into Possession Sound in a sea kayak and was never seen again."

"He drowned?"

"Presumed drowned. Declared dead after seven years."

Ingrid swallowed. "His body was never found?" She snatched a breath.

"Nope. Never found."

Ingrid closed her eyes and let the news sink in for a moment.

"You still there?"

"Sure." The game was still on. She tried to remember what theory about Cory Ellis she and McKittrick had been discussing just before she'd called Mike and discovered Ellis was supposedly dead. But her foggy brain just wouldn't cooperate.

Dammit.

"Mike, OK if I call you back in a little while? This news has sent me into a bit of a tailspin."

"Just as long as you rehearse your speech of infinite gratitude and endless thanks first."

She hung up. Now she really was pissed. If Mike Stiller hadn't told her Cory Ellis was dead in the first place, she might not have wasted all morning trying to identify an alternate candidate for Highsmith's killer. Sometimes Mike tried just a little too hard to be indispensable. Ingrid looked up at Jennifer, who was hovering nearby her desk.

"Are you OK?" She walked around Ingrid's desk and stood next to her, touching her gently on the shoulder. "Only you had your eyes closed just now, I thought maybe you were in pain. Can I get you some painkillers?"

Anything that might make her head even a little less clear was something Ingrid wanted to avoid. "How about a strong black coffee?"

Jennifer was staring over Ingrid's shoulder at her computer monitor. "A long black, right?"

"Make it a double espresso. I need a jump start."

"If you're sure." The clerk couldn't seem to take her eyes from the screen.

"What is it?"

"Why are you looking into Barbara Highsmith?"

"It's connected to a case I'm investigating."

"Which case?" Jennifer sounded a little affronted there was something going on she didn't know about.

Ingrid didn't know where to start. She decided not to. "It's a little complicated."

Jennifer continued to read what was on the screen. "She's dead?"

"She was murdered last May."

"Oh my God."

"You knew her?"

"No. Not exactly." Jennifer ran back to her own desk and yanked open a drawer. She pulled out a thick hardback book and flipped to the index at the back. When she'd found what she was looking for, she waved the front cover at Ingrid. It featured a dramatically lit portrait of Ambassador Frances Byrne-Williams sitting at her desk right here at the embassy.

Jennifer dumped the heavy tome on Ingrid's desk and stabbed a finger at the entry for Barbara Highsmith in the index. There were at least a dozen page references.

"Frances is a huge fan of Barbara Highsmith. She didn't mention anywhere in the book that the congresswoman was dead." Jennifer then quickly checked the date of publication at the front of the book. "This edition was printed November 2011. I guess it wasn't updated." She shook her head. "I've read so much about her, how she was an inspiration to Frances, more of a mentor, really, that I feel like I do know her."

"How did they meet?"

"At Wellesley College. Frances was doing some part-time teaching there when Barbara Highsmith was a visiting lecturer."

"When?"

"I'm sorry?"

Ingrid had just remembered the conversation she'd had with McKittrick about Cory Ellis, specifically, why he hadn't left town straight after murdering Matthew Fuller. The fact that he hadn't finished what he came to the UK to do. "Which year were they both at Wellesley College?"

Jennifer flipped back to the index then leafed through the pages until she found a section on the ambassador's college years. "They were both there for the academic year 2003–2004. Why do you need to know, anyway?"

Ingrid worked out Cory Ellis would have been twenty-four at the time. Was it possible he'd made some connection between the two women? Could he have been in Massachusetts at the same time?

"What is it, Ingrid? Can I help with anything?" Jennifer was wearing her concerned girl scout expression. Ingrid was getting a little sick of it.

Then Isaac jumped up from his desk. "What's happening? Anything I can do to help?"

Ingrid wanted to shout at them to shut up and sit down. All she needed was just a little time and space to think. "Jennifer—you can get me that coffee I asked for?"

Jennifer nodded meekly.

"And Isaac—find out anything you can about possible links between Ambassador Byrne-Williams and Barbara Highsmith outside of their college connection. Anything at all. Though I'm most interested in any link the ambassador may have to Washington state."

"Washington State?"

"Any connection to the US Attorney's Office there."

Isaac hesitated.

"You understand what I'm asking you to do?"

"Sure. I'm on it."

Both Jennifer and Isaac slunk away from Ingrid's desk. Ingrid leaned back in her chair and exhaled. Was it possible Cory Ellis did plan to kill someone else in London? Could the ambassador be the next victim on his list?

THIRTY-EIGHT

After the double espresso had been duly delivered by an unsmiling Jennifer and drunk in two gulps by Ingrid, a good thirty minutes had passed. So far Isaac had found no connection between Highsmith and Byrne-Williams except for Wellesley College. Ingrid's own search was just as unsuccessful. She got Jennifer on the case too.

"Can I ask why we're looking for a separate link?"

Ingrid decided not to go into the details. At this stage, the ambassador's possible connection to her investigation was so tenuous she didn't want to risk saying it out loud and triggering an overreaction. "It's just a little theory I'm working on."

"Hey—did you know Highsmith was poisoned by peanuts?" Isaac called over to Jennifer.

"She was?"

"She had an allergy."

"Poor Frances. She must have been so devastated when she found out."

"*And* her killer is still on the loose." Isaac seemed a little too ghoulish in his revealing of the facts.

"Is that the investigation you're working on?" Jennifer asked Ingrid. "Are you looking for Barbara Highsmith's killer? Does that mean he's here in London?"

"I can't go into the details right now." Ingrid glared at Isaac, who seemed completely oblivious. "We're still looking for a link, remember," she told him. "Details about the murder are irrelevant."

"Not if he's planning to poison someone else," Isaac said.

If Frances Byrne-Williams had nothing to do with the Henry Ellis case, there was no reason to think she would be on Cory Ellis' hit list. But it was possible they just hadn't found the link yet. Ingrid grabbed her cell from her desk and headed for the door. "Carry on with that research," she told Isaac and Jennifer as she left the room.

Halfway down the corridor she called Sol. Running her crazy theory past him was the sanity check she needed. If he felt the ambassador was in any danger, he could decide to contact the Regional Security Officer, who in turn could ramp up Byrne-Williams' security detail.

Her call went straight to voicemail. She thought about leaving a message, but it was just too complicated to explain. Instead, she called DI Mbeke. He was more than due an update.

"Ingrid. You've been very quiet," Mbeke said in place of a simple 'hello'.

"I've been a little tied up." She then proceeded to tell the detective inspector everything she'd learned about the Henry Ellis case, his son Cory, the very definite connection between the Fuller and Highsmith poisonings, and the possibility that Cory Ellis was still in the country because he hadn't finished yet.

"How long have you known all this?"

"Is that relevant?"

"I thought we were sharing everything, as and when."

"Like I say, I've been tied up. It was impossible to call any sooner." Ingrid really didn't need to be given a hard time by Mbeke.

"And you think this Cory Ellis is still here in London?"

"I'm saying it's a possibility. We've discovered a link between the woman he poisoned in Savannah and…" She hesitated. Could she even voice her theory to Mbeke?

"Yes?"

"The ambassador."

"Your ambassador?"

"It seems Highsmith was something of a mentor for Frances Byrne-Williams."

"But have you found a connection between the ambassador and the original Ellis fraud investigation?"

"Not yet. We're working on it."

"But you've raised the ambassador's protection level while you do your research?"

"The whole thing seems a little far-fetched to me. I figured I should have a more robust connection before I go spreading panic."

"Better to be safe than sorry, surely."

Ingrid had been wrestling with that question for a while now. She really needed to locate Sol. "You think?"

"I suppose I'd do it just to cover my own arse. Imagine if you did nothing and something happened to her."

"Point taken."

"I have a little news of my own," Mbeke said.

"You do?"

"Two things. Patience Toure has contacted me. Initially all she would tell me was what a good man Miguel Hernandez was, how she was sure he wouldn't hurt anyone. How she didn't want to get him in any trouble. Eventually she told me she was calling about the picture on the front of the *Evening News*."

"She'd already seen that photograph."

"Not the photograph—the artist's impression. She said maybe it looked a bit like Hernandez. With some more encouragement from me, she was prepared to admit that it looked a lot like him. She apologized for not recognizing him before, told me he'd always been very good to her, then rang off."

"So we have a motive for Ellis to kill Fuller, and a witness confirming the man seen at the Latvian's apartment was also the cleaner at Fisher Krupps. It's all fitting together."

"But we're still no closer to finding the perpetrator."

"I've created a profile of Cory Ellis that you might be interested in taking a look at. Might help you work out where he could be holed up. I'll email it to you."

"I suppose I should liaise with the team investigating the Latvian's murder. You're sure Ellis is responsible for that death too?"

"As far as I can be. Let me contact the team first. Like I said before, I've been a little tied up. I need to bring them up to speed."

"Are you all right?"

"Why wouldn't I be?"

"You're slurring your words a bit."

"I am?"

"I wasn't going to mention it."

"I had a night at the hospital. But I'm fine now."

"You don't sound fine."

"Fully recovered. Right as rain. One hundred per cent."

"I hope you're managing to convince yourself."

"What was the other thing you wanted to tell me?"

There was a long pause, as if Mbeke had forgotten. "Actually, it's some good news for once. The maintenance man, Colin Stewart, has been released from hospital. He's made a full recovery."

Ingrid couldn't quite believe just how good that news seemed. She felt like she needed something to go right. "That's great. Really great. Thank you for telling me. "

"My pleasure." He said goodbye and hung up.

As she'd already walked as far as the elevator, Ingrid decided to pay Sol a visit.

She stepped out onto the fifth floor and hurried to his office. His door was open and the office was empty. She tried calling him again. Got the voicemail again. Patrick Mbeke's words had started to haunt her a little. What if she did nothing and something bad happened to the ambassador? Without Sol acting as her sounding board she felt lost and adrift. The fact that her head was still so foggy didn't help the rational decision making process one little bit. She headed back to her office.

"Have you found any other connections between Highsmith and the ambassador?" she asked before she was even through the door.

Isaac and Jennifer shook their heads.

"Maybe it would help if you could tell us why we're looking for one," Jennifer unhelpfully suggested.

"Do you think the peanut poisoner wants to kill the ambassador?" Isaac asked. He glanced at Jennifer who scowled back at him. It seemed to Ingrid as if they'd discussed the matter between themselves and then agreed not to raise it. Isaac had just broken ranks.

Ingrid took a deep breath. "I don't want to rule anything out."

"We should tell the RSO—Frances' protection should be increased," Jennifer said.

With the risk that Jennifer or Isaac might act unilaterally and contact the head of diplomatic security without her knowledge, Ingrid had no choice but to do something herself. "It's OK—I've got this covered. You carry on looking for a link, I'll deal with the RSO."

In Sol Franklin's absence, she headed for his boss' office. Thankfully, when she arrived, she discovered Amy Louden, the deputy chief, sitting behind her desk. Taking her time, making sure to enunciate as clearly as possible, Ingrid outlined in brief what she had discovered so far.

"You think there's a clear and present danger?"

"That I can't say. We don't have a concrete reason why Cory Ellis might consider the ambassador a target. But I thought it better not to take any chances." As Louden stared at her and said nothing, Ingrid was acutely aware that the potential threat she'd just outlined must have sounded crazy to any rational individual. She tensed, waiting for Louden's final verdict.

"You've done the right thing. I'll have a quiet word with the RSO, the ambassador need never know anything about it."

Ingrid rocked backward on her heels. She hadn't anticipated such a sympathetic hearing. She supposed that now a potential threat had been raised, maybe Louden was just covering her own ass. She couldn't just ignore it. It was hard to tell if the deputy chief was pissed at her, or genuinely pleased she'd brought the matter to her attention.

"Well done, Ingrid."

"Thank you, ma'am."

"Close the door on your way out."

By the time Ingrid stepped out of the elevator onto the third floor, she could already sense something had changed. As she passed fellow Feds, Marines and Diplomatic Security agents in the corridor, she felt each of them had a little more purpose in the way they moved. A tangible sense of urgency had somehow filled the air. Amy Louden sure worked fast. The RSO must have set some protocol in motion immediately. Ingrid couldn't help wondering if it was all a terrible overreaction.

She returned to the office and slumped heavily into her chair, her limbs as exhausted as her brain. She was starting to question the wisdom of returning to work so soon. She shook her head in an attempt to clear the cobwebs from it and only succeeded in making herself feel slightly dizzy and a little nauseous. She closed her eyes and took a few deep breaths.

"Man, it's harder to get into this building that the goddamn White House," a voice called from the other side of the room. Ingrid's tired brain had started to play tricks on her. That voice didn't belong here. She opened her eyes and turned her head slowly toward the doorway.

No way.

With a suit carrier slung over his shoulder, a huge grin plastered across his face, Marshall Claybourne sauntered toward her.

THIRTY-NINE

Marshall dumped his bags on her desk, leaned over and planted a kiss on her open mouth.

"Hey, honey, aren't you pleased to see me?"

Ingrid glanced over his shoulder to see Jennifer and Isaac staring at them, their jaws dropped lower than hers. "What are you doing here?" she managed to say in an urgent whisper, once she'd recovered the power of speech.

"I'm not sure that's any sort of welcome, honey."

She jumped up and grabbed his hand, then marched him straight out the office. She dragged him all the way down the corridor and into a small kitchen area before she let go. Once she had, he took the opportunity to wrap his long arms around her, pinning her arms to her sides, and scooped her off her feet. He squeezed her hard and rocked her from side to side. Eventually he returned her to the ground and kissed her again.

She took a good look at him. He'd gained a few pounds since she'd last seen him five months ago. His sandy hair was a little thinner too, at the temples. There were definitely more lines around his eyes and mouth. As they stood there for a moment, looking each other up and down, she supposed he was thinking the same thing about her. Sprinkled across his nose, Ingrid noticed the start of dark golden summer freckles. Somehow it still seemed kind of cute.

"Aren't you pleased to see me?" He looked a little crestfallen.

"I'm just so surprised you came all this way."

"I'd be a pretty crap fiancé if I didn't come see you after some lowlife tried to kill you. I love you, baby." He kissed her on top of her head. "You're using a new shampoo. I like it."

Marshall hadn't been this attentive even before she left the US. It was unnerving her. She wasn't sure she would have jumped on a plane and crossed the Atlantic if the same thing had happened to him. Which made her feel as guilty as hell.

He searched her face some more. "You look a little tired, honey. I can't believe you're back at work so soon."

"Wouldn't you be?"

He grinned at her. "I guess."

"I still can't believe you've just dropped everything and come all this way. I told you on the phone last night that I was perfectly fine."

"I was already at the airport when I spoke to you. You think I was just going to stay home when somebody tried to kill you?"

"When did you leave D.C.?" It suddenly occurred to her that Marshall may have found out about her continuing investigation into the Darryl Wyatt case.

"I just said—I was at the airport when we spoke. Why?"

Ingrid thought it through. There was no way he could have found out about the progress she was making on the case. She'd only found out herself that Cory Ellis might still be alive a few hours ago. She couldn't help but smile. Marshall couldn't have known about the case and yet here he was, in his six feet three, two hundred and ten pound glory. In exactly the right place at exactly the right time, slap bang in the middle of a minor crisis that needed solving. It was quite a knack.

"What's going on around here, anyway?" he said, "has there been a terrorist threat? There were so many armed

Marines manning the reception I thought there'd been an invasion."

Ingrid really couldn't face the prospect of explaining everything she'd discovered. As soon as she'd finished, she knew Marshall would insist on taking over. She stared at the floor and said nothing.

"Honey? What is it?"

"There's probably some stuff you should know." Ingrid then spent the next ten minutes bringing Marshall partially up to speed. Although she confirmed a man fitting the description of Darryl Wyatt had been seen visiting the dead Latvian, she stopped short of revealing what she knew about the Henry Ellis case and the connection to Matthew Fuller's death. She felt she had to keep a little something back for herself.

"And the ambassador has a direct link to Barbara Highsmith?" Marshall asked once she was through with her little speech.

"She does. But I'm not one hundred per cent convinced that makes her his next target."

"Does she have an allergy?"

"No—not as far as I know."

"But he may choose a similar method. He could be right here in the embassy cafeteria. Or maybe working in the kitchen of the official residency. Has anyone interviewed the kitchen staff?"

"We literally just got the ambassador's protection ramped up moments ago. Nothing else has happened. Not yet."

"We should put the kitchen and cafeteria into lockdown. Plus the kitchen at the residence."

We?

As Ingrid had feared, Marshall was taking over. It was second nature to him. She wasn't even sure she blamed him. But she sure didn't have to like it. "Just because he once poisoned someone in a restaurant, doesn't make that his M.O. I mean, look at what he did to the Latvian woman."

"You still think that was him?"

"I'm certain."

"How long have you known about Wyatt's presence here?"

"What's that got to do with anything?"

"Why didn't you tell me?"

"Wait a minute. I tried right at the beginning. You crapped all over my theory." Her earlier vaguely warm feelings toward her fiancé were rapidly cooling. It wouldn't be long before she was just plain mad at him again.

"But I'm listening now. What a stroke of luck I should be here when this all kicked off." He was grinning at her like a big idiot. "Aren't you pleased for me, honey? All the hard work, all the promotions and the commendations, they're all for you, you know. For us." His smile grew wider. "I'm making a better future for us both."

It had never felt that way to Ingrid and she certainly didn't want to think about their future together right now. She wasn't sure they even had one.

"I booked into the same hotel as you for my stay. I wanted to get you all moved into my suite while I'm here, but someone must have screwed up with the reservations or something. The manager said you moved out a couple days ago. I told him he didn't know what the hell he was talking about. Stuck to his story though. Fool."

This was not the way Ingrid had intended telling Marshall she was planning to extend her stay, but in the circumstances, she could hardly *not* mention it. She took a deep breath. "I moved into my own apartment."

"What?"

"The heater with the leaky flue that nearly killed me? That was in *my* bathroom."

"I assumed it was a friend's house."

She shook her head.

"Well, heck, honey. When were you planning on telling me?" He stepped back from her and narrowed his eyes. "Does this mean you're making the job permanent?"

"No! I don't know. Not permanent. But I do want to stay for at least another six months."

"And when the hell were you gonna share that with me? What about the wedding? Are you expecting us to get married and then live four thousand miles apart?" His cheeks had started to flush.

"No! I'm not expecting anything—" She pulled up short. They couldn't have this conversation here. She didn't even know for sure how she wanted the conversation to go. They had a job to do. They needed to focus on it. Bring their personal relationship into the equation, and things would get too messy to work around. "We can talk about everything later, when all this is over. Sitting down, in a calm environment. I'll buy you dinner, huh? The biggest steak in London, how about that?"

His face softened a little. He opened his arms wide. "I'm sorry, honey, you've been through a traumatic experience. I should be a little more understanding. It's OK now—I'm here to protect you." He took a step forward, but Ingrid was too fast for him, she ducked sideways and away, and left him hugging nothing but air.

He quickly recovered and clapped his hands together. "I need to get started." He turned on his heels and headed back toward the office.

"Where are you going?"

"I'll need some help. But I don't want to exhaust you. What's the name of the skinny black kid sitting in the corner?"

"Kid? He's a twenty-three-year-old grown man. You need to treat him with some respect. His name is Isaac."

"Good, I'll use him as my assistant for the time being. I need to speak to the RSO, find out exactly how secure the ambassador is. And we'll need to stop any food that's come from the kitchen being consumed by her."

"Or anyone else," Ingrid interjected.

"What?"

"If you genuinely think it could be poisoned, no one should be eating it."

"No, of course not. I'll see to that. Plus we have to interview all the staff." He shook his head. "My God—it's a huge job."

"You really think Wyatt is right here inside the embassy?"

"He got himself pretty embedded in the restaurant in Savannah."

"But security is so tight. There's no way he could be here."

"Why take chances? Who do I need to talk to? I've got to get the kitchen staff isolated."

"I thought you were here to see me."

"You need to take it easy. I'll keep coming back to check on you. OK, honey?" He pecked her on the top of the head.

"You're wrong about this, I'm sure of it." Ingrid was controlling the urge to punch her fiancé square in the jaw.

"We'll see, I guess." He smiled at her, screwing up his eyes the way he did when he wasn't really smiling at all.

He marched her back to her desk, grabbed Isaac and headed for Deputy Chief Louden's office. Ingrid was pretty sure Amy Louden wouldn't go for Marshall's scheme. She was content to let him fall flat on his face. It'd make a nice change.

As she watched him hurrying away, an awestruck Isaac trailing behind him, Ingrid decided she'd get back to basics. If Cory Ellis was still in London because he had someone else to kill, maybe studying exactly who was involved in his father's arrest and conviction would yield some piece of information that might actually help her track him down.

FORTY

"So that's your fiancé, huh?" Jennifer stared at Ingrid, her expression hungry with the need for information.

Ingrid blinked. She sat back down at her desk.

"How long have you been engaged?"

"I'm sorry, Jennifer, I'm just too busy for a girlie chat."

"Me too. I'm really busy." Jennifer flicked through a stack of Post-It stickers to prove it. "There's a message here for you." She unstuck the little yellow note from the pile and read it aloud. "Please call DC Fraser."

"Did he say what it was about?"

"He couldn't have—or I would have written it down."

Ingrid quickly found his number on her phone and dialed.

"I thought you'd lost interest," Fraser said when he picked up.

"I've been a little… indisposed. Do you have news about the case?"

"We think we've identified her. Name of Marija Jansons, family haven't heard from her since January. Her brother's flying over tomorrow to make the formal ID. You can speak to him if you like."

"Thanks. Thanks for letting me know. I appreciate that." Ingrid took a deep breath. "I guess you've been pretty busy getting lots of calls about the picture on the front of the *Evening News* yesterday?"

"Not as busy as I might have expected."

"I have a name for the murder suspect, but I doubt very much he's using it now." Ingrid went on to repeat everything she'd told Mbeke. Apart from the current presumed threat to the ambassador. There was no way Fraser should know about that.

"So you think he's killed, what... three people?"

"It could be more."

"Jesus. And he's not left the country yet?"

"That's the hunch we're working with at the moment. It's possible he's not finished yet."

"Bloody hell. I'll need you to put all that in writing. And you should probably speak to the DCI too."

"Sure." *But it won't be anytime soon.*

She threw her phone on the desk and thought about the dead woman. Marija Jansons had gotten involved with the wrong man. Ingrid supposed Bella Townsend in Savannah was damn lucky to be alive. If she'd stumbled across something she shouldn't have, presumably Ellis wouldn't have hesitated to dispatch her in much the same way. What Ingrid still had trouble understanding, was the fact that Ellis had left the details of his old bank account accessible to Jansons in the first place. The man was a meticulous planner. That just seemed too sloppy. It didn't fit with his profile. Every move he made was deliberate, carefully prepared in advance. Maybe Marija Jansons was smarter than he'd given her credit for.

Her cell phone buzzed. She glanced at the screen as it gently vibrated against the desk. It was McKittrick, no doubt wanting to know how she was doing. Ingrid hesitated before picking up.

"I'm fine," she said, before McKittrick even got a chance to inquire after her health.

"That's nice. So am I. That's not why I called. I've just got off the phone. I've been talking to a certain chief inspector working on an attempted murder case I think you might be interested in."

"Oh yeah, whose?"

"Whose? Yours, you daft cow!"

Although Ingrid's sore temple and fuzzy head had been bothering her all morning, she hadn't given much thought to what had caused them in the first place. "They finally found some of those goddamn arrows?"

"What? No. No, I'm talking about the investigation into the *second* attempt on your life. The arrows I can't help you with."

"So what do you have?"

"I'm trying to tell you."

"Have they identified a suspect?"

"Not exactly. They've been speaking to the other estate agents who were working with your lettings man on Monday afternoon."

"Has he turned up yet?"

"No—they didn't have any new information on him, but they did tell the chief inspector that a bloke with an American accent—claiming to be your husband, can you believe it— tipped up shortly before five p.m. He and the lettings agent left shortly afterwards. That was the last anyone saw of them."

"My husband?"

"The theory the DCI's working on is that this mysterious American chap—seemed to know all about you, by the way— lured the agent somewhere, somehow got him out of the way, then presumably went to the flat, tampered with the boiler, left the keys on the main door, where you found them, and... well, you know the rest."

"'Got the agent out of the way,' you just said. You think the guy's dead?"

"I'd put money on it. Expect a call from DCI Renton later this afternoon. He wants to ask you some more questions. In the meantime, you've got to work out who this American bloke might be. Someone so intent on bumping you off, that he's not at all worried about collateral damage. Poor bloody agent just happened to be in the wrong place at the wrong time."

Ingrid's breath got caught in her throat as she tried to speak. She coughed and tried again. "Did the realtors provide a description of the guy?"

"They were a bit sketchy about the details. But they were both certain he was just under six feet tall and quite slim. But he was wearing a baseball cap too low for them to get a proper look at his face."

"I guess they didn't see his left arm?"

"You mean the rose tattoo? They didn't mention it. So you are thinking what I'm thinking—that it was Darryl Wyatt?"

"Darryl Wyatt, Cory Ellis, Miguel Hernandez. Whatever the hell he's calling himself today."

"I thought Cory Ellis was dead."

"There have been some... developments."

"He's alive?"

"He could be."

"And you didn't think to tell me?"

"It's been a little hectic around here." Ingrid glanced up at Jennifer, who quickly looked away. "Marshall turned up about an hour ago."

"He did what?"

"He's right here at the embassy. He's taken over the investigation."

"Can he do that?"

"It's complicated. And too long a story to get into right now."

"At least nothing untoward has happened so far today. Unless there's something else you're not telling me."

"What's special about today?"

"Bloody hell—don't you remember? I think it's fair to say you may have lost your edge. Should you even be at work? "

"What are you talking about?"

"Today's the 15th of May. The killer's preferred kill date. You didn't think I paid attention, did you?"

Ingrid gasped in a breath. How could something like that slip her mind? She had to shape up, and fast.

"So with Marshall on the scene, I suppose you won't be staying at my place again tonight? I was planning to go to Marks and Spencer and pick up a few treats for dinner."

Ingrid thought about the suite Marshall had booked at the hotel. The way she felt right now she couldn't even bear to look at his face. "Thanks—I'd like that. I'll call you later to let you know when I'm leaving." She hung up and carefully placed the cell back on the desk. She sat very still and pondered what McKittrick had just told her. She'd never known her brain feel this sluggish. But then she'd never suffered carbon monoxide poisoning before. She took a deep breath and considered the facts calmly and objectively.

An American man, same height and build as the man seen at Marija Jansons' apartment, lured away the realtor, most probably to his death, in order to get into Ingrid's apartment to tamper with the boiler. He knew all about the apartment. He must have been following her since she set off from her hotel last Saturday to go apartment hunting with McKittrick. If he stayed around long enough to remove the poisoned soap from the restroom, there was every chance he'd seen her at the murder scene at Fisher Krupps. Had he been following her ever since then? Had he been watching her when she visited Marija Jansons' apartment?

Ingrid tried hard to remember who she'd seen on the street that evening. She was pretty sure there were only two other people around. A dog walker and some guy washing his car. Ellis could have been either of them.

Then it struck her.

Maybe Ellis hadn't been careless with his bank details. Maybe he wanted Jansons to access the account to test the response it provoked. Then sure enough, less than an hour after the account was accessed, the FBI agent he'd seen at Fisher Krupps turned up at the apartment in Dulwich, using some lame story to get inside.

Ingrid suddenly felt very stupid. And, if she allowed herself a moment's self-indulgence, not a little scared.

FORTY-ONE

Ingrid grabbed her phone and jumped up from her desk. She hurried out of the office, trawling through her contacts list as she went.

"Nick?"

"Hey—I didn't expect to hear from you so soon. Are you on the move? Want some back-up?"

Ingrid sucked in a breath, trying to calm her nerves. "Not yet, I'll call again later. Just thought I'd update you on developments." She briefly explained the investigation she'd been working on and who she thought was responsible for the two attempts on her life. She then gave him as detailed a description of Ellis as she could. "But I'm just going by the eye witness report that resulted in the artist's impression on the front page of yesterday's *Evening News*."

The line went very quiet. Ingrid could hear Angelis breathing. "Are you OK about this?"

"Sure."

"I read the article. I know what he did to that woman. The man's a vicious bastard. Do you have protection where you are right now?"

"Of course not. Ellis won't be here inside the embassy." Ingrid quickly remembered that was exactly where Marshall was supposing Ellis, or as far as he was concerned, Darryl Wyatt, was right now. Her stomach somersaulted. She coughed as a reflux of acid tried to make it all the way up into her mouth. Whatever Ellis had been planning and wherever he intended to execute that plan, it was likely to happen today. Ingrid felt as if time was running out.

"Presumably this Ellis bloke will have changed his appearance again?"

"He has a distinctive rose tattoo on his left forearm."

"So as long as he's wearing a tee shirt I won't have any problems."

"It was worth mentioning."

Angelis sniffed. "Of course it was. Don't mind me, I'm just worried about you."

"I'm fine. There are dozens of armed Marines patrolling the building."

"I can come in—I don't have much on today. I wouldn't be any bother. Just sit me in a corner with a good book."

"That won't be necessary. But thanks for offering."

Ingrid made her way back to the office, frustrated Sol still wasn't answering his phone. She got there to discover Marshall sitting at her desk, tapping away at her keyboard. Jennifer was leaning over the desk, thrusting her breasts toward him.

Dear God.

"Is there anything else I can help you with, Marshall?" Jennifer said.

"No—that's all for now. Thank you." Marshall looked up and smiled at Ingrid, who was hovering in the doorway. She felt like turning right around and leaving again. Instead, she marched purposefully toward her desk.

"Where's Isaac?" she asked and watched as Jennifer sashayed back to her own desk.

"I sent him on an errand to find Sol Franklin. We can't get him on his cell," Marshall said.

"You do know Isaac doesn't actually work for you?"

"For today he does. I squared it with Deputy Chief Louden."

"So what do you want with Sol?"

"The deputy chief said Sol would be able to authorize any extra manpower I'll need to maintain security at the cafeteria and kitchen."

"How long has Isaac been gone?" She glanced at her watch. Her tone was a little harsher than she'd intended.

"What's wrong, honey?" Marshall grabbed her hand.

Ingrid tugged it away and glanced up at Jennifer. The clerk was watching them closely. Now was neither the time nor the place to list all her grievances.

Marshall stood up. "I guess you want your desk back. I'm heading to the kitchen soon to start interviewing the staff."

"You're just fine where you are. Sit down." With that, Ingrid spun around and left. She tried Mike Stiller on her cell phone and headed in the direction of Sol's office.

"Hey, Mike. How many miracles is it so far today?"

"Whatever it is you want, make it quick. I do actually have other work to do."

"I'm looking for a connection between Ambassador Frances Byrne-Williams and the original Henry Ellis investigation."

"The ambassador? You've got to be kidding me. Are you saying she's mixed up in all of this somehow?"

"Actually I'm trying to prove the opposite. I don't think she is. But I do think Cory Ellis is still right here in London and he hasn't finished what he came here to do." She reached the elevator as the doors opened. A half dozen Marines marched out, heading toward her office. No doubt they were on some fruitless mission for Marshall.

"You know how impossible it is to prove a negative?" Mike said. "I guess you could look at all the main players involved in the investigation. See how many of them are still alive, see if any could conceivably be in the UK."

"OK—I guess Cory Ellis would have targeted the man who actually killed his father."

"The prison guard?"

"Can you find out what happened to him?"

"What's the matter? Your computer stop working?"

"I'm not at my desk. It's been... commandeered by somebody working the Byrne-Williams angle."

"OK—you remember the name of the guard?"

Ingrid struggled to remember. Amazingly, the name popped into her head. Maybe her mind was finally clearing a little. She spelled the name out to Mike Stiller and stepped out of the elevator on the fifth floor. She reached Sol's office. Again it was unoccupied. Only this time she noticed Sol's cell phone sitting in the middle of his desk. No wonder she wasn't having any luck calling him. Maybe he'd just popped out to the restroom. She heard a whistle at the other end of the line. "Mike?"

"Well, as you may have already guessed, the guard responsible for killing Henry Ellis is no longer with us."

"How'd he die?" Ingrid wondered if Ellis had plumped for poison.

"He was shot dead. Three shots to the chest, two to the face. Point blank range."

That didn't match Ellis' profile at all. To be so close to the victim at the time of death? Plus he carefully planned and executed the killings. That just sounded like a wild shooting spree. And how did it have anything to do with a weakness or vulnerability in the victim? At the end of a gun, everyone is vulnerable.

"Perpetrator was never found."

"Can you tell me anything about the guard himself? I'm looking for some kind of weakness he might have had. Something that maybe most people didn't know about him."

"It's hardly likely to turn up in the police report, if nobody knew about it."

Ingrid felt like she was flailing. She reminded herself that, despite his claims, Mike Stiller wasn't actually a miracle worker.

"But I can tell you something about the poor schmuck," Mike said.

Ingrid waited. Knowing Mike he would want to pause a beat for an imaginary drum roll.

"The guard was shot in his bed, naked, handcuffed to the headboard."

FORTY-TWO

"The guard had a sex addiction?"

"Maybe, but that's not the perceived weakness I was shooting for. According to the regular bartender at the local gay bar, on the night he died, the guard picked up some dark handsome stranger and took him home with him. Something he never did. Because of his job, he was always real cautious. Seems the dark stranger made him an offer he couldn't refuse."

"Ellis?"

"Can you think of any more likely candidates?"

"How did Ellis even know he was gay?"

"All he had to do was follow him for a few nights. If the perpetrator is as smart as you seem to think he is, it wouldn't exactly have taxed his intellect to discover the guard's little secret."

"What year was this?"

"Two-thousand five."

"And the date?" Ingrid had a feeling she knew the answer already.

"May 15th. Just like Highsmith and David Brite." Mike paused again. "Wait a minute. That's today's date."

Ingrid closed her eyes.

"OK—let's look at exactly what we've discovered so far," Mike said. "Holy crap."

"What is it?"

"I've got a meeting I should be getting to."

Ingrid took one last look around Sol's office and left the room. Where the hell was he? "Any help you can give me, Mike, you know I appreciate it."

"I've only got a coupla minutes."

"We have four victims either directly or indirectly involved in the Henry Ellis investigation. The investor who testified against him, the investor's son, the prosecuting attorney and the prison guard who shot him dead." Ingrid was more convinced than ever that there was no connection between Cory Ellis and Frances Byrne-Williams. She should go and speak to Marshall about it.

She headed for the cafeteria in the basement.

"Listen, I'll call you back," Mike whispered down the line. "My boss just walked in the room."

Ingrid reached the entrance to the cafeteria. A Marine was standing sentry. She waved her security pass at him, followed by her badge. Eventually, he stood to one side and let her enter.

All the harsh overhead lights had been turned on in the cafeteria. Ingrid recognized some of the counter staff sitting at the tables, sipping at cans of soda, nibbling on candy bars and potato chips. All of them looking royally pissed off. Then there were lots of faces she didn't recognize, judging by the way they were dressed, they had to be kitchen staff. They looked severely pissed off too. None of them, however, looked in any way tense or guilty. No one was trying to leave. They just seemed resigned to their fate, as if this sort of thing happened every day.

"Excuse me." A woman dressed in a white tunic and checkered pants stood up and touched Ingrid on the arm. "Do you have any idea how long this is going to take? Only I have some slow-cooking pot roasts in the ovens. Pretty soon, they're going to start burning."

"I'll look into that for you," Ingrid said, without the slightest intention of doing any such thing. She needed to find Marshall, try to convince him again how wrong he was. At the far end of the cafeteria was a small office used by the restaurant manager. From what Ingrid could see through the window in the door, it seemed Marshall was using it to interview the kitchen and cafeteria staff. Another armed Marine was guarding the door.

Ingrid's cell phone started to buzz in her pocket. She pulled it out and answered quickly.

"When are we going to get our cell phones back?" one of the kitchen staff asked, the tone of her voice somehow managing to be accusatory and defeatist at the same time.

Ingrid ignored her. "Mike, did you get out of your meeting?"

"I'm joining them in five minutes. Now, where were we?"

"Trying to work out the identities of other possible victims on Ellis' list."

"Sure. If we work backwards, I guess we should look at who the arresting officers were. Who was investigating Henry Ellis before he even got arrested."

"Was it a cop or a Federal agent? Should have been a Fed, in that kind of fraud case, shouldn't it?"

"Just looking that up now."

Ingrid's left ear was suddenly filled with the sound of nasal breathing coming all the way from Washington D.C.

"Holy shit."

"What have you found?" Ingrid started to edge closer to the small room Marshall was occupying, and the six feet something Marine standing to attention outside.

"Tell me you're sitting down."

"Please don't make me go through all of that again. Is it someone you know? Someone I know?"

"I can't believe it, but here it is in black and white."

"Goddammit, Mike, who?"

"Special Agent Solomon Franklin."

Ingrid stopped in her tracks. "Sol? You're sure?"

"He led the team of investigating agents. It looks like it was quite a coup for him at the time. Got a juicy promotion out of it."

"I've got to go, Mike." She hung up and tried Sol's cell phone again. It switched to voicemail. Just like it had every other time she'd attempted to speak to him today. The phone was probably still on the desk in his empty office.

Ingrid marched up to the Marine guarding Marshall's interview room. "I need to speak to SSA Claybourne," she declared, "right now."

"He's a little busy."

She flashed her embassy ID and her FBI badge. The Marine wasn't impressed. Ingrid stepped to one side and banged a fist against the door, and kept on banging until the armed guard physically restrained her. Marshall turned around and yanked open the door.

"What the hell is it?"

FORTY-THREE

Ingrid pushed into the makeshift interview room, glanced at the man dressed in white tunic and checkered pants sitting very upright in front of the desk, then turned her attention to Marshall.

"For God's sake, what do you think you're doing?" Marshall was trying to keep his booming voice down and failing.

"You need to stop this charade right now." Ingrid could feel the Marine's hot breath blasting against the back of her neck. He was standing just inches away. In theory, one word from Marshall and he could have her bundled away.

"Charade? What the hell are you talking about?" Marshall glanced at his interviewee, a hint of embarrassment on his face. "These interviews are highly sensitive. They have to be handled in the right way."

"And I'm telling you to stop."

Marshall grabbed her arm, walked her past the Marine and straight out the office. He didn't let go until they were in the corridor outside the cafeteria. "Were you deliberately trying to humiliate me in there?"

"I can't worry about hurting your feelings, you're wasting your time interviewing these people. The ambassador is not the target."

"You have nothing to back that up."

"The target is Sol Franklin and I have plenty to back it up but no time to explain. We've got to find Sol. I haven't been able to reach him for hours. The killer will strike today. Maybe he already has." Ingrid drew down an unsteady breath. "We can't waste any more time."

Much to her amazement, Marshall seemed to be considering what she'd said. He was chewing the inside of his cheek as if it were a plug of tobacco. Then he shook his head decisively. "If I didn't know better I'd think you were trying to… sabotage this operation. Just because I've come here and—"

"Taken over?"

"Exactly."

"You seriously think I'd put the ambassador's life in jeopardy out of… some petty resentment?"

He shrugged at her. "I know you never say anything, but it's got to be hard seeing me get promoted over and over. It's only human. I don't even blame you." He gave her a patronizing smile with the corner of his mouth.

She wanted to slap it.

"Listen, Marshall. I am one hundred per cent sure about this. I need the manpower you've been assigned to search the building for Sol."

"You think the suspect intends to poison Sol?"

"Poison? No!" She hadn't had time to consider what method Ellis might use. "I don't know how he plans to do it. Just that he will. We have to find Sol." She grabbed Marshall's thick arms and squeezed them, hoping that might somehow make him take her more seriously.

"I love you, honey, but you're just not making any sense. You obviously came back to work too early. Why don't you go back to the hotel and I'll join you there just as soon as I can."

"Goddammit, I don't have time to argue with you. You have to help me."

"Explain to me properly why I should, and I'll consider it."

"I've already told you—we don't have time."

"I'm not going to let some crazy, half-assed theory get in the way of my investigation. Take it up with Deputy Chief Louden if you're not happy about it."

Ingrid let go of his arms and strode away. She called Louden. Maybe the deputy chief would agree to some resources to help her search. The call switched straight to voicemail. Ingrid wasn't going to get any help there.

Time was against her. Left to search on her own, it would be practically impossible to find Sol. He could be anywhere in the building.

She ran toward the elevator, not really knowing where she would go when she got there. She passed another armed Marine guarding the door to the stairwell.

"What are you doing here?" she asked him.

He stood a little taller and raised his chin. Ingrid showed him her embassy ID and FBI badge. "Please, tell me why you're here."

"To ensure none of the kitchen or cafeteria staff leaves the basement. There's a man stationed at every exit."

"Really?"

"Orders from above." He looked toward the ceiling.

Typical. Marshall Claybourne overkill. Trying to prove how much power he could yield. What a waste of resources.

"I'm guessing it's OK for me to leave the basement?"

"Yes, ma'am." He opened the door for her.

Ingrid got through the door, heard it clang shut behind her, and wondered what the hell she was going to do next.

Sol had to be inside the building. No way would he go anywhere without his cell. If Ellis really was within the embassy, was it possible he'd forcibly taken Sol some place? Wouldn't somebody have noticed? Sol would have put up too much of a fight. It was much more likely that wherever Sol had disappeared to, he'd gone of his own accord. But then what had happened? And it still didn't explain what his cell was doing on his desk.

Ingrid was finding it hard to believe that Cory Ellis was working within the embassy. But then he had gotten on the cleaning staff at Fisher Krupps without any problems. Maybe he'd done the same thing at the embassy. She'd seen all the cafeteria and kitchen staff, and none seemed to fit his description. Perhaps he was part of maintenance and engineering, or the janitorial team.

She had to remind herself that it was still possible Ellis wasn't on staff at all and was planning to kill Sol outside of the embassy. Some place Sol was more vulnerable and exposed. But the fact that she couldn't track down the assistant deputy chief made her fear that something had already happened to him.

An audacious attack within the walls of one of America's most prestigious embassies fitted Cory Ellis' profile too—how much of a coup would it be to kill a Federal agent right inside one of the most secure buildings in London?

Ingrid hesitated. Should she head up or down? She tried hard to fit together everything she knew about how Ellis operated when he was working through one of his kill plans. The method of execution would have something to do with a weakness he had discovered about Sol.

Ingrid wasn't sure she knew Sol well enough herself to have discovered any weaknesses. Maybe he didn't have any.

The creak of a door opening sounded from the floor below. Someone coming in from the parking lot, presumably. She waited for whoever it was to make their way up the stairs and pass her. But no one came. Maybe they'd gone down instead of up.

She waited a few more moments then shut her eyes tight and pictured Sol in as much detail as she could. What immediately sprang to mind?

What did she see, hear, feel?

She snapped her eyes back open. The strongest sense of Sol she had was his aroma. He always stank of cigarettes. Plus he had the worse smoker's cough she'd ever heard. Surely his

Achilles' Heel had to be more significant than a nicotine habit. But then if it was something else she had absolutely no idea what it could possibly be.

She tried to picture where he was most likely to go for a smoke. Apart from the courtyard out back and Grosvenor Square itself, she was at a loss. He had mentioned some place inside the building he'd found for himself. A little niche, he'd said. But where?

Another noise sounded from below. This time she heard someone moan. The long, low moan of pain.

Ingrid's immediate thought was of Sol. She flew down the stairs to the lower floor. The small landing area leading out into the basement parking lot was empty.

She heard the moan again.

She raced down another two flights.

Then she saw him.

Not Sol.

Isaac. He lay in the doorway leading to the third basement level, clutching his stomach with both hands. The heavy fire door had trapped him where he lay. His pants and his shoes were covered in thick dark blood. A pool of blood was spreading across the floor. His eyes flickered open and he looked toward her. He moaned again.

Ingrid bent down low and put her head close to his. "It's OK, buddy. You're going to be OK. We'll get you some help." She started to move away.

Isaac moaned again. Louder and more insistent this time. "Sol," he managed to whisper.

Ingrid had retrieved her cell from a pocket and was dialing for assistance. Her fingers fumbled with the phone. "It's OK—help'll be on its way real soon."

"You... gotta... help Sol."

"What about Sol?"

"He's... killing him." Isaac looked down at his hands, both of them slick with red. He swallowed. "Help... him."

"Where? Where is he?"

Isaac's eyes closed. His head lolled heavily to one side.

Oh no, dear God.

Ingrid looked at her phone. She wasn't sure who she could call to get the response she needed. Everything would take just too long to explain.

Then she remembered the armed Marine two floors up.

There was nothing she could do for Isaac now. But she might still be able to save Sol.

FORTY-FOUR

She sprinted up the four flights of stairs and threw open the door. "I need you to come with me. Now."

"Ma'am?"

Ingrid flashed her badge at him, just in case he'd forgotten her from ten minutes ago. "Come with me."

"I have orders to secure the stairway on this level. The kitchen and cafeteria staff are in lockdown."

"I realize that. But I'm ordering you to come with me."

"Supervisory Special Agent Claybourne outranks you. I'm staying exactly where I am."

Screw this.

"Give me your gun."

The Marine's hand automatically flew toward the holster in his belt. "Step away, ma'am."

Ingrid puffed out a frustrated sigh. She didn't have time to argue with him. Still looking him square in the eye, she brought up her knee hard and fast and slammed it right into his crotch. As he doubled over, she kicked him hard under the chin. His head snapped backward at the same time his knees buckled. He fell to the floor like a puppet with its strings cut, folding in on himself.

Ingrid prodded him with the toe of her boot. He was out cold. She popped open his holster and yanked out a Glock 27. Not the model she was used to. But it would do just fine.

She shoved open the door to the stairway and clattered back down toward the level three basement, her feet only lightly touching the edges of the steps.

She quickly reached Isaac. Why the hell did Ellis have to hurt him? He must have just been in the wrong place at the wrong time. More collateral damage Ellis didn't give a crap about.

Ingrid blinked hard and pushed open the door, unable to avoid jarring Isaac's body. In the dim basement light, she could just make out a trail of blood smeared along the floor. It led away from the door, deep into the corridor beyond. The corridor that carried all the services to the rest of the building. Thick insulated pipes ran along the low ceiling as far as she could see.

Ingrid struggled a little for breath, it was so hot and airless down there. She stepped over Isaac Coleman's dead body and gently let the door rest once again against his ribs.

She inspected the Glock 27, and quickly unclipped the safety. She hated relying on a weapon she hadn't personally tested, but she didn't have a lot of choice. She held the gun outstretched in both hands, two index fingers resting lightly on the trigger. A gentle squeeze would be sufficient to let off the first round. She hoped to hell she wouldn't have to use it.

She continued to tread slowly and carefully, glancing down at the trail of blood every now and then, but mostly keeping eyes front, staring into the gloom, watching for movement.

Now she knew where she was headed, her destination was obvious. The only place inside the building not fitted with smoke detectors was the bunker on basement level three. It had its own water, power and oxygen supply. And it was never used. Sol's little smoking 'niche' was a nuclear fallout shelter.

The bunker had to be at least another hundred yards ahead of her. Its entrance was set into the wall of another corridor that ran perpendicular to this one. Cory Ellis could be anywhere between there and here. Assuming he was here at all. It was quite possible he'd done what he'd come to do, watched Sol die a slow and painful death, and escaped completely without detection.

Ingrid blinked the moisture from her eyes. She wasn't sure if it was caused by sweat or tears. She glanced up toward the ceiling, at the thick pipes covered in insulating foam. It really was hot down there.

After a few more yards she stopped for a moment and listened. All she could hear was the deep, insistent thrum of the generators.

She picked up a little pace, conscious Sol could very well be struggling for his last breaths just a hundred or so feet away. She forced a little more air into her lungs and continued down the corridor, keeping her eyes fixed on the end, now just thirty or so yards away, occasionally glancing left and right toward maintenance access doors as she passed each one. Sweat was dribbling between her breasts and making her shirt stick to her back.

Finally she reached the last few yards of the corridor. She pressed herself against the wall and edged sideways, barely daring to breathe, not wanting to make too much noise. She got to the end of the corridor, where it met the one running perpendicular to it.

From her position, she could just make out the innocuous painted wooden door set in the wall of the corridor beyond. The door that led to the fortified bunker. She struggled to remember the layout on the other side.

As far as she could recall, this door actually opened onto a square, ten feet by ten interior room. The bunker itself was situated on the other side of a twelve-inch thick titanium reinforced hatch that looked like something from a ship or a submarine—a circular handle set into its center, a punch code security pad on the wall to the right.

Ingrid steadied her breath for a moment.

She had no idea whether Ellis would be armed. He could quite easily have overpowered a Marine the same way she had.

Only one way to find out.

Gun in one hand, she inched forward and reached the wooden door. She bent her head in close. She listened. The blood pumping in her ears pretty much drowned out anything else. She tried to swallow, but her mouth was too dry. Her lips were stuck to her teeth.

She pushed down on the handle. When the latch released, she pushed open the door wide and shuffled sideways, pressing her back flat against the corridor wall. No sound came from within. She waited another couple of seconds then stepped through the doorway. Gun outstretched, she swung left, then right.

The anteroom was empty.

The shiny reinforced hatch leading into the bunker itself was ajar. Ingrid stepped toward it. She peered through the gap.

She couldn't see much, but about thirty feet away, half obscured by shelves of dried goods and eight-gallon water containers lining both sides of a narrow corridor, she could see into another room, beyond another submarine-style shiny metal door that was open wide. She'd never seen inside the interior room before. She could just make out a figure stooping low, his legs straddling a large object on the floor.

Ingrid slowly opened the hatch in the anteroom wider and stepped into the long, thin corridor that stored the supplies. As carefully as she could, she started walking down the shelf-lined passage, toward the inner room, her eyes fixed on the stooping figure she could see through the open hatch. It was definitely a man. He straightened suddenly.

Ingrid froze.

How had he heard her? She'd been so quiet.

The man started to turn.

"Show me your hands. Now!" she yelled, running along the remainder of the corridor toward the open hatch and the interior room. "Hands over your head!"

He didn't move.

"I won't ask you again."

He turned a little more, one hand gripping his thigh, the other behind his back. As he moved, Ingrid caught a glimpse of Sol's lifeless body lying at his feet.

"Get away from him."

"What are you going to do, Agent Skyberg?" Slowly, he turned to face her.

He didn't look like the photograph or the artist's impression. His hair was cut in a short crop, close to his scalp. His chin and cheeks were covered in two days' blonde stubble.

"Hands over your head!" she said again.

He smiled at her.

She suddenly felt vulnerable, standing in the middle of the room, and backed up closer to the hatch, keen not to get locked inside.

"You really think I'm going to do what you say? Haven't you done your research? You should stop wasting your breath." He let out a little laugh. "Your friend here stopped wasting his a short time ago."

"Step away from him."

"You shoot me, I win. I've done everything I came here to do. You don't shoot me, you die." He pulled his right arm from behind his back, his right hand wrapped around the handle of a ten-inch screwdriver.

She couldn't let him have what he wanted. Suicide by cop? No way.

He jabbed the screwdriver toward her. But he was still more than ten feet away. He stepped closer.

"Drop your weapon."

"Haven't we just been through that? Weren't you listening to me? I guess I should make allowances—the carbon monoxide still preventing the oxygen getting to your brain, huh?" He smiled again. "I was pretty pissed when your friend turned up to save you, but then if she hadn't, I guess we wouldn't be enjoying this moment together now, would we?"

The sweat from Ingrid's forehead was sliding into her eyes. She didn't dare blink.

"Drop your weapon."

"Isn't that getting a little tired?"

"This is your last warning."

He laughed at her and took a deep breath, his shoulders almost shrugging up to his ears. Then he exhaled and his whole body seemed to go limp.

A second later he launched forward, hurling himself toward her.

Ingrid squeezed the trigger. She saw the effect of the bullet before she heard the deafening crack. Ellis jerked backward, but didn't fall. A long moment passed. The screwdriver slipped from his hand. Then he came at her again.

She fired.

He stalled. Dropped to his knees. Pitched forward. He landed just a couple of feet from her. Blood started oozing onto the floor beneath him. His arms and legs twitched.

Ingrid turned back toward the door and searched for the panic button, her eyes still misted with sweat. She located the big red plunger switch and thumped her fist against it.

A piercing wail erupted from loudspeakers in the corridor outside. Ingrid skirted around Ellis' twitching body and kneeled next to Sol. She kept her gun trained on Ellis' back.

But Cory Ellis wasn't going anywhere.

And neither was Sol.

FORTY-FIVE

Three days later

Marshall opened the door, but refused to look at Ingrid as she entered the room. He was still pissed at her for being right. The way things were between them at the moment, it seemed he might never be able to forgive her. The fact that she'd broken off their engagement the night before seemed much less important to him than what he perceived as her attack on his professional capabilities.

She couldn't worry about Marshall's feelings. She was right and he was wrong. They both needed to move on.

Right now she had to stay focused. She was about to conduct the most important suspect interview of her career.

She stood at the viewing window and stared at Cory Ellis. He was staring right back at her. Beneath his tee shirt, his entire right side, all the way from his shoulder to his hip, was covered in strapping and bandage. Even though Ingrid hadn't been on a shooting range for over six weeks, her aim had still been accurate enough to miss the major arteries and his heart and lungs. His shoulder blade would need a lot of reconstructive surgery. But that wasn't her problem. She'd been determined he wouldn't use her the same way his father had used the prison guard. Suicide by cop was never going to be an option.

"I could have gotten him to talk. I just needed a little more time," Marshall said.

He'd been telling her that for the last two days. But the chief had lost patience and given in to Ellis' demands: he was pleading the fifth unless Ingrid interviewed him herself.

The door to the observation room opened and the deputy chief of the FBI mission, Amy Louden, came in. She nodded to Ingrid and Marshall, settled herself in a chair, and stared toward the prisoner.

"They're always much smaller than you think they're going to be," Louden said, turning to Ingrid.

"Ma'am?" Ingrid glanced at Ellis, who was grinning toward the glass now.

"In my experience, at any rate." Louden raised her eyebrows expectantly. "Shall we get this started? I have a feeling it may take some time. Remind me—what's the current estimated death toll?"

Ingrid opened her mouth to speak, but Marshall beat her to it.

"We've identified at least five people connected to the imprisonment of Ellis' father who have died either in unexplained accidents or unsolved homicides," he said.

"Are we expecting to add to that list?"

"At the moment we'd like to get confirmation he's responsible for those killings. He might volunteer further information in the course of questioning."

"And the killings here in London?"

"As far as we know, in addition to the City trader, there were two fatalities outside of embassy property—the Latvian woman and the realtor. We're not pursuing those as a priority. We'll liaise with our London colleagues, of course." Marshall glanced at Ellis. "But there's no way we're handing him over. He's coming back to the US to face trial."

Louden had tilted her head impatiently. Ingrid winced a little inside. Marshall was stating the goddamn obvious. The deputy chief turned away and leaned her elbows on the table in front of her. "When you're ready, agent."

Ingrid did her best to cover the discreet earpiece wedged into her left ear with her hair. But it wasn't really long enough to do the job. She stepped out into the corridor and took a deep breath. She hadn't interviewed a suspect on her own for nearly a year. She wanted to ensure Ellis wouldn't pick up on any potential weakness in her technique. If she went into that room presenting anything other than supreme confidence, he'd be able to detect it in a heartbeat. She straightened her collar, tugged at the bottom of her jacket and opened the door.

Striding into the room, she stared into Ellis' face and didn't take her eyes off him as she lowered herself onto the plastic and metal chair opposite his, determined not to be the one to blink first.

After a few seconds Ellis smiled at her. "OK—you win." He dropped his gaze toward the single handcuff tethering his one functioning hand to the table. "Where would you like to start, Ingrid?"

"How about the beginning?"

"Why be so conventional? Why don't I talk to you about the assistant deputy chief, huh? Wouldn't you like to hear how he pleaded with me to spare his life? Or maybe I should tell you all about how he and his fellow agents harassed my family for months before my father's arrest?"

"Was that when you decided you'd kill him? All those years ago? Most teenagers would have been dating girls and hanging out at the mall."

"Most teenagers weren't hounded out of high school."

"What is this? Am I meant to feel sorry for you?"

"Not as sorry as I feel for you."

Ingrid maintained a neutral expression.

"I mean," he continued, "it can't be easy for you carrying all that pain around. There's no escaping it, is there?"

"I think you may be mistaking me for somebody else."

"Not at all. I can see the suffering in your eyes."

"Don't let this slip out of your control," Marshall murmured into her earpiece.

She thought about removing the device from her ear. A running commentary from Marshall wasn't going to help anyone.

"How naive do you think I am, Ellis? I know what you're trying to do. This isn't *Silence of the Lambs*, we're not playing a game of quid pro quo. Either you're going to tell me what you've done, or you're not. It doesn't really matter to me one way or the other." She relaxed back into her chair. "We have enough forensic evidence to convict you of at least two murders. Your DNA has been detected on the clothes of Isaac Coleman. Plus there's all the evidence found at the restaurant in Savannah. Two murders is more than enough to put you away."

Ellis tilted back his head and yanked at the metal cuff. "You can't deny it. Something happened to you When you were a child maybe. Or a teenager, like me. You must have lost someone like I did. I can see it in your eyes."

She studied his face. There was no expression there to read. Ellis was on a fishing expedition. Everyone had pain some place in their past. If he thought he could unnerve her with a carnival fortune teller's trick, he was sorely mistaken.

"Stay focused, agent," Marshall said in an urgent whisper.

Ingrid supposed he was putting on a show for the deputy chief. She wished he would shut the hell up.

"What I'd be interested in knowing," Ingrid said, leaning forward a little, "is why it took you so long to do anything. I mean, your dad was shot dead in 1992, and yet you waited a whole *decade* before you acted."

The muscles in his jaw flexed and bulged. It was the first real sign she was having some impact.

"Oh wait, maybe it took your *mother's* suicide for you to finally grow a pair, huh? Two parents who chose to end their lives. That's got to make you feel pretty unloved and abandoned, I guess."

Ellis blinked slowly at her but said nothing.

"Nice of your mom to end it all on the anniversary of your dad's death. I guess she was just thinking of you. You'd only have one day in the year to truly dread."

He licked his lips.

"Even then, you still waited to make your move. It couldn't have taken you that long to track down the prison guard. But then I guess it was a big step—your first kill. Must have taken you months to summon the… I was going to say courage… but there's nothing brave about shooting an unarmed man in the face at point blank range."

"You know nothing about it."

"But that's why I'm here, isn't it? For you to enlighten me." She pulled the miniature speaker from her ear and laid it on the table. "You have my undivided attention."

Ellis stared into her face, searching. Ingrid stared right back at him.

"No," he said emphatically. He blew out a breath. "I've changed my mind. You don't get to know. I won't give you the satisfaction. I'm not telling you anything." He stared toward the mirror set into the wall. "This interview is terminated."

FORTY-SIX

Frustrated as hell, Ingrid scooped up the earpiece and marched out the room. She threw open the door into the observation room.

"That went well," Marshall said. "Maybe the combative approach wasn't the right one after all." He was clearly trying to embarrass her in front of the deputy chief.

She ignored him. "I'm certain he'll come around, ma'am."

Louden raised her eyebrows.

"If we leave him to stew a while, the need to boast about his achievements will overwhelm him. He'll be begging to speak to me again."

"How long are we going to let Ellis dictate the timetable?" Marshall said, his face and the tips of his ears reddening. "Maybe someone else should have a crack at him."

Deputy Chief Louden tensed as he raised his voice. "The BAU guys have profiled him. I assume you've read their report?"

Both Ingrid and Marshall nodded back at her. Ingrid had been surprised and hesitantly self-satisfied that their profile matched the one she'd compiled almost point for point.

Louden turned to face Marshall. "So I suppose you know Agent Skyberg's approach is the one they've recommended?"

"Yes, ma'am." Marshall was balling his fists and breathing fast. Ingrid knew that if he didn't shout at someone or punch a wall soon, he risked exploding.

"He still hasn't requested a lawyer," Louden said. "Ensure someone asks him if he's still happy with that situation."

"I get the feeling he wants a one on one... a gladiatorial contest." Ingrid regretted making the interview sound like a boxing match as soon as the words left her mouth.

"I think you're absolutely right," Louden said. "Are you happy to continue to be his opponent?"

"Absolutely, ma'am."

"Let's hope he decides to start talking again soon." With that Louden left the room.

As soon as the door closed behind her, Marshall turned to Ingrid. "Are you trying to sabotage my career?"

Ingrid started to move toward the door. Marshall blocked her path.

"Come on, Marsh, let's not get things out of proportion."

"You can call me SSA Claybourne while we're in a work environment."

The way he was acting, Ingrid sure as hell didn't want to be in any other kind of environment with him. She was waiting for him to relieve his pent up frustration by shouting at her. "About last night... we didn't really finish the conversation—"

"I am *not* discussing that matter here. Besides, there's nothing more to discuss."

"I never intended to hurt you. I just couldn't let things go on—"

"Shut. Up." He turned and flung open the door. Ingrid watched him stride down the corridor.

She felt relieved that the termination of their fourteen month engagement had gotten to him a little. She also felt a little sorry for him. He disappeared around the corner and she let out a long breath and sucked in another. Right now she had more important matters to focus on. She returned to her desk and reread the case files.

Less than ninety minutes later, Ellis told the Marine guarding him that he wanted to speak to Agent Skyberg again. Louden, Marshall and Ingrid reconvened in the observation room ten minutes after that.

"You're confident you can handle this?" Louden asked.

"One hundred per cent." Ingrid tried to make her tone convincing. Everything depended on whether Ellis had truly decided to cooperate. If he had, Ingrid supposed she wouldn't be much more than an over-qualified note taker. But if he still wanted to play games, there wasn't much she could do to stop him.

She entered the interview room without the earpiece she'd been wearing earlier. Ellis had made it a condition of their meeting. Which was fine by Ingrid. She was relieved to be free of Marshall's unhelpful interjections.

She sat down slowly and rested her hands in her lap, keeping her upper body as relaxed as she could. All her tension had transferred to her thighs, which had started to twitch. Thankfully they weren't visible beneath the table.

"I guess you're wondering why I changed my mind and decided to talk to you?" he said.

"I'm not, but feel free to enlighten me."

"A sense of completion. I've achieved everything I set out to. I think that deserves a little celebration."

"I left the balloons and party poppers at home."

"We can make our own fun."

Ingrid's legs twitched a little harder under the desk. She wanted to get this over with. Fun and games Cory Ellis style she could do without.

"Where shall we start?"

"Why not be conventional and choose the beginning?"

"Way back then?"

"I don't mean the first kill. When did you decide there would be any kills at all? Was it after your mom committed suicide?"

Ellis tilted his head sideways and stared hard into her face. The muscles in his cheeks flexed. Any mention of his mother seemed to hit a nerve. "There wasn't a specific tipping point. I'm sure I don't have to tell you that these things fester and ferment over time. Must have been the same for you, with the loss you suffered."

Ingrid had already decided that if Ellis started to make things personal, she'd terminate the interview. She ignored the comment. "OK, let's move on to your first kill."

"I made a plan for every single one long before that."

"You drew up a list?"

He nodded back at her. "I like to be thorough. I worked out an exact plan for each one back then too. Obviously, I had to adjust and amend the details over the years. But it was good to start out with a blueprint, a framework. The outcome was the same, no matter the exact execution method."

"Each one based on what you saw as a weakness in the victim?" Although it was petty, Ingrid wanted Ellis to confirm another of her theories.

"I had to make it a little challenging for myself. There would have been no fun in gunning them down with a semi-automatic, now would there?"

"So, getting back to the prison guard."

"Thomas Greerson. That name haunted me right through my teenage years."

"That was 2002. Exactly a year after your mom's death."

He tensed again, this time across his shoulders. "No better way to honor her memory, wouldn't you say?"

Ingrid held his gaze. Raised an eyebrow. "And when you shot Greerson in the chest and the face… how did that make you feel?"

"I'm giving you a comprehensive list, not participating in a counseling session. It's none of your goddamn business how I felt."

Ingrid leaned forward in her seat. "OK—tell me about David Brite."

"He was called David Fuller when I killed him." Ellis' nostrils flared as if he'd just smelled something unpleasant. "If Brite had kept his mouth shut, none of this would have had to happen." His eyes sparked with an intensity Ingrid hadn't seen before. "Brite was making a fortune. And it was my dad who made it possible."

"He was breaking the law."

"No one really got hurt. Lots of people were making a lot of money."

"It wasn't sustainable." Ingrid wondered just how deluded Ellis was about his dad's illegal investment scheme.

Ellis shrugged.

"So you killed David Brite in 2003. What happened in 2004?"

"Nothing."

"But you had a plan."

"I was busy making a living. I worked on Wall Street 2004 through 2007."

"Really?"

"Have you any idea how expensive these operations can be? I had to get some cash together."

"So what happened in 2008?"

"Plenty."

Ingrid shifted in her seat. She'd meant to remain perfectly still, hoping to appear supremely in control. So far she felt as if she'd been wriggling around in her chair like a five year old. Ellis, meanwhile had barely moved. Mostly he seemed relaxed, almost Zen-like in his repose.

"I could see what was around the corner," he continued. "The crash was so inevitable it's amazing it took anyone by surprise. Time to get out of finance. I'd made enough not to have to work again. Enough to dedicate myself to my... mission."

For a moment Ingrid thought he was going to say 'art'.

"Who did you kill in 2008?"

He pulled a face. "Highsmith was asking for it. To have the audacity to run for Congress after what she did to my dad? She might as well have waved a red flag. Taunting me that way."

"Her allergic reaction in the restaurant in D.C.? That was you?"

"Would have killed her then if her aide hadn't been carrying a spare EpiPen. How could I have known a thing like that?" He shook his head, the bitterness fierce in his eyes. "No aide to save her the second time." In an instant the bitterness transformed into something approaching glee. "But I'm skipping ahead. You want strict chronology, I'm sure." He leaned back in his seat and yawned. "In 2009 I eliminated the FBI agent who was second in command in Sol Franklin's team. Agent Franklin had left the country by then, so I plumped for the next best thing—his able lieutenant. Not the order I'd planned originally, but over the years I've learned to be flexible. Sometimes you have to improvise." He stared into her eyes. "Were you quite close to Sol? I saw a little tension around your eyes just then, when I mentioned his name. Was he a mentor maybe? A father figure?" He searched her face.

Ingrid was determined not to react. When Ellis realized he wasn't going to get the response he wanted, he eventually looked away.

"There I go, skipping forward again," he said. "Where were we?"

"Twenty-ten."

"Oh yes, 2010 it was the turn of the reporter from the local paper. That bitch hounded my mom after Dad was convicted. She wouldn't quit. Finding new angles to write about, anything to twist the knife just a little more." He shook his head. "Then I found out why she was so diligent in her work. Her dad was one of the investors who lost money. It was a personal vendetta. Got so bad Mom couldn't take it anymore. We moved towns. Ended up some place Mom had no friends, no job, no life. All she did was look after me." He looked down toward the table. Ingrid thought she'd detected a slight moistening of his eyes. "She could have been so much more." He sat motionless for a few moments and said nothing. Then his head snapped back up and the gleeful glint was back in his eyes. "I guess we're nearly through. I dispatched the defense attorney in 2011."

"The attorney who defended your dad?"

"He had to be the most incompetent lawyer ever to pass his bar exams. Assuming of course he actually did. A better lawyer may have gotten my dad off."

There was no doubting Ellis' dedication to his task. He certainly had been thorough.

"So, we're practically up to date." Ellis sniffed. "That bitch Highsmith last year. And Sol Franklin just three days ago. A complete set."

"What about Matthew Fuller?"

"He was a bonus I wasn't expecting. He hadn't actually made it onto my list. He was only a kid at the time of the conviction. I came here to eradicate Franklin. But when I discovered Matthew Brite was in London too—some people really are careless with what they post to their social media accounts—it seemed too good an opportunity to pass up. Especially when I discovered he was suffering from OCD. Got my creative juices flowing."

"So you got yourself a job at Fisher Krupps?"

"Do you know how easy it is to get into all sorts of places when everyone sub-contracts their cleaning and maintenance work? You should maybe check who else you have working here at the embassy. You might be surprised. Shocked, even." He glanced over Ingrid's shoulder toward the glass. Ingrid pictured Marshall scrambling for the phone, demanding a list of all the staff.

"And that's it," Ellis said. "A full wrap. I'll of course provide methods, dates, times. Everything you need for the complete picture."

"What about everyone else who got killed along the way?"

"Collateral damage. Unavoidable."

"Do you even remember them all?"

"Sure—I can make you another list. The only one I truly regret is Marija. She was a great gal. But I needed to test the FBI response, as I'm sure you've worked out by now. Marija was the best way of doing that." He slumped back in his seat. "A shame, but unavoidable." He flashed a smile at Ingrid. "I guess we're done. I won't say it's been a pleasure, Agent Skyberg. But I do rather admire your determination, not to mention your apparent cockroach-like indestructibility. I hope there are no hard feelings between us. You were getting in the way just a little too much. I couldn't have you jeopardizing what I'd come here to do. And ultimately, you didn't. So it all worked out for the best." He smiled more broadly at her.

Ingrid scraped back her chair and got to her feet. "I would maybe tone down the smugness, if I were you."

"Oh please, allow me a little self-congratulation. Twelve years ago I had quite a to-do list. And I've achieved everything I set out to. How many people can say that about their miserable lives?"

"Not quite everything." Ingrid smiled down at him. "And there's absolutely nothing you can do about it now." She pulled out her phone and scrolled through her photo gallery.

Ellis frowned up at her, his chest rising and falling a little more rapidly. But he said nothing.

"Oh come on," Ingrid said. "You're dying to know what I'm talking about. Admit it."

He glared at her.

"Now that you've… unburdened yourself, I thought it was the least I could do to keep you up to date with the latest developments. I thought you might appreciate that."

"What could you possibly have to say that would interest me?"

"Something that'll change your whole perspective. It'll certainly destroy your sense of... completion."

"Don't bother trying to play games—you're no good at it."

"I wouldn't dream of playing games with you. I just thought you'd be interested to know Assistant Deputy Chief Franklin says hi."

Ellis started to laugh, but as the pain in his shattered shoulder took hold, the laughing abruptly stopped. "Really? Is that the best you can do? And you expect me to believe you?"

"Sol Franklin regained consciousness a little before you did on Wednesday afternoon."

"You're lying."

"Now I expected you to say that. So I came prepared."

She turned her phone around and showed Ellis a picture of Sol Franklin smiling up at the camera from his hospital bed with a copy of yesterday's *Washington Post* lying across the bed covers. It had taken all of Sol's will power and determination to pose for the photograph. He was completely exhausted afterward. But it had been worth it for this moment. Worth it to witness the bewildered, distraught look on Ellis' face.

"I guess you didn't achieve what you set out to do after all," Ingrid said. "And you never will."

About the author

Eva was born and raised in London. She's been a local government worker, web editor, dot com entrepreneur, portrait artist and singer. She wrote her first novel in 2005 and has never looked back.

In 2011 Eva won the inaugural Lucy Cavendish Prize for Fiction for her first published novel, *The Loyal Servant.* The book was also shortlisted for TV's People's Novelist Award. Eva lives in Sussex and London, and loves to spend time in the US.

You can catch up with Eva on her website: evahudson.com, on Twitter: https://twitter.com/Eva_Hudson and Facebook: https://www.facebook.com/evahudsoncrimewriter.

Acknowledgements

Big thanks to my editor, FC, my copy editor/proofer, Lucy and my early readers, Jose and Hilary.

Printed in Great Britain
by Amazon.co.uk, Ltd.,
Marston Gate.